The Ruins of Anthalas

The Ember War Saga Book 2

RICHARD FOX

For Kristy, My Darling

CHAPTER 1

The silent city around Lieutenant Ken Hale felt like an empty crypt. After the alien Xaros wiped the planet clean of all human life and nearly scoured away the last traces of civilization, the city of Tucson, Arizona reflected the Earth as a whole.

Once home to millions, Tucson was now a few dozen square miles of high-rise towers and sprawling commercial centers surrounded by scrub desert. Highways leading in and out of the city cut off neatly into tumbleweeds and pampas grass. Several towers were missing perfectly cut sections, like God himself reached down to cut away a slice. The Xaros drones had deconstructed most of the surrounding city with arcane technology, transforming every scrap of human-made material into a tactile form of energy dubbed Omnium.

Deep within the city, the fire of humanity kindled.

Hale ran down a street, careful not to leave boot prints in the small sand dunes washed against the curbs. He passed a sporting goods store, the interior covered in mold, racks of clothes rotting on their hangars. Perfect holes the diameter of his fist perforated the building, evidence of a disintegration beam fired by the Xaros drones that had killed whoever had taken refuge in the store decades ago.

The disintegration holes allowed nature easy access to the buildings that hadn't been removed by the Xaros. Mother Earth would reclaim the land slowly, and as surely as the Xaros technology had erased the rest.

"Where did you see it?" Hale asked, speaking into his IR net. The infrared broadcaster in his helmet and armor connected him to the Marines around him, the beam weak enough not to be detected by their quarry.

"Over the baseball stadium, maybe a mile away," Gunney Cortaro said.

Hale raised his gauss rifle and sidestepped across a blind alley, glancing up to scan for threats.

"Watch your corners. Damn things are tricky," Hale said. "Bailey, you have a firing point?"

"One sec, sir," Lance Corporal Bailey said, the smack of her chewing gum carrying through the IR net as she swiped and pinched on a screen attached to the back of her left hand. She double-tapped, and a section of the map popped up inside Hale's helmet. A dashed line traced from the building to the distant stadium.

"The fifth floor?" Hale asked.

"You want me to make the shot or not … sir?" she asked. Hale tapped his fingers against his gauss rifle, then caught himself. His Marines would spot the nervous tic, and the last thing an officer should ever do was portray indecisiveness. Bailey, short and squat, cradled a gauss carbine in her arms, the two halves of her rail rifle strapped to her back.

"Sir," Cortaro said through a private channel, "she'll hit it. I've seen her put two rounds in a quarter twice that distance away."

"It's the escape route I'm worried about," Hale said to Cortaro. He switched to his team frequency and sent the building to his Marines with the swipe of a finger. "Here's our sniper's nest. Let's move out. Standish, take point."

Standish, the lanky corporal, ran ahead without one of his usual quips. He stopped aside a building parallel to a four-lane street and took a quick glance up and down the road.

Maybe Standish is ready for sergeant's stripes, Hale thought. Torni, their team hacker, kept up with Standish, staying a few steps behind him.

"Face-first into battle, Marines!" Standish said as he sprinted across the road.

Maybe not.

Cortaro and Bailey waited until Standish and Torni found cover on the other side of the road, then crossed.

Hale glanced at the last two Marines: Yarrow, the medic, and Orozco carrying the Gustav heavy gauss rifle. It hurt to replace the Marines he lost to the Xaros, but the reality of war demanded a fully manned squad. He joined the new Marines and sprinted across the roadway.

Urban combat alternated between offering excellent cover and concealment among the buildings and debris, and being exposed like a sitting duck while racing from building to building.

Hale fell back and slid, his armor scraping against the concrete as he slowed to a stop next to Cortaro.

"Show off," the sergeant muttered. "Target building is right there." Cortaro gestured to a commercial building, its glass walls obscured with mold. The upper floors were stripped away, and steel beams jutted into the sky like broken bones through punctured skin.

"Let's go." Hale ran for the building, passing a car missing its rear half. A family of cats bolted from the car as the Marines made their way to the building, silent but for the slap of their boots against the concrete.

Hale stopped in front of the double glass doors and raised his rifle as Torni and Standish dug their fingers into the seams between the doors. Hale braced himself as they struggled to slide the door along the rusted-out runners. The new gauss rifles could fire armor-penetrating, cobalt-jacketed tungsten rounds as fast as he could pull the trigger, and each shot would kick like a mule against his shoulder.

He pressed a thumb against the activator on the special launcher attached to the bottom of his gauss rifle. The launcher held a single quadrium round, one of the few weapons that could incapacitate their foe for a few seconds. After the battle for the Crucible, the alien jump gate in orbit around the dwarf planet Ceres, quadrium rounds were few and precious.

The doors slid open with a tortured shriek, and Hale winced as the sound echoed up and down the block. If their enemy was paying enough

9

attention, the sound would serve as a giant spotlight on their location.

The first floor of the building was nothing but decaying reception desks, rotted-out leather chairs and a piece of modern art that looked more interesting as time and nature ground it into dust.

"Next time just go through the glass," Orozco said. He aimed his Gustav heavy gauss rifle down the street and slammed his rear heel against the ground. Clamps against his lower leg snapped to the ground, and servos whined as the clamps anchored him to the ground. The new version of the Gustav packed enough punch to shatter a drone with a single shot, but the human body wasn't the ideal chassis for the weapon.

"How about next time you tell that good-idea fairy on your shoulder we're on a stealth mission?" Standish asked.

"Shut your traps and get up those stairs before I save you the trouble and punt your ass up there," Cortaro growled.

Hale jogged through the waiting room of

what remained of a legal firm and found the stairs. He eased the door open with his hip and swung his rifle up as he scanned the stairwell. The stairs cut off in open air, an overcast sky above them.

"Fifth floor," Hale said. He took the stairs two at a time and even with the pseudo-muscles built into his armor to aid him, he was huffing from exertion by the time he got to the upper levels. Hale swore to spend more time on physical training once this mission was over.

A conference room took up the whole side of the building with a sectioned, ornate oak table running through the middle of the room. High-end holo projectors that once cost more than Hale made in an entire year lay covered in dust.

"This'll work," Bailey said from behind Hale. "Someone cut out the glass while I put Bloke together." The sniper swung the rail rifle off her shoulder and set the pack on the conference table. She unzipped it and began reassembling the weapon with a practiced ease. Fully assembled, the rail rifle was taller than Bailey. She ran a cloth down the bisected rails that served as the weapon's barrel and gave the tips a quick pat.

"Table," she said to Standish. The Marine grabbed a segment of the conference table and pulled it parallel to a gap in the glass wall that Torni was cutting out with a suction cup and a motorized hand saw.

Bailey unsnapped a plastic case from her lower back and grunted as she raised it up over the table. It slipped from her hands and thumped against the wood, a corner kicking up splinters. Standish winced as it fell to its side.

"Seriously?" he asked.

"Damn battery pack is heavier than my mother-in-law," Bailey said. She scrambled onto the table and ran a power cable from the battery pack into the butt stock of her rifle. A whine filled the room. Bailey went prone and settled against the table, scanning for her target through the weapon's scope.

Hale tapped into the feed from Bailey's scope and saw the distant stadium. A shadow wove between rusted-out billboards and came to a stop just beyond the foul pole, an orange streamer still flapping in the breeze. An oblong black drone hung in the air, stalks twitching and scratching at the air around it.

"There, next to the Tesla ad," Hale said.

"I've got it," Bailey said. She slid a cobalt bolt the size of her forearm from the weapon's carry sack and set it atop the rails. The electric hum grew louder and the bolt quivered as it floated in between the rails held aloft by magnetic fields.

Bailey spat out her gum and let out a slow breath.

The rail rifle fired with a clap of thunder. Glass shattered and blew out into the empty city as the hypersonic round seared through the sky, igniting oxygen in its wake and leaving a thin trail of fire that burnt out within seconds.

The clink of falling glass echoed through the building with the fury of a monsoon's downpour.

Hale looked through the window frames ringed by jagged glass. Pigeons and doves spooked by the blast flit through the air. The stadium had a new burning hole through two sides of its walls.

"Did you get it?" Hale asked.

"I'm sure of it. Won't be anything left to see after Bloke here is done. … What the hell?" Bailey peered through her scope, then her head shot up. "Contact."

A drone rose from behind the stadium and flew straight for them.

"Take it out!" Hale shouted. His Marines took careful aim and fired, their gauss rifles snapping with each shot. The drone jinked through the air, untouched by the shots.

"How could I miss?" Bailey asked aloud.

"Baily, set your charge. Forty-five seconds until it gets here," Hale said.

Bailey rolled onto her side, unplugged the battery from her rifle and took a green cylinder off her belt. She twisted the cylinder hard until something within it clicked, then she attached it to the power cord.

"We should leave," Bailey said. She rolled

off the table, scooped up her carry bag and ran for the door.

The Marines followed her, tromping down the stairs like the hounds of hell were on their heels. Hale vaulted over the railing and let gravity take him down the last fifteen feet. He hit the ground and rolled forward, rising with his rifle ready and watching for the drone to swoop down on them.

He made it to the outer wall and stopped. A timer ticked down against his visor.

"Forty-three … forty-four …," he said.

The building shook as the rail rifle battery case overloaded and blew the top two stories into fragments. Flaming debris rained down onto the street, wrecking cars and shattering what glass had survived Bailey's earlier shot.

Hale waited two seconds after the last hunk of what remained of the conference table bounced across the asphalt, then he backed up and ran through the glass wall. Slivers of glass scraped against his armor and crunched beneath his feet as he ran onto the street. His full body armor could take a direct hit from a gauss rifle—broken glass was hardly a concern.

He swung his rifle up and looked through the sky, no sign of the drone. Maybe his gambit worked and the explosion took out the drone as it reached the building.

"Get to the extraction point. No use keeping quiet now," Hale said.

They had to make it to an overgrown football field half a mile away and signal a drop ship to make their escape. Hale kept glancing at the sky as they ran, his confidence rising as no drone appeared.

They followed a highway leading beneath an overpass that cut off against the encroaching desert. Hale took a signal flare locked against his utility belt and popped the cap off. He turned from the overpass to address his Marines.

"OK … we need to—"

Hale ducked and swung around as Yarrow raised his weapon and fired a shot over Hale's shoulder. A drone clawed its way around the side of the overpass and fired a ruby-colored ray of light over his head. Hale fired off a hip shot but the bolt glanced off the side of the drone and bounced against the side of the overpass. Two more bolts of light lanced through the air around him. Hale hit the drone again and it collapsed against the desert.

"Everyone alright?" Hale asked as he turned around. His Marines lay sprawled across the road, still.

He felt a vibration through the air and looked up. A drone hung over him, tendrils swaying against an unseen current. A blast of light hit him in the chest and his armor locked. Hale fell to the ground, his visor flashing KIA over and over again, accompanied by a nerve-grating buzz. He'd been Killed In Action, and Hale cursed himself for the series of mistakes that had led to this.

"End exercise," a baritone voice said.

Air shimmered and warped around a humanoid form as it moved to Hale. The cloaking field fell away, revealing an alien standing six feet six in Marine fatigues. Wisp-thin, sand-colored feathers ran over its head and aside a flattened snout. Greenish-brown scales served as skin around its reptilian eyes and over its mouth.

Steuben of the Karigole species reached down with its four-fingered hand and picked Hale up with ease. The Karigole set Hale on his feet like he was fallen toddler and held the Marine up. The claw points at the ends of his fingers tapped at a forearm computer and Hale's armor unlocked. Hale pulled his helmet off and wiped a hand across his sweaty face. The Karigole looked Hale over and he smacked his lips.

In the months since the Karigole had begun training the Marines, Hale had never found a good way to read their expressions but he was pretty sure this one was unhappy. Hale unlocked the armor for the rest of his Marines and they stirred, their complaints overlapping through the IR net.

"You have failed this training event," the Karigole said. He looked up at the drone still floating overhead, an Ibarra Corporation construction droid outfitted with training lasers and an armor façade to mimic a Xaros drone. The faux Xaros zoomed away on its antigravity engines.

"Damn you, Steuben!" Bailey got to her feet and ripped her helmet off. She stalked toward the alien, her hands balled tight, and squared off against the alien, her head barely at his chest level. She wagged a finger at him.

"You cheated! You had that drone move before I could kill it and made me miss!"

"Stand down, Marine!" Cortaro said as he ran toward the confrontation.

"Admit it, you shonky poofter!" Bailey demanded, her Australian accent coming to the fore as her anger rose.

Cortaro grabbed her by the collar and tugged her back from the Karigole.

"The little one is correct. I did interfere and alter the parameters of the exercise," he said.

"'Little one'?" Bailey struggled against Cortaro's grip but couldn't get loose. Cortaro pulled her around the corner of a building as she protested and hurled more insults at the Karigole. Her shouts fell away and Hale could hear Cortaro's stern tone in the air.

"Rest of you, gather 'round," Hale said. The rest of the Marines were quiet, eyes downcast. Hale wasn't sure if they were bothered more by their failure or Bailey's loss of control. They formed a semicircle in front of the alien. Orozco stuck a wad of chewing tobacco into his lip. Standish and Torni drank from water packs slung over their shoulders.

"Steuben," Hale said to the alien, "would you please explain what happened."

Steuben, as the Karigole preferred to be called, looked over the Marines, his face inscrutable.

"Your team infiltrated the target area successfully and chose an appropriate firing position for a long-range engagement. The conditions of the exercise were then altered. I wanted to see how you would react to the unexpected," Steuben said.

"I'd say we've already had plenty of experience with the unexpected," Standish said.

Torni jammed an elbow into his side.

"You destroyed the drone under the overpass, but then you all made the same error." Steuben pointed a clawed finger to the sky. "You did not look up. You must always look up. The second drone killed every last one of you with ease because you had tunnel vision. Your evolution is as a terrestrial species. You perceive your battles in two dimensions. But the Xaros can fly, maneuver in three dimensions with ease."

Steuben extended his finger toward the burning building where black smoke rose and tapered into the wind. His head turned around nearly backwards as the alien looked at Hale, his eyes blinking slowly and one at a time, the lids moving from side to side instead of up and down.

"You," Steuben said to Hale, "you blew up my training area."

"It worked, didn't it?" Yarrow asked. The Marine was young, barely out of his teens, and his close-cropped red hair stood out against a pale complexion that suffered beneath the Arizona sun.

"The maneuver has merits," Steuben snapped.

"It was a good idea, Yarrow. Keep them coming," Hale said. The Marine beamed at the compliment. Hale scratched his face, suddenly unsure of just how much paperwork he'd have to fill out for the loss of equipment and destruction of civilian property, not that the owners were around to claim compensation.

"Had I not redirected other drones to intercept you, I'm sure you would have made it to the extraction point without issue," Steuben said.

The Marines groaned and shook their heads.

"You cheated," Standish said. "We would have been just fine but you went and cheated."

"I do not know this word, 'chet-ed,'" Steuben said.

"It means you didn't follow the rules that were laid out," Hale said.

"Rules? In war?" Steuben flicked a claw beneath his chin and clicked needle-sharp teeth. "What rules do the Xaros follow? What do rules serve in any fight for survival? The purpose of this exercise was to put your squad under stress so you learn something." The alien pointed a finger at Hale. "Did it succeed?"

"Yes," Hale said.

"If you had completed the exercise with ease, you would have gained nothing and I would have failed in my mission to prepare you hairless apes for what is to come," Steuben said. "Rules, chet-ed, foolish notions of a species that thinks it is fighting for anything but its very existence."

"Thank you, Steuben. We are better for this lesson," Hale said.

Steuben clicked his teeth together and looked at the smoking building.

"The next squad will be here in two hours. I must adjust the exercise," the alien said.

"Mr. Steuben Karigole, sir," Bailey said from behind him. Steuben turned his head around a hundred and eighty degrees to look at the sheepish Marine, Cortaro a step behind her, his arms crossed. "I want to apologize for my behavior. I am a shame to myself, my team and my Corps. I acted innap—"

"Accepted," Steuben said. "Now leave, all of you. I have work to do."

Hale called up their true extraction point, a battery recharge station five miles to the east, and sent the way point to the squad.

"Double interval, march pace. Yarrow, take point," Cortaro said. The Marines put their helmets back on and peeled away from Steuben, weapons pointed to the flanks of their formation as they walked into the desert.

Hale walked next to Cortaro and opened a private channel to his head enlisted Marine.

"What was that all about?" Hale asked.

"She's a hothead, sir. Doesn't care to have her talent called into question. She isn't real happy about 'taking orders from an alien' either," Cortaro said.

"The Karigole aren't the Xaros," Hale said.

"She's not the only one that thinks that way. Plenty of people out there who'd like to throw the Crucible into the sun and Ibarra with it," Cortaro said. Marc Ibarra, the genius industrialist who'd engineered a plot to keep a sliver of humanity alive and defeat the Xaros that conquered the solar system, had died during the invasion, but his consciousness lived on inside some sort of alien probe. Hale had led the team that rescued the probe from where it hid from the Xaros occupation, and even he wasn't sure if he fully understood what Ibarra had become.

"She need to see a chaplain?" Hale asked.

"She'll sit down with one when we get back to Phoenix. Plus, she's got a 'group of mates' from her home country she meets up with most nights," Cortaro said.

"Aren't they the Australians that get drunk and break things a couple times a week?"

"We all grieve differently, sir. You still want her with us on this mission? We could find another sniper before we leave," Cortaro said.

"We're not going to give up on her. There's not a Marine, soldier or sailor in this fleet that didn't lose someone to the Xaros. She can do the job, baggage or not. What about the others?"

Orozco lifted up the edge of his visor and spat a wad of tobacco juice into the dust.

"Big guy's deadly with the Gustav, doesn't say much, stays out of trouble and is on time for everything. Give me a dozen more just like him and I could have reconquered Taiwan," Cortaro said. "Yarrow follows you around like a damn puppy dog and he's so new he squeaks, does a good job too."

"Torni and Standish holding up?"

"Torni spends a lot of time at church. I see her at every morning Mass I manage to make it to. Standish ... he's just Standish," Cortaro said.

"You good?"

"I've got this. My Marines. We've all got shit to work through," Cortaro said. The Gunnery sergeant lost his wife and four children to the Xaros, more than anyone else Hale knew. Every time Hale had tried to offer a sympathetic shoulder, Cortaro had thrown up his defenses and changed the subject as quickly as he could. Hale didn't think this time would be any different.

Hale closed the private channel and went back to the squad frequency.

"I'm telling you," Standish said as Hale joined in mid conversation, "they killed all the crows too."

"You're so full of it your eyes are brown," Torni said. "Crows didn't have cities, language, or an Internet full of cat videos. Why would the Xaros wipe them out?"

"Because crows can use tools," Standish said. "When I was a kid back on the farm, I saw one jimmy open a lock with a piece of metal. Zoologists have known about that since the turn of the century. Heck, crows even have—had regional dialects. The Xaros had to know they were kind of intelligent. That's why they killed them all."

"What makes you think the Xaros did that, corporal?" Yarrow asked.

"You seen any crows since we've been out here? Has anyone seen one since the fleet did its little time jump—skip, whatever we're calling it— to sidestep the invasion?" Standish asked. "I asked

27

some of the guys that went to scout out the other surviving cities and none of them saw crows. The Xaros wipe out anything that uses tools. That's my hypothesis."

"I don't know how crows would be any threat to whatever those things were doing on Ceres or what they had planned for Earth," Yarrow said.

"Look, kiddo, just admit I'm right about the crows—or we make a bet. You see a crow in the next month and I give you a month's pay. No crows and you give me a month's pay," Standish said.

"We're about to leave the solar system for God knows how long and you want him to take that bet?" Torni asked.

"Thank. You. Ms. Torni." Standish kicked a pebble at her.

"Are we getting paid again?" Yarrow asked. With all the world's banks and electronic records wiped out by the Xaros, reestablishing a working economy had taken a backseat to rebuilding the only remaining city of Phoenix and repairing the fleet after the Battle of the Crucible. With every human either in the military or part of the Ibarra Corporation that provided for all its employees' needs through robot labor or 3D printing factories, there hadn't been much of a need for currency and trade.

The Marines looked over their shoulders at Hale, expecting an answer from the captain.

"Let's worry about getting back from Anthalas before we worry about bank accounts," Hale said.

CHAPTER 2

Euskal Tower, once the headquarters of the Ibarra Corporation, was the de facto center of human government. It was the largest remaining building on the planet, and its utility infrastructure had remained intact through the Xaros occupation. A thin layer of quadrium metal ran beneath the city, which, for reasons no one had ever explained to Hale, had made it the last place the Xaros targeted for removal. In the sixty years he'd colluded with an alien probe, Marc Ibarra had planned ahead.

Hale avoided the tower whenever possible. He'd lost two Marines to the Xaros there, and while the battle damage had been repaired, feelings of loss and guilt still nagged at him every time he walked down the hallways lined with plush carpets and restored art. The robot workers had returned everything to its original state, which was at odds with the military nature of its new occupants.

Hale and Cortaro walked past a coffee pot set up outside the conference room and pushed through the heavy doors. The stadium seating of the conference room was almost full of sailors and Marines. Conversations rumbled through the air as Hale caught sight of Captain Valdar, master and commander of the *Breitenfeld*, surrounded by the chief officers of the strike carrier.

"I'll leave the brass to you, sir. I'm going to find our Marines and make sure Standish and Bailey don't try to heckle whoever's going to speak to us," Cortaro said. Hale left him with a nod and went down the stairs to where the senior officers were gathered near the front rows.

Captain Valdar greeted him with a quick wave, then turned his attention back to Commander Janessa Ericsson, the ship's executive officer, and the data slate she carried. Valdar, Hale's godfather, was gaunt, his face stretched tight against his skull, his uniform looking like it belonged to a bigger man. A cluster of new officers, replacements for those lost in the Battle of the Crucible, stood near the ship's captain and XO, answering any questions snapped at them.

On the outer edge of the group, Lieutenant Marie Durand glanced at her watch every few seconds. Her flight suit stuck out like a sore thumb amongst the Marines in their fatigues and the sailors in their black pants, ties and collared shirts.

"Marie," he said to Durand.

"Lieutenant Hale," she said, stressing his rank.

"Pardon me, lieutenant. How are the new fighters?"

She gave him a quick sidelong glance and pulled a data slate from her pocket. She flicked through messages then put it back in her pocket. She looked at him again, seemingly annoyed that he was still there.

"The new rail cannon capacitors are guaranteed not to overload my ship and turn it into a slow-moving target. I will note that none of those engineers who're incorporating the improved technology will be on this mission or will ever fly the mark two Eagles into combat," she said stiffly. "Now, is there anything of military necessity that I can help you with?"

"Marie, come on, we can talk about this—"

"Here? Now?" She put her hands on her hips. He and Durand had been an item before the Xaros invasion. A few days after the Battle of the Crucible, when things aboard the damaged *Breitenfeld* had calmed down, she told Hale in no uncertain terms that their relationship was at an end and they'd conduct their business as professional officers and little else. She and the rest of her squadron left for the aerospace base outside Phoenix for retraining and reassignment, and she hadn't answered a single message he'd sent her in the months that followed.

"No, never mind," Hale said.

The auditorium's lights dimmed and brightened several times, alerting everyone that the briefing was about to begin. Hale took a seat far from Durand and pulled out his data slate to take notes.

A senior chief petty officer marched onto the stage and stopped at the position of attention.

"Room! Attention!" the sailor shouted.

The room went silent and the assembled servicemen and women rose to their feet and stood at the position of attention.

Admiral John Garret strode onto the stage and walked over to a podium.

"Take your seats," he said, the microphone in the podium projecting his words across the auditorium. There was a brief rustle as his order was followed, then a rapt silence endured.

"Let's skip the crap and get to business you all know where you're going." Garret clicked a control and a hologram of a world covered in jungle, worn mountains and small, shallow seas formed on the stage next to the admiral. "Anthalas.

Habitable world with a breathable atmosphere two thousand light-years away from Earth. Currently under Xaros occupation. You've busted your asses to get the *Breitenfeld* back up to snuff and get her ready for this mission. Now I'm going to tell you why you're going there."

He clicked the control and the hologram blinked into a scroll of light, perpendicular to the stage. The image was basic, simple, like the message imbedded in the old Voyager space probes that were supposed to signal to any alien that came across them how to find Earth and gave fundamental information about humanity—a monumentally foolish act in retrospect. Although the Xaros drones had followed Earth's first radio broadcasts back to the planet, they didn't come across the first objects humans sent beyond the solar system. Another aggressive and advanced species could have come across the Voyager probes, if the Xaros had left any in their wake.

A pixilated humanoid figure with a black stripe across its waist stood at the top of the scroll.

Below that was the same figure lying on its side. The next image was of a different figure, this one missing the dark stripe and raising its arms over its head next to the prone figure. The final image showed the two figures standing side by side, both of them with arms raised. Below them was a grid with a mélange of tiny black and white squares.

A woman in her late twenties wearing an Ibarra Corporation jumpsuit walked onto the stage. She took the control from Garret with a trembling hand and stood behind the podium. Her hands grasped the wooden edges like it was a life raft and she bent close to the microphone.

"Hello, I'm Helena Lowenn," she said, her voice throaty as she spoke too closely to the microphone. "I'm a doctoral candidate—well, I was—in anthropology and sociology at the university of … doesn't matter. What you're looking at is an image broadcast from Anthalas across the electromagnetic spectrum several thousand years ago. We believe that whoever was sending this out from the planet was promising a cure for death, or some sort of transfiguration into eternal life. That's what you see." She pointed the control at the image and a red dot wavered over the top image. "Someone alive, then dead, then resurrected by another person.

"The grid at the bottom is a code, which, when deciphered, is an energy reading," she said. She clicked the control and the hologram shifted to a cube of energy, spinning slowly on an axis. Murmurs ran through the audience.

"Many of you have seen this here on Earth," she said. "We're calling it Omnium. As the Xaros erased our cities, they converted all of that matter into Omnium. Our estimate is that a little over ninety-eight percent of every man-made thing on Earth was converted into Omnium, and much of that was used to make the Crucible. There's still a significant amount here on Earth, Mars, the moon. Somehow, the Xaros can change matter into Omnium, then change energy into any other kind of matter."

She handed the control back to Garret and

tried to scurry off the stage. Garret snagged her by the arm and kept her next to the podium.

"We think whoever was on Anthalas knew the secret to Omnium and was trying to get someone's attention with it. Dangling eternal life and the means of unlimited energy were pretty decent incentives for a visit to the planet. I'll turn the next portion of this briefing over to a subject-matter expert," Garret said.

He stepped aside and a silver needle of light grew out of thin air. The audience shifted nervously in their seats as the light grew stronger. Shouts of alarm shot from the men and women seated behind Hale, but he wasn't stirred. Hale knew exactly who, or what, was about to speak to them.

A cloud of light broiled out of the needle, then solidified into a silver and blue approximation of a slight man in his early forties. Ripples ran up and down the man's surface as he looked across the audience.

"Hello everyone," the shimmering man said, "I'm Marc Ibarra and I'm sure this is just a little bit odd for most of you." Ibarra looked right at Hale and winked. "The Alliance, the same people that sent a probe to Earth to try to save you all, sent another probe to Anthalas. It was going over there to try to get them to shut the hell up and figure out if they really knew how to use Omnium, which is a trick only the Xaros seem to know. On the way to the system, the probe encountered a message."

The hologram switched to a two-dimensional screen. An alien with tiny, calcified horns jutting from beneath deep-blue skin, it's lower jaw thick and with a pronounced underbite, wearing simple spun robes spoke to an unseen camera. Its words were guttural, a series of modulating barks that grated against Hale's ears. What bothered Hale the most about the alien was its eyes, glowing with a golden light.

"Spirits of the galaxy," a monotone translation came over the alien's words, "Anthalas offers you eternal life and freedom from want. Come and be exalted in the light." The image froze.

"That," Ibarra said, "and only that, was

repeated for several years. That species, which called itself the Shanishol, isn't native to Anthalas. They're from a system a couple light-years over. What's unusual about their presence on Anthalas is that they were barely at 1950s–era technology when they figured out how to pick up the original broadcast from Anthalas—that scroll of images you saw a few minutes ago. Somehow, this species jumped from barely knowing how to use nuclear power to claiming godlike powers in just a few decades."

The hologram flickered back to the planet.

"Unfortunately," Ibarra said, "we weren't the only ones interested in the planet. All transmissions ceased as soon as the Xaros got close enough to be noticed. They beat our probe to the punch by a couple decades. The probe got close enough to get this ...." The image changed to show incomplete rings around Anthalas's equator, same as the rings around Ceres that had moved the dwarf planet from its home in the asteroid belt into orbit around Earth.

Red spots appeared on the planet's surface, each above cities laid out in a neat grid pattern.

"The Xaros didn't remove the Shanishol cities," Ibarra said. "The only time we see this behavior is when the Xaros come across a civilization that's already dead. So all the Shanishol must have hit whatever exaltation failsafe they had and left a bunch of ghost towns for the Xaros. We're confident there's technology we can use on that planet, and that's why we're sending the *Breitenfeld* there."

"How is one ship supposed to fight through an entire planet's worth of Xaros?" someone asked from the darkness.

"The Xaros maintain very small garrisons on worlds they've conquered. Uninhabitable rocks like Mars and Mercury might have a single drone. Places that have supported life in the past might have a half-dozen drones spread across the planet. Why? Best guess is that they're sentinels, making sure intelligent life doesn't reemerge or come in from off world.

"So long as you keep from broadcasting your presence, you should be able to sneak in and out without any trouble," Ibarra said. More than one derisive snort came from the audience. "You leave in twenty-three hours and nine minutes."

"My ship is barely out of dry dock and you want us to leave this soon?" Captain Valdar asked, standing up from his seat in the front row.

Admiral Garret stepped in front of Ibarra to answer. "The laws of physics are dictating our operational tempo." He turned to Ibarra, "Professor?"

"The Crucible can adjust gravity fields within it," Ibarra said. "When the fields are in resonance with another part of the galaxy, we can open a wormhole between those two points. The Xaros are moving Anthalas around the solar system, and that plays hell with any attempt to jump in or out of the system. But, thanks to the orbit of a gas giant in the system and a passing brown dwarf star, we have a brief window into the system. Once there, you'll have less than two days to find the

Omnium tech and jump out, or you'll be there for a very long time."

"Men and women of the *Breitenfeld*," Admiral Garrett said, "if this mission wasn't critical to our survival, we wouldn't put your lives at risk. The Xaros will return. At best, we have a few decades to get ready. Our best weapon against the drones are the quadrium shells, and after the Battle of the Crucible, we barely have enough Q-shells for the fleet to fire a couple shots. When we have Omnium deciphered, we can turn our stockpile into quadrium and just about any other thing we can imagine and give the Xaros one hell of a punch when they get here.

"Now, get back to your ship and get prepped. Every last man, woman and child in Phoenix and the fleet is depending on you. Dismissed."

CHAPTER 3

Hale watched the flight deck of the *Breitenfeld* seething with activity from the upper level catwalk. Mule drop ships and larger Destrier cargo carriers moved through the air on precision anti-gravity thrusters, levitating over unloading ships. The ship's computers maneuvered the Mules and Destriers without human input, though there were still ready pilots in the cockpits in case something went horribly wrong with the ship's computer.

A computer running the flight deck didn't bother Hale as much as the open blast doors on either end of the flight deck. Once the Xaros were defeated, Ibarra gave the remnants of humanity all the technological advances he'd been sitting on since the alien probe arrived decades ago. One of the first upgrades was a force field that allowed the cargo deck to operate in atmosphere. Hale still wore small re-breather tanks on his back and kept an emergency hood in his cargo pocket. The new force fields were supposedly foolproof, but Hale would rather keep an insurance policy handy; he didn't want to die in the void because he trusted too much.

Cortaro put his hands on the rail and checked the tail number of an incoming Mule.

"There, sir. That's them," Cortaro said.

"Let's get them before they wander into a torpedo tube," Hale said. He and his sergeant took the corrugated metal stairs down to the flight deck.

"I still don't get it, sir. Why are we bringing a bunch of army pukes on this mission?" Cortaro asked. They stopped at the edge of the dashed yellow lines along the edge of the flight deck and watched as the drop ship landed at the far end of the runway.

"They've got the skills, and the more warm

bodies we can throw at the planet, the more ground we can cover before the jump window closes," Hale said. They walked down the runway, sidestepping cargo trams hauling Q-shells into the ship's magazines and naval ratings who didn't seem to care for the presence of Marines on their otherwise orderly flight deck.

"Your brother's been around the army. He know any of these guys?" Cortaro asked.

"No, never heard of them," Hale said. His brother, Jared, had opted to follow their father and grandfather's footsteps and join the Marines mechanized infantry once he'd earned his commission. Jared was part of the fleet that survived the Xaros invasion, and the last time he'd spoken to Jared he'd been on the moon, scouring the deep tunnels to ensure a Xaros drone hadn't found a hiding place.

"There's still plenty of Army around, lot more than the Marine Corps—can't expect them to know everyone," Hale said.

The drop ship lowered its rear hatch and a

dozen men and women in army green and brown battle dress uniforms stood in the cargo bay, their gear already slung against their chests and over their backs.

A lieutenant the same age as Hale tromped down the ramp and extended a hand, almost lost in the mountain of gear he carried on his person.

"We've got plenty of kitchen sinks, Lieutenant Bartlett," Hale said.

"Brass said you Marines get by on whatever scraps the navy gives you, told us to bring all our best gear for this mission just in case you're still using crap from the Australian campaign," Lieutenant Bartlett said. He had the look of a warrior, a perpetually tired face with fierce eyes.

"We turned all that in last week," Hale joked. "Gunnery Sergeant Cortaro will take you to your berths. The ship'll shove off under combat conditions, so draw ammo once you're situated," Hale said.

"When do we jump?"

"Three hours."

"Great, we got pegged for this gig first thing in the morning and we'll be up to our eyeballs in Xaros by dinner. It's the assault on the Crucible all over again," Bartlett said.

"This should go a bit smoother," Hale said.

"You hear that, boys and girls," Bartlett said over his shoulder, "a cakewalk." His soldiers chuckled and shifted beneath their gear. "Let me get them tucked in then we can go over what happens after the jump." The lieutenant looked at Cortaro, who led the soldiers from their drop ship. The soldiers all looked exhausted and harried.

Army life is just like the Corps, Hale thought.

"Oh by the way," Bartlett said as he walked away, "got a surprise for you in the back."

The last soldier filed past, and Hale saw a woman he recognized, Helena Lowenn from the briefing in Euskal Tower.

"Oh no," he muttered.

"Hello!" Lowenn waved to Hale and struggled to pick up a heavy-looking pack. She took long steps down the ramp and lost her balance. Hale managed to catch her before she fell face-first against the deck.

"Thanks, guess I don't have my sea legs yet. Or space legs. What do you call them?" she laughed nervously. She pushed errant strands of hair out of her face and smiled.

"Ms. Lowenn, you need to get back on that shuttle and leave right now," Hale said.

"Don't be silly. I have a note for you from Admiral Garret." Lowenn double-tapped a fingernail against the back of her hand and tapped it against Hale's forearm computer. Text files rolled across his display as the chip in her fingernail transferred data. Nail chips were common among civilians, but strictly forbidden for military personnel as they could harbor malware and viruses. One of the files bore the admiral's signature.

"Hey!" the crew chief of Lowenn's drop ship shouted from the top of the ramp. "I've got to button up and un-ass this crate in thirty seconds."

Hale swung Lowenn's bag over his shoulder

and led her off the flight deck by her elbow.

"Ma'am, I can get you on the next ship back to Earth or Titan station. Would you care to explain what it is you think you're doing here?" Hale asked. The deck shivered as her drop ship rumbled into the air on anti-grav engines.

"Why, I'm your science advisor of course," Lowenn said.

Hale tossed her bag atop a cart edged in yellow and black chevrons and grabbed her by both arms. He leaned close to her and spoke slowly and clearly.

"This mission does not need a science advisor. You sit down right here until I find you a ride out of here," he said.

"Do you have someone with advanced degrees in anthropology and archaeology on this mission?" She wiggled free of his grasp and put her hands on her hips.

"Miss, my job is to shoot aliens and break things. There will be no time for science." Hale turned from her and tried to wave down a crewman in a blue vest, an aircraft handler that could help him get rid of this nuisance.

"Well, what about someone that can read Shanishol? Think maybe it would be useful to know which door says 'Super Secret Science Lab' or 'Face-Eating Monsters'?" She grabbed Hale's hand and yanked it back down.

"How can you read Shanishol?"

"The Ibarra probe has their entire language on file and I've been studying it since right after we retook Earth. Very interesting how the Shanishol language patterns match the Inuit trinomial—"

"Stop." Hale held up his hand. "Do you even know how we're getting to Anthalas?"

"Well, we'd better use that jump gate. If we're going by sub-light speeds, then I definitely didn't pack enough."

"No, we're going to do a Low Orbit Low Opening grav chute insertion. There is no way I can even get you to the planet if I wanted to," Hale said.

Lowenn raised her nose slightly. "If you'd bother to look at the files I gave you, you'll see that

I have my civilian LOLO license. I was on my college team and I qualified to Marine standards just last week."

A shuttle roared past them. Hale looked at the files she'd given him and found her certificates.

"What is an archaeologist doing in the fleet? … This says you're a secretary," Hale said.

"I was a personal assistant, thank you very much. Once upon a time, there was such thing as the civilian economy. As much as I loved fieldwork, there wasn't a lot of money in digging through hillsides and trying to convince donors that you needed another six months of funds to find where the Clovis People spent their winters. I would have made more money if I'd majored in medieval French poetry or underwater basket weaving. Girl had to pay the bills somehow. The Ibarra Corporation offered me a spot on the fleet in a menial position and I figured I'd save some money in the colony then come back home," she said. She looked out the open air lock to Earth and a shadow fell across her face.

"Not how I planned it," she said.

"Ibarra. He must have known he'd need you and your skills years before the fleet even left anchorage for Saturn," Hale said.

"And I thought I got the job because the hiring manager had a crush on me," she said with a shrug. "You ever get the feeling that Ibarra, or whatever that probe thing is now, is playing chess and we're messing around with checkers?" she asked.

"All the time. Ms. Lowenn, there's—"

"Helena."

"Ms. Lowenn, there's no way you can keep up with a Strike Marine team or be anything but a hindrance to us in a fight. No."

Lowenn's mouth twisted in anger as she raised a finger in the air. "I'll have you know that I was in the Home Guard and can field strip and shoot a gauss rifle with the best of them. Now, I wanted this to be pleasant but if it's a dick-measuring contest you're after, then you're about to lose to a girl," she raised a finger over the pad on the back of her hand. "One tap and I'll open my direct line to Admiral Garret *and* Captain Valdar where I will explain why you can't seem to follow the simple orders I transferred to you. What's it going to be, jar head?"

Hale sighed slowly. This was a battle he wasn't going to win.

"Come on," he said, walking toward a hatchway leading to an elevator. "You'll need armor and a weapon."

"Wait, aren't you going to help me with my bag?" Lowenn asked.

"Nope."

Lowenn stood next to her bags, staring down the edge of the flight deck. Hale was about to berate her for wasting time when he saw what she was looking at. All four of the Karigole advisors stood together. Steuben and Lafayette he knew; the other two, Rochambeau and Kosciuszko, he'd only heard of. The four stood in a square, hands joined. Lafayette was noticeably smaller than the rest, his bionics much slimmer than the other's bulk.

All had chosen a nom de guerre shortly after their arrival. Their true names were unpronounceable by humans, whose hearing and vocal cords couldn't extend to frequencies the Karigole used for inflections in their speech.

"What are they doing?" Hale asked.

"I don't know. They haven't been very forthcoming about their culture, but this is fascinating to see," Lowenn said.

The Karigole, their eyes closed, pressed their hands together over their chests.

"*Ghul'thul'ghul*," the four said in unison. Each took turns pressing the knuckles of their right hand to the left temple of the others. Once each had received and given the gesture to the others, Rochambeau and Kosciuszko boarded a waiting shuttle.

"Steuben will be on the mission with us, right? I can't wait to talk to him," Lowenn said.

"He's not exactly the talkative type," Hale said.

****

Cortaro pressed his palm against the biometric reader and heard the heavy bolts around the doorway thump. A light above the hatch turned green and he pushed the thick metal door open.

The Central Mechanized Armor Training Room, which the crew referred to as the cemetery, stored the *Breitenfeld*'s armor suits for transit and maintenance. There were a dozen suits of armor, all recent upgrades from the last line that fought the Xaros on Earth and at the Crucible. These suits were more streamlined, and the old head modules that were little more than sensor platforms had been replaced with full helmets that looked like they belonged on a medieval battlefield—were it not for the line of sensors and camera lenses stretching in a line across where the eyes should have been.

Cortaro waited for the door to lock behind him, then he climbed up a rickety stairwell to a catwalk that ringed the room. The armor stood upright, enclosed inside lidless coffin acceleration beds. Cortaro walked past the armor, looking at the breastplate of each for a name. Some had drawings of a Xaros drone with kill marks scratched into the armor.

"Elias? You here?" Cortaro asked aloud, his voice echoing off the walls of the room. He stopped in front of a suit, an iron heart painted over its breast. He raised a hand to knock against the armor, then stopped.

"Elias?"

The suit's head snapped up and Cortaro jumped back in surprise.

"Damn it, *pendejo*! What did I tell you about scaring me?" Cortaro backed against the railing as Elias's armor rolled its shoulders and twisted its head from side to side like it was stretching.

"Sorry, the start-up sequence is a bit sudden," Elias' voice came through the suit's speakers, heavily modulated.

"Yeah, I noticed." Cortaro looked around, double-checking that they were alone. "How you doing? Haven't seen you much since we busted you out of that hospital." The story of how the other two Iron Hearts, Kallen and Bodel, had coaxed Elias out of his coma had gone viral through the fleet, with plenty of details embellished and glossed over in equal measure. Cortaro's role in the event hadn't escaped official notice, but it wasn't part of the tall tale whispered among sailors and Marines whenever they saw Elias.

"New suit. There were some software issues with my … situation," Elias said.

"You look good in the new stuff. Real bad ass," Cortaro said, flashing a nervous thumbs up.

"Not a lot of mirrors in here," Elias said.

"You hear where we're going? Some planet the Xaros have been sitting on. Find us some tech that'll win the war when they come back, or something like that," Cortaro said.

"I've been over the mission specs. The Iron Hearts are in reserve, in case you crunchies run into trouble again." Elias reached an arm up from the coffin and flexed a hand the size of Cortaro's head. Servos whined as fingers tapped into the palm one at a time. "My synch rate is optimal, should be higher by the time you launch."

"You … uh … you think you can ever come out of that suit again?"

"If I unplug, my nervous system will fail," Elias said. "They've got my true body on steroids and electric shock stimulus. I can last for a few more years, unless I catch an infection or the wither sets in." Some armor soldiers had grown too dependent on their suits, their limbs and muscles degenerating as their nervous system attuned to the armor at the expense of their own bodies. In extreme cases, the wither had left soldiers bedridden for the rest of their short lives.

"Come on, Elias, don't talk like that. They can get you in one of those full-body exo-skeletons, let you run around in the fresh air."

"No. There's a chance I could lose my armor synch forever."

"Med tech's getting better all the time now that Ibarra opened up his archives. Maybe you could—"

"No!" The word snapped like a shot from Elias' rail gun. Elias leaned forward. His metal hands wrapped around the top of the railing and squeezed, bending the metal with a tortured groan. "Do you pity what I have become? Some lump of flesh floating in a vat of chemicals and his own piss. Is that all you see?"

Cortaro stood still as Elias' helm came within a foot of his face.

"I am armor. I am armor, Cortaro. This is all I will ever be."

"I'm just worried about you, brother," Cortaro said.

Elias tried to straighten the metal railing and managed to snap the top rung off completely.

"Oops," Elias said.

Cortaro pulled an Ubi data slate from his pocket and held it out to Elias. "I found someone with all of Hideaki Anno's cartoons. I heard you were looking for his stuff."

Elias held a forearm in front of Cortaro and a data entry port popped open. Elias reached for the Ubi and the tiny wire extending from the device. Elias's monstrous fingertips pecked at the wire but couldn't grab it.

"Please," Elias said.

Cortaro plugged the device into Elias's arm.

"It's anime. Cartoons are for kids," Elias said.

"I don't judge." Cortaro pocketed the Ubi. "Nothing personal, but I really hope I don't have to see you on Anthalas. If you're down there, then everything's gone straight to shit … again."

"Cortaro, I never thanked you. For getting me out of the hospital. For saving me," Elias said. A metal hand rested on Cortaro's shoulder, heavy enough to stagger the Marine.

"Sorry, new suit," Elias said.

"No problem. You stay healthy. Maybe we'll find something that'll win the war," Cortaro said.

"Huh, winning the war. I never really think about that. I always thought we'd be at war with the Chinese, not a galaxy full of Xaros," Elias said.

****

Torni and Orozco waited in the *Breitenfeld*'s armory, she leaning against a circular, three-foot-tall bio reader, he scrolling through a data slate. Torni glanced at her watch and sighed loudly.

"They're going to be late," she said.

"They were in med bay, clear on the opposite side of the ship, when we got this 'hey you' tasking," Orozco said. "The ship's about to embark and the crew is going nuts cleaning things and locking doors—whatever squids do. Getting from one side to the other is like swimming upstream."

"Gunney Cortaro isn't a big fan of excuses. He says be somewhere at a certain time, he means exactly that," Torni said. She shook her head at her watch and tapped her forearm computer to make a call. "If they're screwing around somewhere, there will be hell to pay. Standish *knows* he's on probation."

"For what? I thought the lieutenant gave you all a wink and a nod for that business with Elias, that armor soldier, and all those cops," Orozco said.

Torni blushed and crossed her arms.

"I'm not supposed to talk about that," she said.

"I read the police blotter. Theft of military property, kidnapping, disrespect to a commissioned officer, reckless endangerment … what else was there …?"

"Not supposed to talk about it. So I'm not going to say we'd all be in the brig if Elias had stayed in his coma." Torni tapped a foot against the deck, staring at the hatch—which suddenly swung open as Yarrow and Standish burst through, both breathing heavily.

"Twenty … seconds … to go," Standish said, his hands on his knees and his head hanging below his shoulders.

"What were you even doing in med bay?" Torni asked.

Standish pointed a finger at the equally winded Yarrow.

"Sorry, Sergeant," the young medic said. "Lance Corporal Standish's green blood cell count wasn't high enough. He needed a booster."

Exposing the human immune system to an alien world full of potentially lethal and contagious pathogens was a significant risk for anyone who set foot on Anthalas—and the ship's crew once the Marines returned. The Ibarra Corporation had developed nanite bloodstream cleaners decades ago that managed to put a significant dent in infectious diseases, but using the microscopic robots in and around the Xaros was forbidden. The Xaros hacked every computer system they encountered, and no one wanted to find out what the drones would do if they gained control of a human's bloodstream.

The Ibarra Corporation, with plenty of help from the probe on the Crucible, developed green blood cells. The new blood type was a mutated strain of white blood cells that would destroy anything and everything encountered by the host's immune system following inoculation. The green blood cells hadn't gone through the years of clinical trials normally required, but assurances from the alien probe and the immediate need for the green blood cells had cut through the red tape.

"You should hear the docs," Standish said. "'Totally safe! Please report any instances of color blindness, loss of sphincter control and any death or death-like symptoms to your nearest medical professional.' I did not sign up to be a lab rat." Standish rubbed his arm where he'd been injected.

"You want to sniff some flower on Anthalas and have the pollen turn your guts to pudding?" Yarrow asked.

"Listen, new guy, you haven't earned smart-ass remark privileges yet," Standish said. He kept rubbing his arm, then moved his hands to his shoulder and chest. Standish growled through gritted teeth. "I took a shower, but it still itches!"

"Great, Standish, the less we know about your hygiene issues the better off we all are." Torni turned to a control panel next to the bio-mech scanner and tapped in her access code. "Let's get a fresh suit out of storage."

"What? Why?" Standish asked. "We're all fitted to our armor and ready to go."

"Lieutenant Hale says we've got a civilian specialist coming with us and she'll need armor," Torni said. "She's on her way."

"Remember the last time we had to escort some specialist around the battlefield?" Standish asked. "Stacey Ibarra, granddaughter to the great Marc Ibarra, led us straight into a hornets' nest of Xaros—twice—and we lost good Marines."

"And because of her, Standish, we beat the Xaros," Torni said.

"I know. I know. But running around up to my neck in murder droids with space Jesus-ette is beyond my comfort level," Standish said.

"Don't." Torni pointed a finger at Standish. "Don't use His name in vain or make that comparison ever again. It isn't true and you know it."

"Sorry, Sergeant," Standish said. "Bunch of people from that new Church of the Rapture keep pestering me with e-mails, asking me to come testify to what I saw when Stacey vanished into that portal when we were on the Crucible."

"I get them too. Just block them and make your life easier," Torni said. She tapped a command into the control panel. Against the far wall, a number lit up on a storage unit.

"Come on, new guy," Standish said to Yarrow, "we're on heavy-lifting duty." The two Marines went to the storage unit and pulled out a large cube with carry handles on both sides.

"Wow, you guys were there for everything," Yarrow said as he and Standish carried the cube back to the bio-mech station. "You saw the first Xaros on Earth. You got that probe out of Euskal Tower. Assaulted the Crucible. Got to see Stacey Ibarra go to Bastion as humanity's representative. I spent the entire battle deep inside the *Munich*, taking care of civilians. Missed the whole thing."

"You got lucky, kid. Do I need to reiterate the whole horror and imminent death aspect to the tale?" Standish asked.

"No, Lance Corporal, I got that. Why do you think I volunteered to join Lieutenant Hale's squad? You're in the middle of everything. This is the biggest thing to ever happen to the human race. I don't want to be on the sidelines."

"Set this damn thing down next to the reader," Standish said as he and Yarrow made it the last few feet and dropped the cube with a heavy thump. "Careful what you wish for, new guy. All that stuff sounds like fun until you're the one in the middle of it."

"So what did happen on the Crucible?" Orozco asked. He unlatched the cube and inventoried the contents against a checklist on the underside of the lid. "Everything I've heard is secondhand. The Church of the Rapture has a pretty detailed account."

"The only reason they have that is because *someone* blabbed about the whole thing as soon as we got back to the *Breitenfeld*," Torni said, looking at Standish.

"What? Someone asked me what happened … and she was hot. How was I supposed to know Stacey would become the center of some kind of religious movement?" Standish said.

"If you'd ever go to church you might gain a better appreciation for others' beliefs," Torni said.

"Religious events are supposed to happen to other people—not to me—and they were supposed to happen a long, long time ago," Standish said. "I don't want the Gospel of Standish to be part of some holy catechism, especially not if people take my little joke of a religious preference seriously."

"On no," Torni said, rubbing her temples. "Please tell me you're not still talking to Steuben about that."

"He's curious, and the Church of the Flying Spaghetti Monster is, technically, a recognized religion by the Atlantic Union. I'm not sure Karigole have a sense of irony, or humor. … Yeah, maybe I should come clean with him."

"Fresh meat!" Bailey said as she came through the open hatch. Lowenn was right behind her.

"All right, Marines," Torni said. "Standard for fitting a fresh suit to its wearer is ten minutes. Let's get started. Ma'am, please step up on the sensor platform."

Lowenn smiled nervously and did as instructed.

"Hi, everyone. I'm Helena Lowenn. Did Ken tell you why I'm here?" Lowenn asked.

"Ken?" Orozco looked at Torni in confusion.

"The lieutenant," Torni said. "Ma'am, please raise your arms to the side and hold very still."

"You don't have to call me 'ma'am.' Helena is fine." Lowenn held her arms up and a bar rose out of the sensor panel beneath her. The bar ran up and around her body, scanning her with a thin green line of light.

"Hold your breath … done." Torni nodded at the control panel. "OK, need you to get your body glove on."

Standish took a vacuum-sealed packet from the cube. "Let me get you out of your clothes."

Bailey punched Standish on the shoulder.

"By that, I mean, Corporal Bailey will escort

you to the changing room," Standish said, handing the package to Bailey.

Bailey motioned to a door at the end of the room with a nod of her head and took Lowenn away.

"What do you think?" Orozco asked.

"I've got her file here," Torni said. "She's got some training … more orbital jumps than everyone but you, Orozco. So she's got more tactical acumen than Stacey, which isn't saying much."

"No combat experience? That's not good," Orozco said.

"I don't have any either, Sergeant," Yarrow piped up.

"Don't worry about it, new guy," Standish said to the young medic. "I'm sure you'll do just fine on a planet occupied by the Xaros."

"This mission is sneak and peak, not run and gun," Torni said. "I'm more worried about Standish's mouth giving us away than Lowenn's ability to shoot straight."

"You don't think we'll have any contact?" Yarrow asked.

"Once we're on Anthalas," Orozco said, "we'll be hours from extraction or support. We tangle with any Xaros and it'll be a long time before the cavalry shows up. Let's hope we come back with clean weapons and no stories to tell."

"She's ready," Bailey called out. Lowenn, wearing a skin-tight space suit, tried to tie her long auburn hair up into a bun as she and Bailey returned to the rest of the Marines.

"Now I know why you ladies all have such short hair," Lowenn said.

"We'll get you an auto net. It pulls it in tight enough to fit the emergency hoods and your helmet," Torni said.

"Or," Bailey said, tapping a combat knife sheathed on her belt, "we can do a field-expedient solution right here and now."

"No. That's just … no," Lowenn said politely.

"You're wearing an Ibarra Corp

72

environmental layer," Torni said. "It's rated for up to nine hours of hard vacuum. After that you'll start taking radiation—how much depends on your exposure to direct sunlight and how long past your pumpkin time you've been out there."

"'Pumpkin time'?"

"Sorry, Marine-speak for when your radiation protection will start to fail. Let's get you in your muscle suit," Torni said.

Orozco took out a black pair of pants covered by bands of fiber running over the thighs and down to the ankles. He held the pants open and helped Lowenn step into them. Orozco clicked a button on the waist twice and the pants tightened around the waist. A long-sleeved shirt with the same bands went over Lowenn's head. Orozco and Bailey attached the top and bottom to each other while the pieces jerked Lowenn around slightly.

"I feel like I'm a little girl getting dressed by my mother," Lowenn said.

"Step back up on the scanner. We'll get it fitted correctly," Torni said. "The pseudo-muscle layer will augment your strength, pulling with you. It will reduce the fatigue from wearing armor, but it won't carry everything for you. Hold still."

"This is so neat. I saw a demonstration at—" Lowenn gasped and sounded as if she was being strangled as the pseudo-muscle layer squeezed her like a python around its prey. "Tight, too tight."

The suit relaxed and Lowenn looked down at her body, frowning.

"I don't feel like I'm wearing it anymore," the anthropologist said.

"That means it's working as intended," Torni said. "Hop down and we'll get you in armor."

"How strong does this make me?" Lowenn asked.

"*You* won't be any stronger than normal, beyond being able to carry everything we put on you and maybe drag a fully armored Marine. Your suit will have its settings reduced until you've been through the ninety-hour course to learn how to use your suit correctly. For now, that suit just makes you more or less bulletproof," Torni said.

She looked at Yarrow. "OK, new guy, you're on the clock. Get her armored up. Ready? Mark!"

Yarrow hefted a thigh plate from the cube and placed it against Lowenn's leg. It tightened against her quadriceps of its own accord as Yarrow attached wires and tightened straps behind her leg.

"This is the new Mark III armor," Torni said, "enhanced with graphene temperature diffusion that, in the lab, provides some protection against the Xaros heat lasers. Still, try not to get shot. There's no protection from their disintegration beams. You'll notice several knots around your shoulder, elbow, hip and knee joints. Those are tourniquet pulls. Don't play with them. You might accidently activate the tourniquet lines and cut off all blood flow to everything past it."

Armor plates went against her legs, chest, back, shoulders and along her arms. Lowenn felt the weight of each piece as it was attached, then her pseudo-muscle layer rebalanced the load and most of the weight fell away.

"Done!" Yarrow said. He backed away from Lowenn, holding his hands up by his shoulders.

"Nine minutes and nineteen seconds," Torni said. "Let's inspect."

Torni reached under deltoid armor and pulled out a loose connection. "You didn't use the safety snaps on the number six armor point. Drop and give me fifty, Yarrow."

The medic groaned and started doing push-ups.

"Air line under spine plate twelve impinged," Orozco said from behind Lowenn. "Another fifty. Beat your face."

"Yes, Sergeant!" Yarrow's pace increased.

The two non-commissioned officers found four more errors in Yarrow's work, adding to his count with each one.

"Sloppy, Yarrow," Torni said with a shake of her head.

"Damn, new guy, you're going to be down there so long *I'm* going to get tired," Standish said.

Yarrow bent at the waist and took a quick

breath to rest, then went back to doing push-ups.

"Ms. Lowenn," Torni said to her, "this is important. There's an emergency release strap beneath your breastplate. Reach under there and find it."

Lowenn did as requested. "Got it," she said. "Why would I need an emergency release?"

"If you're drowning, or on fire, you'll want to shed the plates. You'll still have problems, but carrying around the extra weight won't be one of them. Pull the release, please." Torni stepped back.

Lowenn yanked the release and her armor shed off, hitting the deck with the clang of church bells.

"When do I get the grav boots?" she asked.

"After your armor is on properly," Torni said. "Bailey, you're up. Ready … mark!"

****

Captain Valdar's ready room was nothing like the rest of the *Breitenfeld*. Valdar allowed his chief petty officers full reign to run the ship while he led it, and the chiefs kept their sections clean and orderly. The ready room was a mess of dirty overalls, an unkempt bed, loose Ubis and data slates that would have brought down the wrath of any noncommissioned officer on a sailor or Marine that let their personal standards slip to such a degree.

Valdar sat on his bunk, looking at the collage of photos he'd tacked to the wall. Pictures of him with his wife and sons: them at a Christmas party, at a family reunion on the coast of Maine, school photos of his boys in ascending grade order, at his last promotion ceremony. In the middle of the photos, lying on a shelf, was a plaster of Paris slate with handprints from his wife and boys, the words "Stay safe, Daddy!" inscribed by toothpick before the molding set.

He spent what little free time he had staring at the photos, holding the plaster his family had given to him right before his carrier battle group deployed to the South Pacific many years ago.

Valdar touched a picture of David, his oldest son, trying to imagine what he'd look like if he were alive today.

The door chimed.

Valdar scowled at the bulkhead. He'd left his executive officer with instructions that he not be disturbed for a few hours. Unless there was a fleet of drones cresting around the moon, whoever was disturbing him would regret it.

Valdar stood up and zipped his overalls shut, hiding a filthy white undershirt beneath it. He slapped the panel beside the door and readied a tirade.

Hale was in the doorway, holding two covered trays of food.

"Uncle Isaac," Hale said. Most of the crew didn't know that Valdar was Hale's godfather, or that Hale and his brother grew up close to the captain and his sons. Hale had tried to keep calling the captain by his rank in private, but Valdar had insisted Hale use the name he'd used since he learned how to talk.

"Ken," Valdar said, glancing over his shoulder at the mess behind him, "now's not a good time."

"Looks like it's time you ate. I've got the finest chicken cordon bleu hockey pucks the ship's food processors can manage." Hale poked the edge of a carton against Valdar's chest. Steam rose around the edges and Valdar's stomach growled.

He took a carton and let Hale in.

"Wow, sir, is this battle damage?" Hale said as he looked around the room for a clean place to sit.

"I have the time to get this ship ready for battle or I can square away my laundry." Valdar ran an arm along the edge of his bed and swept clothes and blankets to the floor. He sat at his desk and popped open the carton. The breaded lump of chicken with rubbery-looking rice and vegetables smelled better than they looked.

"You look like hell, Uncle Isaac," Hale said.

Valdar spooned a mouthful of rice into his mouth and choked it down.

"I've had my ship in dry dock since they were built on Titan station, repaired battle damage to twelve decks and replaced almost two thirds of my crew thanks to casualties and the brass shuffling every last crew in the fleet. I've got new alien tech in my engine room and an alien on my bridge crew as an 'advisor.' So what if I don't shave twice a day?" Valdar poked at the chicken with a plastic knife and shoved the whole tray toward the garbage can at the side of his desk.

Hale snapped a hand out and stopped the carton before it could go over the edge.

"Eat. You don't have to like it. Remember when my mom would try to make apple pie? You asked for seconds every time and I know how awful that tasted."

Valdar grunted. "I didn't want to hurt her feelings." He choked down a lump of chicken and wiped his mouth on his sleeve.

"I heard you went to your parent's house in Maricopa," Valdar said. "You and your brother."

"We did. Got in just before the demolition crews did." Hale rubbed the back of his knuckles against the class ring attached to his dog tags. He and Jared had taken two artifacts from the rotting house where their parents died during the invasion: the class ring and a pair of brass spurs, mementos of their grandfather who'd served in the military at the turn of the twenty-first century.

"At least you had that," Valdar said between bites. "Xaros wiped the entire eastern seaboard clean. All I've got …." He tilted his head to the shrine against the wall.

"Who're you talking to?" Hale asked. "Chaplain Krohe? Another ship captain?"

Valdar shook his head. "No time."

"You need someone, Uncle Isaac. You keep holding all this in and it'll eat you alive," Hale said.

Valdar crossed his arms over his chest and lowered his head.

"I never called them," Valdar said. "I was going to. Soon as I got on board I'd open a channel, tell them I'd be back when they found another captain for this ship. That was the deal I made with Garret. Get the ship to Saturn then I'd be back in no time." He sniffed and wiped a sleeve across an eye.

"Haiden, he understood. Said he wanted a rock from the rings. David, he wouldn't speak to me. Didn't say goodbye at the space port. I didn't hold it against him, I've been in and out of their lives since they were born. I was supposed to stay dirt side for a couple years straight, be there to get them both through high school and see them off to college.

"Garret put the ship on commo blackout before I could call them. Then the Chinese attacked and this ship and the rest of the fleet .... They must have thought I didn't care enough to call them."

"I saw you with your boys when we were growing up," Hale said. "They knew you loved them. I don't know if Haiden ever told you, but he used to bug my father to tell the story how you rescued him and my mother from Okinawa, got them out before the Chinese overran the island. Haiden said he was always happy when you were deployed because you were out there saving people. You were his hero."

"And in the end I couldn't save any of them," Valdar said.

"We didn't have a chance or a choice. The *Breitenfeld* needs you now, Uncle Isaac. It needs you healthy, focused. You can at least finish your dinner every once in a while."

"Ugh," Valdar said, poking through the carton. "If this ship had chefs I'd fire them."

"Someone opened a Thai place in Phoenix. We'll go when we get back, deal?"

"Deal. Now let me get back to a mountain of paperwork the bureau of personnel insists must be completed before I take this ship to the far ends of the galaxy." He picked up a data slate and pressed his thumb against the screen to sign a document.

"I may or may not have your orderlies on payroll to know how much food you throw away. Don't make me come back here," Hale said.

"Shoo, kid, you bother me." Valdar waved Hale toward the hatch with a flick of his wrist.

Hale gave a cursory salute and let himself out.

He turned down a passageway and found Commander Ericsson, the ship's second in command, and Lieutenant Commander Utrecht, the gunnery officer, waiting for him.

"Well?" Ericsson asked.

"He's eating, at least," Hale said.

"He going to make it through this mission?" asked Utrecht, a square-jawed man with a salt-and-pepper buzz cut over his head.

"Captain Isaac Valdar is one of the best officers in the fleet. He'll knuckle down once we're underway … sir," Hale said to Utrecht.

"I know you two are close, but if he snaps, we have to do what's best for the ship and the mission," Utrecht said.

"Planning mutiny already?" Hale asked.

"It's not mutiny when it's a mental health issue," Utrecht shot back.

"Lieutenant Hale," Ericsson said. "I was on the bridge with Valdar at the Crucible. He's got my respect and my trust, but he's had a rough time. We may need you again if he starts to waiver."

"No problem, ma'am. Call if you need me." Hale glared at Utrecht and left.

CHAPTER 4

The control room on the Crucible wasn't
designed for human beings. There were no chairs
for workstations set at almost shoulder level for the
average person. The basalt-like material rising from
the floor glistened with golden motes of light, and
the effect couldn't be traced to any power source or
explained by engineers and physicists that had
visited and examined the station.

Touch screens, holo projectors and raised
platforms—all aftermarket modifications installed
after the last human fleet seized the Crucible in
battle over the dwarf planet Ceres—made the
control room useable. Fleet command had tried to

use the Crucible as a base of operations while Titan station was under construction, but sailors and Marines on the alien station reported strange noises and odd flashes of light and claimed the station would rearrange itself without warning or explanation.

The resident master of the Crucible blamed the alien design, at odds with what the human mind could process. Admiral Garret removed his crew as soon as he could, and no one had clamored to return to the station once they'd left.

From its home in a plinth centered in the control room, the silver needle of light calling itself Marc Ibarra rose into the air. A doorway at the top of a set of too steep stairs didn't open so much as it peeled aside. Three people came down the steps: Admiral Garret; Theo Lawrence, the nominal head of what remained of the Ibarra Corporation; and a woman, gray hair loose against her shoulders. Tatiana Caruthers earned an invitation to this meeting by dint of being the elected mayor of Phoenix. Together, they were the three most powerful people on Earth.

"Garret, Lawrence and Ms. Caruthers, how nice to see you all here for the launch," Ibarra said. A thin sliver of light floated from the plinth and morphed into the shape of Marc Ibarra, younger-looking than when he'd imprinted his mind and memories into the probe on the eve of the Xaros invasion.

"Cut the crap, Ibarra," Garret said. "We could have watched the jump just fine from Titan station without having to wander around this godforsaken haunted house. What do you want from us?"

"So, no tea?" Ibarra asked. He called up a hologram of the Crucible and the approaching *Breitenfeld* with a thought.

"Mr. Ibarra, we agreed to meet here on council business," Lawrence said. "I take it that's why you summoned us."

"Yes, our little council: me, the admiral, the industrialist and the manager." Ibarra directed the last word at Caruthers. "We're a sitcom at the end of the world."

"Ibarra," Garret grumbled.

"Fine!" Ibarra waved a hand in the air. "Fine, no theatrics, no pleasantries. Just business, business, business with you all. I should know better. I hired each one of you."

"You aren't the Marc Ibarra we knew," Caruthers said. "You're some kind of program. Something alien."

Ibarra tapped at the side of his holographic head. "Everything Ibarra ever was, ever thought, is in here. Call me a ghost if you like. Calling me a program makes me feel like a virtual assistant on your Ubis. Can your VA open wormholes to different stars? No? Didn't think so."

Ibarra called up holo screens around the room, each showing population projections, fleet construction schedules, food yield rates from the automated farms around Phoenix. He raised his arms like a circus barker and the holo of the Crucible morphed into a star field.

"May I present to you ... our situation? A

little over 450,000 human beings remain on and around the planet Earth. We'll chop that number down by 700 once the *Breitenfeld* leaves us, hopefully to return soon. The nearest Xaros presence is at Barnard's star, six light-years away. With the time it takes a light-speed message to reach the star and the recorded Xaros speed between solar systems, we expect the next invasion force to reach us in exactly fourteen years and twenty-seven days."

"I already have enough reasons to drink, Ibarra. What's your point?" Garret said.

The star field changed to show a Xaros drone with a graph next to it, one with a line growing higher exponentially.

"If the Xaros follow the model, and they always do, they will arrive with a force of one hundred million drones. Not as many as they showed up with originally, but more than enough to overmatch our remaining fleet." A bar graph showing the current number of capital ships and a projected number of hulls in service by the Xaros arrival popped up on the holo.

"If," Ibarra said, "if we do nothing else but focus all our efforts on building defenses and the fleet until the moment the Xaros return, we have a 0.002 chance of survival."

"Why don't we use a skip drive again?" Caruthers asked. "Let them come, find nothing and think we ran off into the void."

"They may be drones, but they aren't stupid," Ibarra said. "They're wise to that trick now. Don't think we can fool them twice. A simple tachyon pulse through the system would disrupt the field and dump anything out of stasis. Besides, we're plum out of quadrium for the skip drives, and for the Q-shells."

"If the *Breitenfeld* succeeds, won't we be able to make all the Q-shells we need from Omnium?" Lawrence asked.

"That's the plan," Ibarra said. "Our chance of survival rises to just over a whole percent if we have Q-shells."

"Then why are we risking the ship and her

crew for something so negligible?" Garret asked with a sigh.

"What if our fleet had …," the bar graphs on the fleet projection rose dramatically, "this many ships?"

"Impossible," Caruthers said. "There are only so many people left on Earth. Even if every child alive today was put into the fleet, we can't crew a fleet that large. It takes forty weeks to gestate a baby, Mr. Ibarra. Any child born today wouldn't be old enough to be of any use as a sailor by the time the Xaros arrive. The only way to control that many ships is with automation and computer assistance. The Xaros would hack it in an instant."

"Correct!" Ibarra said. "Ms. Doom and Gloom gets the prize. Now, what if I told you there was a way to crew a fleet, and have pilots for wings of fighters, and find men and women for divisions of Marines and battalions of armor by the time the Xaros arrive?"

"I'd say you've been inside that needle for

too long," Garret said.

"Different discussion. No, let me show you a little something." Ibarra clapped his holographic hands together, but there was no sound. He tried again, and his hands passed through each other. "There goes my dramatic moment."

He switched to a singsong voice. "Oh, Mr. Thorsson?"

The holo projection switched to show a tall, Nordic man with blond hair and a full beard. Behind him were rows and rows of cylindrical tanks.

"Sir," Thorsson said. He tilted his head to the side to look around Ibarra and he glanced over his shoulder at the tanks behind him. Thorsson adjusted the camera to remove the tanks from view.

"Don't be shy, Thorsson," Ibarra said. "It's time everyone knew about our little experiment." Ibarra turned his attention back to his guests. "Mr. Thorsson is aboard the *Lehi*, one of my fleet's science vessels. But before I bury the lede ...."

Ibarra raised a hand to the air, and one of the displays floating over a workstation flipped to show a dark-skinned man in a naval uniform talking to a group of sailors standing in a scrub desert.

"This is Commander Clive Randall. He's heading up the effort to salvage what remains of the *Midway* that crashed just south of Phoenix. He's an expert mechanical engineer with several doctorates' worth of knowledge and decades of relevant experience in his head."

"I know him," Garret said. "I'm the one that gave him that mission."

"But you didn't know him before my fleet sidestepped the Xaros invasion, and that's because Commander Clive Randall was born one month ago." Ibarra's fingers wiggled in the air and a picture of Randall floating in a liquid-filled tank took the place of the video. Randall, wearing silvery undergarments, had hoses over his nose and mouth. Wires and tubes ran into a cap covering his skull.

"A clone?" Caruthers asked, her face pale. "God damn you, Ibarra, that's been forbidden for decades."

"Clones? No, don't be so small-minded,"

Ibarra said. "Clones aren't our answer. They'd be a disaster, what with DNA degradation over time, and just imagine the inbreeding disaster we'd have after a third generation of everyone having babies with their genetic brother or sister. Besides, if I grew a clone this quickly, it would be nothing but a flailing toddler once I decanted it.

"No, boys and girls, Randall is something different from a clone. He's the combination of good old-fashioned sperm and ovum collected over decades by the healthcare arm of my corporation. All stored aboard the *Lehi* and combined in artificial wombs to make a baby just as legitimate and unique as the old-fashioned method."

Caruthers backed into a workstation, her lip trembling.

"Ibarra," Garret said, "if that ... thing is really a month old, how can it know so much? When I talked to him, he remembered going to college, raising the wreck of the *Reagan* off the California coast."

"An excellent observation. Tell me, admiral,

how much data does your brain hold at this point in your life? If I could watch every second of life that you remember, how long would it take?" Ibarra smiled and jiggled his eyebrows.

"I'm not a neuroscientist," Garret said.

"A little over two petabytes, that's how much data you've got in your gray matter. Taking in the vagaries of head trauma and substance abuse, we could cull a movie from your memories that would last about nineteen years. Fascinating how three pounds of brains can hold so much. But this is the twenty-first century. I can store all that data on a chip the size of a fingernail. And I did!"

Screens across the control room popped to life, first-person camera footage of class rooms, military training, waiting in line at the DMV and more and more facets of life, both the fantastic and mundane, appeared around the room.

"As soon as the smart phone became popular, recording every aspect of a person's life became easy. It became even easier when almost everyone in the Western world had one of my Ubis in their pocket. Hundreds of millions of people gave me almost their entire life story—not with their knowledge or consent, but that hardly matters now. I used that data to create virtual lives inside quantum computers. I can procedurally generate a person's entire life, all their memories and skills I need them to have, and upload it to a natural body flash grown in a tube. Not one identical by genome or memory to another.

"In six months I can have an entirely new crew for the *Midway*, all with the necessary and unique training for every sailor in their heads. They'll all remember growing up in the Atlantic Union and their lives before the Xaros invasion, and they'll remember fighting to take back the Earth." Ibarra tried to snap his fingers, uselessly.

"Ibarra, you can't play God like this," Caruthers said. "These aren't real people. We can't just let them … mingle with us."

"Someone has to play God, my dear," Ibarra said. "I set humanity down a very narrow path to survival the night I met this probe in the desert. All we have left are the embers of what we once were. This is how we rekindle the fire. This is how we beat the Xaros when they return. A fleet to match their swarm full of men and women no less human than you are."

"They don't have souls," Caruthers said. "They're procedurally generated abominations. If we let these things loose, there won't be any true humans left within a few generations."

"Why don't we leave the theistic discussions to the clergy, yeah?" Ibarra said to her.

Lawrence cleared his throat. "Morality and ethics aside, how are we supposed to incorporate these kinds of numbers? There are only so many humans left, and we don't all know each other. If we reshuffle the personnel on ships and in departments, we could infiltrate a couple of these procedurally generated people—"

"They're not people!" Caruthers shouted.

"Shut up, Tatiana," Lawrence snapped at her. "To get the force numbers you want, people will notice."

"For once in my life, I'll advocate complete honesty. Tell everyone what's happened. If I did my job right, no one will know if they're an actual survivor from Earth or grown in a vat," Ibarra said.

"There will be riots. We can't expect people to just accept these things," Caruthers said.

"How long?" Garret asked.

"Finally, a pragmatic question," Ibarra said. "There are one hundred and thirty-seven tubes on the *Lehi*. Each tube can produce a fully trained man or woman in nine days. There's an expansion facility under construction in Hawaii. The quantum computer banks are the only limiting factor for now. Once we ramp up, we'll cross the statistical threshold for surviving the Xaros fleet in ten years, so we'll have a few years to spare."

"You aren't considering this, are you?" Caruthers asked Garret.

"Using these procedurally generated— proccies, from now on they're proccies. Using proccies makes my skin crawl, but I've been through the simulations. We could barely beat a thousand drones right now, and we won't be much stronger when a hundred times that get here in a few years," Garret said.

"And you?" she asked Lawrence.

"Incorporating them will require some finesse. We'll need a plan, a cover story of some kind," Lawrence said. "Have you even done a study on their long-term viability and stability?"

"There were a few issues with the initial batch, but the second is doing well under field testing," Ibarra said. "Earth's population grew by seventy-five people in the last two weeks, and no one even noticed."

"This is—I can't even ...." Caruthers stalked off and slapped her palm against the door until Ibarra opened it for her.

"She'll be a problem," Ibarra said. "I knew it was a mistake to hire her."

"Continue work on the Hawaii facility," Garret said. "We'll work on Caruthers, at least keep her quiet until the deployment is so far along that it can't be stopped. And I want a list of your ... test subjects."

"Ah, ah, ah," Ibarra said, waving a finger at him. "Can't have you poking around my double-blind experiment. Let's see if any come to your attention as proccies. Validate my hypothesis that they're indistinguishable from any true-born humans."

"Marc," Lawrence said, "could you bring someone back? Load a record of experiences into a new body?"

"No," Ibarra's hologram flickered, "the body grows along with the mind as it's created. Now shall we watch the *Breitenfeld* make the maiden voyage through our jerry-rigged wormhole lens?"

****

Ibarra, Lawrence and Garret watched the hologram of the *Breitenfeld* approaching the gaping center of the Crucible. The gigantic interconnected thorns of the Crucible morphed and slid against each other, twisting gravity fields in the center of the station's wreath. While the Crucible writhed against itself, not even the slightest vibration disturbed the control room.

+You lied to them,+ the probe said to Ibarra, the words coming to Ibarra's consciousness like a whisper from darkness.

Why aren't you concentrating on getting that ship to Anthalas? Ibarra sent back to the probe, their conversation hidden from Lawrence and Garrett.

+Conversing with you requires a minimal amount of processing power. Are you evading my observation because of … guilt? You are free of your body's hormonal restrictions and evolutionary conditioning. I don't understand why you continue to lie.+

Of course I lied to them. I've been lying to them for years, kind of hard to stop now.

+Why? We could bring some humans back. They won't be perfect but they will meet all expectations.+

You don't understand humans, Jimmy. Hope

can pull us through the worst things imaginable, but it can destroy us too. If they believe, true or not, that I could bring a revenant of their loved ones back, everything will spin out of control. We won't have the fleet we'll need to beat the Xaros—we'll have another planet full of victims.

+Hope. Grief. I don't understand why you biologics remain encumbered with such notions.+

We can't all be sentient programs. This is why you keep my mind locked inside you, to keep the plan going, the long game.

+So why did you recreate Martel? Which spectrum of your retained emotions led to that decision?+

Martel has a special set of skills and divorced herself from emotions long before I recruited her. The decision was pragmatic, not emotional.

+Deception detected. You had a history of physiological reactions to her presence noted at the following dates and times. Number one—+

Shut up, Jimmy. Just be glad we have

Martel. We'll need her soon if we can't get
Caruthers to see the light.

A shimmering field materialized over the empty space within the Crucible, a riot of colored static like a dead TV channel from Ibarra's youth. The *Breitenfeld* passed into the field and hung motionless for a moment, then shrank into nothing. The field dissolved and the Crucible stopped moving.

"Gentlemen, the die has been cast," Ibarra said.

CHAPTER 5

The *Breitenfeld*'s bridge was eerily silent. Crewmen wearing void helmets and strapped into their workstations looked around, as if they just heard a strange sound.

Sitting in the captain's chair, Valdar slowly opened a single eye and kept the other squeezed shut. He looked around, then tapped his helmet.

"Was that it?" he asked.

"That wasn't so bad," Ericsson said from her perch by the tactical plot.

"Astrogation," Valdar said to the ensign to his right, "are we where we're supposed to be?"

"I've got readings from six different pulsars

… and visible constellations match with what the Ibarra probe predicted. We're in the Anthalas system, sir," the ensign said. Camera feeds from around the ship fed into the astrogation pod. The ensign adjusted angles with a small joystick and tapped a keyboard to take screenshots of the star field around them.

"Any sign of Xaros?" Valdar asked.

"Negative, sir. Spotters on all decks report clear skies," Ericsson said. "Shall we launch the fighters we have on standby?"

"Not yet. Lower blast shields. Let's see what we're dealing with," Valdar said.

Heavy graphene-reinforced armor plates slid from the windows around the bridge and wan red light flooded in, strong enough that Valdar had to throw a hand up in front of his face. He flicked a dial on the control panel attached to an armrest and the window opacity adjusted to block out the offending light.

"Wow," someone said.

A ruddy star burned in space, dark spots

dotting its surface like scabbed-over wounds. For the first time, humans bathed in the light of an alien star.

The star was much older than the sun, larger and cooler as it neared the end of its life. There were only a few hundred million years left before the star went supernova or collapsed into a black hole.

"Lafayette," Valdar said to the Karigole aside the engineering station. The alien wore only a helmet over his head; the rest of his biomechanical body didn't need the protection of a space suit. "What's the status on the ZPE drive?"

"Fifteen percent and charging. We can transit back to Earth in ... thirty-five hours. At the soonest. The gravity wormhole will be stable for the next four days and should remain undetectable to the Xaros until we're ready to leave," Lafayette said.

"And if they detect it before then?" Valdar asked.

"It will be a very long thirty-five hours,"

Lafayette said.

"I've got Anthalas, sir," the astrogation ensign said. "Forty-three mark negative twelve from the prow."

"Show me," Valdar said. He pulled a flat screen up from the side of his chair and swung it flat over his lap. On the screen was a picture of Anthalas surrounded by artificial rings of brass-like metal around its equator, the Xaros rig used to move celestial bodies. A small moon the color of smeared blood orbited the planet.

"It's … a bit farther than we'd projected," the ensign said. "Transit will take twelve hours with grav drives. If we go full burn, then we can be there in less than an hour."

Valdar ran though time tables in his head. As the captain, he was responsible for the success or failure of this mission, but there were levels of risk he wouldn't accept.

"Set course under grav drive. Set us in at a Lagrange point with the moon between us and the planet. No need to risk a drone catching a glance of us if we can help it," Valdar said.

"Sir," Commander Utrecht said, "take a look. Forward flak cannons saw it first."

A blurry image of a crown of thorns over Anthalas' southern pole popped on Valdar's screen. Another Crucible jump gate.

"Lafayette, what does this mean?" Valdar asked.

"Curious, I had no idea the Xaros had built such a facility in this system," Lafayette said.

"Answer the question."

Lafayette shuffled his hands around. "I don't know. We've never seen the Crucibles in use before. I have no idea how long it would take for the gate to become active, or how long it might take to bring in reinforcements."

"Let's get in and out of here without poking that hornet nest," Valdar said. He flipped a cover off a button on his control panel and held the bottom down with his thumb.

"Now hear this. Now hear this," echoed through the ship.

"*Breitenfeld*, this is your captain. The ship is in the Anthalas system and we are underway to take up orbit around the planet's moon. We will remain under silent running conditions until further notice. Ground insertion will commence once IR buoys are in place. Remain alert and ready. *Gott mit uns*." Valdar ended his address with the ship's motto.

"Astrogation," Valdar said to the ensign, who had a pile of slide rules and a large tablet out on his workstation. The ensign looked up at the captain, sweat on the young officer's face. "You can do the Lagrange point calculations without the computer," Valdar stated.

"Yes, sir, of course. It's just manual celestial mechanics of an unexplored solar system. Give me an hour," the ensign said. He squinted at the equations on his tablet, grimaced, and then erased something.

"I have full faith in your abilities," Valdar said quietly. His last astrogation officer, Stacey Ibarra, could do the equations in her head. He'd been spoiled by such a talented officer. Yet, from everything that happened on Earth and on the Crucible, there'd been much more to her than met the eye.

"Silent running, everyone," Ericsson said to the bridge. "One wrong electromagnetic fart and we'll be up to our neck in Xaros. Think quietly, just to be careful."

****

Bastion, as Stacy Ibarra had decided to call the space station where she represented the human race to the amalgam of sentient species allied to fight the Xaros, did its best to make her feel comfortable. The temperature and humidity of her quarters were always perfect, like she was in a Hawaiian bungalow and not crammed deep within an alien fortress that fed her recycled air. The food was whatever she desired, but no matter how much pecan and caramel ice cream she ate, she never seemed to gain any weight. Sleep came uncharacteristically easy for her, despite bouts of insomnia brought on anytime her mind caught on to some new and interesting idea. If there was one thing Bastion had to offer, it was the new and interesting.

Despite all the creature comforts, Stacey always felt ill at ease, as if something was constantly watching her beyond the edge of her vision. The harder Bastion tried to make her comfortable, the more the artificial nature of her surroundings stuck out.

Walking the hallways made it worse, always.

Stacey held a data slate against her chest as she turned down a long hallway. The slightly domed ceiling reminded her of the interior of the Crucible where a Xaros drone had killed a Marine right in front of her and had almost torn her apart to get at the alien probe embedded within her hand. The lighting was natural, as if she was walking around her alma mater at the California Institute of Technology, which was not the truth. She should have seen the planet Bastion orbited, an enormous gas giant with an atmosphere so active it made

Jupiter's look like drying paint in comparison, out of every window on this side of the station.

"Bastion, set windows to true view," she said. The station complied and the gas giant appeared.

The station always did exactly as she asked, even changing its name from Rendezvous to Bastion at her request. After a few days on the station and learning its purpose, the new name seemed more fitting.

Another ambassador came down the hallway, and it looked like a perfectly normal human being. He was in his mid-thirties, losing some hair and had a slight paunch. The ambassador nodded and smiled to Stacey as they passed by.

What the ambassador truly looked like, Stacey had no idea. She could have stopped and chatted with him, and Bastion would have translated her image and words to perfectly convey what she said to the alien in terms and language it could understand. Thanks to Bastion's conversion field, that's how it was here: every other ambassador looked like a human to Stacey. And every other ambassador saw her as one of its own species.

She'd made the mistake of disabling the conversion field once and decided to walk around and see the ambassadors as they really were. The first one she saw looked like an eight-armed slug with a fanged maw and four eyes attached to stalks. She managed to hold her composure, then she turned a corner and nearly ran into a floating alien that was a gaping skull held aloft by writhing tentacles.

She'd screamed. She'd ran. She screamed louder when the skull chased after her, asking in a very human and caring voice what the matter was. She shuddered from the memory, as much out of embarrassment as fear.

Thankfully, there were several humanoid species on Bastion, and she was going to visit one now.

She knocked on the door, a slightly domed impression against a beige wall, and waited.

It slid aside without a sound, revealing

absolute darkness within.

"Pa'lon? You in there?" Stacey asked.

"Come in. I have a holo running," a man's voice answered.

Stacey stepped into his room, and the door slid shut behind her. She was in total darkness for a moment, then the floor fell away. She found herself surrounded by stars and nothing else. She froze, too shocked to move a muscle. She could still feel a floor beneath her feat, but other than that she was standing in deep, dark space.

"Pa'lon! Damn you, give me a floor!" Stacey shrieked.

"Oh, my apologies." A walkway appeared beneath her feet and led toward semicircle of waist-high control stations. A Nordic-looking man smiled to her and waved her over. "I thought you were a spacer, Stacey. Why the panic?"

"Space is just fine when I'm in a suit or surrounded by a giant cozy pressurized ship." She held her hands out for balance as she took small steps toward the control stations. She glanced over the edge of the walkway and saw that it was a very long way down. Her mind knew the reality of her situation—she was in her friend's quarters surrounded by a very safe space station—but her eyes saw something very different and for now her senses were overriding what her brain knew to be true.

She jumped the last two feet and let out a sigh of relief.

"It is nice to see you again," Pa'lon said.

"Same, I figured I'd come say hi as you're about to portal home for a little bit, right?"

"That's right. Bastion came up with a solution to an agricultural issue that should boost food production by nine percent. The planet we're on isn't friendly to agriculture from my home world, but a slight tweak to a protein combination will act as a natural insecticide to a species of mites," he said.

"Oh boy … mites." Stacey raised her eyebrows and nodded slowly.

"Not everything is a life-or-death struggle

against the Xaros, young Miss Ibarra."

"For me it is," she said.

"I admire your conviction. I was born in a colony ship long after the Xaros took my home world. I was fortunate enough not to see the devastation firsthand," Pa'lon said. "Perhaps that's why I like your passion."

"Right, lucky you. What are you doing and why is your conversion field up? I thought we had an agreement. Bastion, drop his visual field," she said. An error buzzer sounded from the ceiling.

"Member species has requested conversion field remain in place," a modulated voice said.

"It's fine for her," Pa'lon said, tilting his chin up slightly.

The hologram over his body vanished, revealing a five-foot-tall, green-skinned Dotok. Thick black tendrils fell back from a high forehead and his mouth was a blunt beak with a point centered on a slight underbite. Despite not having a visible nose, the skin on the upper half of his face and his eyes was almost human.

"Are you shy?" Stacey asked.

"Cultural habit. We wear masks when we mingle with other groups in a political setting. Keeping the field up at all times feels appropriate," he said.

"I didn't come here for politics. Thought I might ask you a few questions about the next assembly," she said.

"Ask away." Pa'lon swiped a fingertip over a screen and the view shifted wildly, zooming in on a shattered comet, its tail stretching deep into space. Gas and dust boiled away from the giant lumps of rock that had a semi-coherent shape of a single large comet core.

"Ugh ... I'm going to be sick," Stacey said.

"Wuss," Pa'lon hit a button and they slowly moved closer to the comet.

"Did your species evolve with a cast-iron stomach? Anyway, there's a vote next assembly about contacting a species named ...." She looked at her data slate and frowned. The name was twenty letters long and contained no vowels.

"Yes, I know it," Pa'lon said.

"I'm not on the voting list, and neither are you."

"We wouldn't be. The species will encounter the Xaros in the next two hundred years, but it is on the far edge of Alliance space. There is no way Earth or my world can send aid to, or receive aid from, that world before the Xaros reach us. Even with jump engines there's no way we can interact with that species before the issue is largely moot."

"You mean the Xaros will wipe us out, or them out, before we can help each other," she said.

"Yes, we can still participate in debate, but we can't vote."

"Why?"

"It stops any ambassador from convincing others to waste resources. You vote on what you can affect, and that's all." Pa'lon twisted a dial and the approach to the comet grew faster.

"Realpolitik over interstellar distances," Stacey said.

"That doesn't mean you can't make an impassioned plea for or against a vote. I did it for your species, managed to sway a few votes toward sending the probe that your grandfather met," Pa'lon said.

"Humans thought we were alone in the galaxy for so long, that we were responsible for our destiny. Yet a committee and popular vote is what sealed our fate."

"We provided a little help. You did the rest. There are those who view the Xaros as the galaxy rebalancing itself, removing sentients who meddle with the laws of physics and destroy worlds as it suits them. But I don't care for those people," Pa'lon said.

"Then what do you believe the Xaros are?"

"If you can fight against something, it isn't fate. The Xaros aren't the same as what happened to the species we're about to see." The shattered comet grew closer and Stacey finally got a sense of scale. It wasn't a comet—it was a shattered planet.

Multihued gas mingled with evaporating ice,

creating a corona around the continent-sized chunks of rock.

"What is this?" she asked.

"An ancient recording from one of the first probes the Qa'Resh sent out. A billion or so years before this, a passing singularity upended the system's planetary orbits. This planet, about the size of your Pluto, wandered too close to a gas giant and was broken apart by gravity sheer and set on an elliptical orbit around the primary. Then … something wondrous happened."

They zoomed close to the surface of one of the larger rocks. A thick smog of gasses diffused the distant primary star into a smear across the sky.

"Life." Pa'lon pointed into the distance where three balls hopped toward them on spindly legs. "Fascinating, aren't they?"

The creatures were deep red and covered in short curly hair, each almost the size of a basketball. They hopped past the two observers, twirling and clicking at each other.

"What are they called?" Stacey asked.

"The Qa'Resh don't bother with names. These have a quantum state designation and nothing else."

"Are they talking to each other?"

"Oh yes, they were quite intelligent. Watch." Pa'lon tapped his control panel and their view shifted to the inside of a deep crater. Nests dug every few feet contained piles of eggs, hexagon patterns over the chrome shells. At the edge of the crater, the round creatures formed a tight chain, their bodies touching the creature on either side, all of them swaying from side to side.

"What is—"

"Shh!"

A sonorous trill began, joined by multi octave notes that stretched together like a symphony.

"They're singing?"

"That's right. They're welcoming their young."

Eggs cracked open and miniature, naked creatures crept out. Their tiny legs shook off fluid, then each wondered toward the edge of the crater seemingly at random.

"The hatchlings can tell which is their parent by how they sing." The alien smiled, the gesture similar to humans except that Pa'lon exposed long eyeteeth as his lips pulled apart.

"Human birth is more … scream-y and painful. So I've heard." Stacey said.

"As is Dotok." The image blurred and they were in a field of small asteroids, hordes of the creatures leaping from one asteroid to the other in a cacophony of chirps and squawks. "They had songs for phases of their home's transit around the sun. Molting, breeding, such things. They had no concept of war or even conflict."

"Are they here? On Bastion?"

"No," Pa'lon frowned. "They've been extinct for millennia."

"What happened? The Xaros?"

"No, celestial mechanics. The elliptical orbit was unstable. The same gas giant that gave birth to the world as you see it nudged it off course to send this entire ecosystem and this species into the sun. The probe that recorded this could do nothing to save them, and it didn't interact. But … they knew. As the planet broke apart even further and burned away, they all joined together and sang again, a song that the probe had never recorded before."

"You heard it?"

"No, I don't have the heart to listen to it just yet."

"Don't tell me this is the first time you've been here. Why are you doing this to yourself?"

"It helps me focus on the ultimate threat—extinction. My people were fortunate. A probe found us before we could develop radios and announce ourselves to the Xaros. We wasted a century arguing whether or not the probe was some sort of cosmic charlatan, then we listened to a species a few stars over as the Xaros came to their system and annihilated them.

"By that time, the Xaros were too close for us to build and crew a credible navy—we breed far too slowly. So we created ark fleets and ran. The first fleet was grand, dozens and dozens of ships carrying the best minds and warriors from our entire population, sent out to a world like our home. Those who weren't chosen stayed until smaller colony fleets were built and sent off to less desirable worlds. My parents were of the less desirables, and I was born in transit to Takeni.

"Takeni was the first world we settled, but the grand fleet and others haven't reached their destinations yet. Bastion needed an ambassador from us, so ... here I am. But, extinction. If we'd stayed behind, my people would have been wiped out. So we cast chance to the stars and run from system to system while the Xaros catch up, and they will eventually. There's only so much room left in the galaxy. While I may be from an insignificant world of few people and resources, it is a candle against the night that I must maintain, or all will be darkness."

Stacey reached up to touch a baby as it crawled over its parent, her hand passing through it. The baby poked at its parent's skin then scrambled aside as the parent scratched at the irritation. The baby repeated the game several times until the parent flipped over and tickled the baby until it squealed.

"Bad enough when species go extinct through no fault of their own. You ever wonder why the Xaros are doing this to us?" she asked.

"If we knew the *why*, would it do us any good?"

"Maybe we could get them to stop."

"They've overrun ninety percent of the galaxy. Never a single communication or demand. We've never even been able to examine one as they disintegrate on death or capture. For all the species who've encountered them, we can only guess what they truly want." Pa'lon ended the hologram and his Spartan quarters filled the room around them.

"Come," he said. "Let's go to the Assembly and see if we can keep another light burning."

****

Hale had to walk almost doubled over as he

made his way through the air vent. A fine layer of dust that seemed impervious to the ship's air scrubbers was caked along the walls. He made a mental note to add "cleaning the vent" to a list of approved extra-duty punishments for any of his Marines that warranted a meaningless punishment to eat up their spare time, yet one miserable enough to deter future events of whatever minor infraction led to the punishment.

But, if he wanted the air vents clean, it would mean he'd been in the air vents, and that begged questions he didn't want to answer.

The air vent rumbled as a fighter roared into space from the flight deck beneath the vent. At least he was going the right direction. There were enough jokes about lost lieutenants that he didn't need to add to the legend by accidentally falling into a maintenance bay or requiring a search party to cut him out of the air ducts.

Hale turned a corner and found the spot he was looking for—an air grate overlooking the flight deck. He also found Steuben, his legs curled beneath him, sitting by the grate. The Karigole brought the tip of a plastic wand to his mouth and exhaled blue smoke that faded into nothingness.

"Lieutenant," Steuben said.

"How ... what are you doing here?" Hale looked over his shoulder to make sure no one else was there with them.

"I wished to speak with you, but Gunney Cortaro feigned ignorance as to your location. I followed your scent and found where it was strongest. By the way, you took a wrong turn three corridors back," Steuben said.

"I have a scent?" Hale sat beside Steuben and stretched out his back.

"Chlorine. You spend a great deal of time swimming and reek of it." Steuben took another drag from the wand. Smoke wafted through a secondary set of nostrils aside the alien's nose. "The smoke detector in this section is inoperative. Most convenient."

"What've you got there?"

"*Tamkoolak* in concentrated form. I'm down

to my last juice cube, inevitable and unfortunate. I'd offer you some but it would cause a seizure and loss of bladder control."

"Thanks anyway," Hale said. He took a tube, the size and shape of cigarette, from a pocket on his shoulder and twisted a brass ring to activate it. "You must have quite a habit if that's your last cube. I figured you'd bring more with you when you arrived."

Steuben took another drag.

Hale puffed his e-cigarette and took in a deep breath of nicotine-doped water vapor. While water vapor wouldn't set off smoke detectors, some moralist in the fleet decided the devices should detect a number of airborne substances as an additional function. Nicotine was at the top of the list.

They watched as a pilot climbed up a ladder and crawled into the cockpit of an Eagle Air/Space superiority fighter. Crewmen removed battery charging lines and made last-second maintenance checks, yanking away red streamers labeled

REMOVE BEFORE FLIGHT from rocket pods and the gauss Gatling cannon slung beneath the fighter's nose.

"You come here often," Steuben said. "There are layers to the chlorine smell."

"Before every mission. It helps me clear my head to see that things can happen without me."

"Gunney Cortaro is a fine Marine. He seems fully capable in his duties."

"He is. Most of the time when I tell him something has to be done it's already finished. I'm lucky to have him."

"Yet you feel every decision is your responsibility?"

A crewman in a yellow vest stood in front of the Eagle and raised two lit wands. He led the Eagle away, directing him toward the launch ramp. Upgraded battery capacitors had replaced the treadmill system the flight deck used to have; now each plane could use its own internal power to launch from the ship.

"I am the officer in charge. Success and

failure are my responsibility."

"We are more egalitarian. When the Karigole go on a mission, each and every one of us knows the desired end state and acts in unison to achieve that goal. We have no need for officers or rank. Your system seems derived from a landowner/serf relationship remaining from your feudal period. Odd that you haven't evolved since then."

Hale chuckled. "You try to get three Marines to agree on pizza toppings, see how that works out for you. So what brings you to my once-secret hiding place?"

"There is something about this ship and crew that Lafayette and I don't understand. You are the most levelheaded human we have access to, so we decided to approach you with the question," Steuben said.

Hale tensed, his mind racing through what little he could remember from the primer on the Karigole he'd skimmed through.

"The phrase *Gott Mit Uns* appears many

times, which I understand to mean 'God is with us.' I've seen it on the ship, stenciled on armor. I see it on at least three fighters on the flight deck. Your planet's history has several wars of religion, to include a crusade in Europe that displaced the entire Islamic population from the continent. There are twelve different religious groups on the *Breitenfeld*, most denominations of Christianity with some … pagans?"

"Yes, they're a blast on shore leave."

"And one adherent to the Church of the Flying Spaghetti Monster."

Hale shook his head. "Standish."

"How is it that so many religions can accept that a singular god is with them? Do you have an overarching deity that you are invoking with *Gott mit uns*?"

"No, Steuben. For the most part, humans tolerate the presence of other religions. Things are different when one religion decides that they're the only way to believe and forces those nonbelievers around them to convert or suffer. There's a tacit agreement through the ship that the *Gott* means the god of whoever is saying *Gott mit uns* and no one tries to make it about only their god."

They sat quietly for a few seconds.

"You humans are very complex."

"Thanks, I think. You mind if I ask you a question?"

"You just did, and without offense."

"Then can I ask you another—" Hale shook his head. "I saw you with the Karigole on the flight deck before we left orbit. You all said something together."

"*Ghul'thul'thul.*"

"Yes, what does that mean?"

Steuben folded his wand in half and rolled to his feet. He stomped away, bent beneath the top of the air vent.

"Sorry," Hale said.

****

Lieutenant Durand looked through her canopy at the stars cape beyond. The Anthalas system was deep within the Milky Way, and the galactic center was three times as wide and twice as luminescent as what could been seen from Earth.

A bluish-gray nebula dominated space on the other side of her canopy, nascent stars shining from within the stellar nursery.

Years ago, she'd bought into the Atlantic Union military recruiter's promise to see the solar system. This was more than she'd ever bargained for.

"Gall, there's a comet dorsal side," Choi Ma, her wingman, called Durand by her call sign through the IR net.

Durand flipped her Eagle over, a simple maneuver in the void as small thrusters on her wingtips pulsed. In atmosphere, flipping over ran the risk of rushing blood to her head and disorienting herself to the point where she risked a sudden "air ground interface."

The comet burned silently, its tail stretching out for a million miles. Starlight coursed through it like sunlight through a dusty room stirred up after years of isolation.

"We're coming up on the dark side of the moon. IR buoy ready," heavily accented English came over the IR.

Durand sighed and rolled her fighter over again. The Condor bomber between her and Choi's fighter wagged its wings. Durand craned her neck at the moon, a heavily cratered rock as unremarkable as Mercury or Luna.

"All right. Filly, Nag, drop the buoys every five hundred kilometers as we slingshot around the moon. Stay ballistic. Keep course corrections to grav/anti-grav thrusters so we don't send out a heat plume from the engines for the Xaros to see," Durand said. The IR buoys would transmit messages from the *Breitenfeld* to the Marines once they hit the planet. Keeping the moon between the ship and the planet helped with operational security. The infrared lasers that transmitted communications were weak enough not to be detected by the Xaros, but they needed to circumvent the moon.

"Stop calling us that," said Mei Ma, the pilot

of the bomber. "Just because 'Ma' translates as 'horse' doesn't mean we want clever nicknames."

"When you defected to the Atlantic Union, you agreed to our militaries' customs and courtesies. No one gets to pick their call sign. Isn't that right, Glue?" Durand said, calling out the other Eagle pilot.

"We did not defect!" Mei shouted and Durand had to suppress a chuckle. Some buttons were just too easy not to push. The Ma cousins were captured after a Chinese attack on the *Breitenfeld* just before the fleet vanished from space and time. Durand recruited them to fly in the assault on the Crucible, and the three women had integrated into her squadron after the battle.

A stern admonition in Chinese shot over the IR from Choi.

"Buoys ready," Mei said, suddenly calm. "Drop in three … two … one. Mark."

A cylinder tumbled away from beneath her bomber and the tiny thrusters along the buoy brought it to a halt. The sides of the buoy opened and formed into a teacup shape, baffles to keep any IR radiation from spilling over when the beams hit the receiver.

Zhi Ma, sitting in the weapons control seat in the bomber, reoriented the buoy toward their course around the moon. She was the only one who had to concentrate for the rest of this mission as she had to connect each buoy to the other as their three-ship formation swung around the moon.

Durand flexed muscle groups from her toes to her face one at a time to keep sensation in her body and remain alert. It would take hours to traverse the moon, hours exposed to any Xaros on the side of the moon that the *Breitenfeld* couldn't see once it jumped into the system.

They swung around the light-side edge of the moon, and Durand kept her eyes to the horizon, watching for any threats. Anthalas came into view quickly, deep orange and reddish clouds meandering through its sky, its surface mostly green blotches of jungle between worn mountain ranges. She could have sworn there were some seas on the planet from the mission briefings, but she couldn't spot any.

Zhi deployed and oriented the buoys with ease. Test messages sent to and from the *Breitenfeld* were clear and secure.

"All right, ladies, two more and we can head back to the *Breitenfeld*," Durand said.

"Um … what is *that*?" Choi asked.

Durand's heart jumped in her throat and a cold wave of adrenaline coursed through her veins. She looked over both shoulders for whatever Choi had seen.

"Where? Where?" Durand asked as the memory of Xaros disintegration beams slicing past her canopy prodded her to fire up the Q-shell launcher within her fuselage.

"Ten o'clock, on the horizon," Choi said.

There. Durand saw a glint of light, straight and uneven lines of a beige structure that extended beyond the curve of the moon. Straight lines, as a rule, had no place in nature. Whatever they could see had to be artificial.

"It's not on our course plot," Mei said.

"What the hell is it?" Zhi asked.

As they flew closer, they could make out perfect cubes floating over the moon's surface, thick, straight lines ran from one cube to the others without obvious rhyme or reason. Some of the cubes had dozens of lines running in and out of them; others had only one. There were hundreds of cubes arrayed in a flat plain. Starlight faded between the cubes, as if they were looking at a bright light through fog.

"How big are they?" Durand asked, her words tinged with awe.

"Given our distance …," Zhi said and Durand heard the keys on a manual calculator clicking, "each cube must hold three times the volume of the *Breitenfeld*. That structure is larger than every void ship in service before the Xaros arrived."

"Is it a ship?" Durand asked.

"I don't see any engines," Zhi said. "Do you think it's Xaros?"

"They've already got a Crucible and the displacement rings around the planet," Durand said. "Why would they need a bunch of cubes?"

"How about we not go find out? Just drop our buoys and get back to the *Breit*," Choi said.

"Open a channel to the ship. Captain Valdar will want to see this," Durand said.

CHAPTER 6

Valdar and his senior officers clustered around the tactical plot, a printed-out screen capture of the cube ships tacked against Anthalas' moon. Flight recordings of Durand's flight past the cube ships ran on a loop on data slates left on desks around them. Hale, bulky in his void armor, stood next to Durand, still in her flight suit with her helmet under her arm. Lowenn, also in void armor, looked as natural as a dog in a tutu. Steuben, clad in armor that looked like overlapping scales, and Lafayette stood behind the humans.

"Lafayette, Steuben, is this cube ship like anything you or the Alliance have seen before?"

Valdar asked.

"It doesn't conform to any known race," Lafayette said. "Strict adherence to such basic geometric shapes is typical in species with limited imaginations or love for aesthetics. The Shanishol were known to appreciate stone carvings and to imitate shapes seen in nature. This does not appear to come from them."

"Maybe some other species heard their invitation and decided to stop by," Ericsson said.

"But it's not Xaros," Valdar said to Lafayette.

"No. Xaros will combine into larger structures to overwhelm an enemy, but they always revert back to single drones as soon as they can."

Valdar stood up straight and picked up a photo sheaf of Anthalas. "Let's not lose focus. We came here for what's on the planet, not what's in orbit." He flipped through pictures taken by Durand's reconnaissance mission and laid out the photos on the table, creating a tableau image of the light side of the planet. Identified cities and structures were in blow-up boxes, yellow lines tracing from the city images to where they corresponded to the map.

"Ms. Lowenn, you're the expert. What are we looking at here?" Valdar asked her.

"Well, there are still cities, so woo-hoo," she raised her voice for the last two syllables and wasn't met with similar enthusiasm. "Um … the cities are all equidistant from each other, which is odd as most civilizations build their cities along rivers or coastlines, places that make transportation easier. These Shanishol—and I'm assuming they're Shanishol—settlements are in some lousy spots— the middle of jungles, one is in the center of a mountain range, all very isolated from each other— and there are no roads linking any of these places. The IR buoys will show us the other side of the planet once it rotates into view, but I think the pattern will hold."

"Is there some kind of capital? Some place we should go first to find Omnium?" Valdar asked her.

"Well, given that this city," she said, pointing to a circular settlement with wide avenues lined with stepped pyramids, all leading to a straight-sided pyramid at the center, "is the largest and the central structure definitely looks to have some sort of significance, I'd say we start there."

"Go to the biggest placc? Did you have to go to college to learn that?" Commander Utrecht asked her.

"Did you not learn about Occam's Razor at Asshole University?" Lowenn fired back.

"Stop," Valdar said. "I've got six recon teams on this ship, and I'm not going to send them all to one spot, not when we've got a limited time frame. Hale, Ms. Lowenn will accompany you to this capital city. Bring another team with you. Cut your search time in half. If you come up empty, I'll spread the other teams around until we do find something."

"I'll take the Rangers. They've got the most experience," Hale said.

"Fine, get prepped for your jump. Avoid

contact with the Xaros at all cost, but don't be afraid to call in the cavalry when you need to," Valdar said.

Hale saluted, and Valdar nodded in return. The navy did not salute or return salutes while aboard ship like the Marines, and Valdar suspected the Marines kept that incongruous standard just to annoy naval officers.

"Oh, look at this!" Lowenn pointed to a trench running around the capital. "Can I see a close-up shot of this?" Hale grabbed Lowenn by the carry handle on the back of her armor and pulled her away from the table.

"No?" Lowenn stumbled back and was gently but firmly led off the bridge by Hale. Steuben went with them.

"Still leaves us with what to do about these cubes," Valdar said. He tugged at his mustache, deep in thought.

"If I may," Lafayette said "Omnium has an energy signature, one we could detect if we were close enough to it. If we could get a passive sensor, something that won't alert the Xaros, into the cubes, we might find which ones are carrying Omnium."

"It might be none," Valdar said.

"There is that risk." Lafayette said.

"Sir," Ericsson said, "we have no idea if there's any kind of atmosphere in those cubes. Any engineering team we send over will be in hard suits for a hell of a long time."

"Not an issue for me," Lafayette said. "I can operate in vacuum indefinitely. I just need air." The alien tapped his metal fingers together.

"You're the only one on this ship with that … advantage," Ericsson said.

"No." Valdar squeezed the bridge of his nose. "There are others."

****

Valdar and Lafayette found the Iron Hearts in the cemetery, all three suited up and waiting in their coffins.

"You want us to what?" Elias asked.

"Go with Lafayette to the cubes, find any

Omnium technology, and bring it back," Valdar said.

"Sir … we're killing machines, not engineers," Kallen said from within her armor.

"Your armor is void hardened. Lafayette will handle the tech side of things. You're along the ride for security and to help him out however you can," Valdar said.

"What about the ground teams? What if they get in trouble and we're busy dicking around in some alien latrine?" Bodel asked.

"Another team is going through med prep to suit up, the Smoking Snakes, Brazilians," Valdar said.

Elias looked to the armor on either side of him.

"They aren't bad," Elias said.

"But they aren't us," Kallen added. "We'll need our exo-packs for this."

"MacDougall is waiting for you on the flight deck. He'll get you kitted out. Get down there as soon as you can." Valdar turned and walked for the door. "Lafayette will fill you in on the details."

Lafayette tried to smile and flashed shiny canine teeth.

"I am looking forward to this mission," the alien said. "I've been meaning to come see you all and—" Elias scooped Lafayette up by the waist and brought him close to the armor's breastplate.

A vision slit snapped to the side and Elias's true face pressed close to the synthetic diamond window. Elias' milky eyes looked over Lafayette's cyborg body.

"Is this some human greeting I'm unaware of? What should I do to remain polite?"

"What happened to you?" Elias asked.

"I was hit by a Xaros disintegration beam. My armor mitigated some of the effects, but the damage to my body was severe. I required augmentation and replacements to survive," Lafayette said.

Elias tapped a finger gently against Lafayette's chest, the two metal surfaces clinking against each other.

"You have a heart of iron," Elias said.

"Technically it's a … oh, I see what you mean. I suppose I do."

Elias set the Karigole back on the catwalk. The three suits beat their chests as one, the noise ringing through the cemetery like a church bell. Lafayette repeated the gesture.

"Let's go," Elias said. "We have work to do."

****

Hale took a deep breath, sucking stale air from the drop ship's airline. He felt lightheaded as the super-oxygenated air hit his system. It never hurt to have a bit more fuel in his bloodstream, especially when the air reserves he carried within his armor had a small margin of error for this jump.

Like it or not, portions of his armor were manufactured by the lowest bidder and trusting the factory specs for any gear wasn't something Marines did easily.

"Hale," the ship's pilot said through his

helmet comms, "almost there. I'd get you closer but there's too much risk of a heat-plume detection. Xaros come for us, and I'll have a hell of a time picking you up on the way down."

"Roger, do what you can."

"The Ranger chalk adjusted their landing zone. Their LT didn't like the weather patterns."

Hale cursed under his breath. Changing a LOLO jump wasn't something done on the fly. He'd have a talk with Bartlett soon as he found him. A private channel icon flashed on his visor. Lowenn.

"Yes," he said to her.

"You've … done this before, right?" she asked, her voice weak and jumpy.

"Jumped from orbit down to an alien planet full of killer robots? This will be a first."

"But you've done a LOLO jump into enemy territory at least, right?"

"No, and that's why I'm going first." Hale switched to his squad frequency. "All right, Marines, brace for gravity."

Red lights pulsed twice, stayed lit, then pulsed again, warning of gravity's impending return. Floating at the top of the drop ship's cargo bay when the gravity plating came online would be unpleasant.

Weight returned to Hale's body and his stomach lurched as a standard gravity pulled him against his seat. The drop ship's rear hatch opened, revealing the sunset hues of Anthalas. Hale unsnapped his restraints and stood up. He locked his rifle against his back and watched as his team made ready for landfall.

"Remember," Hale said, "the IR buoys will guide you to the landing zone. Follow the waypoints and let gravity do all the hard work for you."

He crouched slightly, then sprinted for the opening.

"*Gott mit uns!*" Hale launched himself from the drop ship and dove headfirst into Anthalas' atmosphere. At almost a hundred miles above the planet, his freefall felt no different than if he'd been floating motionless in the void. He twisted slightly to look back at the drop ship and saw starlight glint off the armor of his team as they followed his lead. The drop ship's pilot sent him an all clear, which meant Cortaro hadn't had to throw Lowenn out of the ship like the gunnery sergeant and Hale had planned in case their technical advisor developed second thoughts about the mission. Hale didn't want her on this mission, but he needed her.

He straightened out and looked to the planet. The IR buoys around the moon triangulated his position and the landing beacon appeared on his visor, a silver pillar of light at the edge of a green gnarl of vegetation.

The anti-grav linings on his boots flared to life and shot Hale toward the beacon. The press of acceleration through his body made him feel like he was leaving orbit, not falling deeper into a gravity well. He maneuvered over the beacon and cut the acceleration once he felt the first tugs of atmosphere against his armor.

The atmosphere on Anthalas would slow

him to terminal velocity soon enough, no point in wasting his armor's batteries when there was no chance of getting a resupply on this mission.

A Marine streaked overhead and zoomed past Hale. The Marine cut his anti-grav lining and rolled over to give Hale a quick salute. He reignited his boots and shot toward the planet, evidently in a real hurry.

Standish.

Hale shook his head and spread his arms and legs slightly as wind from the atmosphere's troposphere layer buffeted him off course. The curve of the planet's surface moved beyond the periphery of his vision as he fell closer. He tried twisting his arms and legs to guide him back toward the beacon, to little effect.

A timer on his visor counted down the distance until the surface, the distance shrank alarmingly fast, seconds until impact.

A gale of wind toppled him through the sky, the planet and space tumbling end over end through his visor as he fought to right himself. The black of space faded into a reddish gold as the atmosphere grew thicker.

Hale grit his teeth and activated his boots. He opened his legs and managed to stop the end-over-end tumble. Then he fell into a cloud. His world turned into a yellow haze like he'd jumped into the methane atmosphere on Saturn's moon Titan.

There was no sign of the beacon and no connection with the buoys, his IR connection lost in the cloud. The altitude meter on his visor went blank then flashed an error message. The air around him darkened as he fell deeper into the thick cloud and rain snapped against his visor.

Panic clawed at Hale's mind as he tried to remember just how far above the surface he was supposed to deploy his parachute.

A bolt of red lightning cracked through the air, leaving a burning line across his vision. Thunder boomed around him and tiny bits of ice and sleet fell against him in waves, driven by wind from the thunderhead around him.

If he opened his parachute now, the risers would turn him into a giant lightning rod. If he didn't open his parachute, gravity's embrace would turn him into a curious smudge for whatever life was on the surface to investigate.

The cloud broke and Hale found himself in a rain storm. He slapped his hand against the release on his chest and his parachute billowed into life. The parachute jerked him out of his rapid descent like he was a sparrow caught in a hawk's claws.

He looked up to check his canopy and saw a bolt of lightning claw along the underside of the deep blue thunderclouds. He looked down and saw a forest, a forest as far as he could see and mere seconds from away.

Hale let loose a string of curses that would have made a sailor's mother blush and pulled his arms across his chest and his feet and knees together. The forest just below him was thick with pointed branches and thorny vines. Anthalas welcomed him like a shark's mouth welcomed a fish.

Branches gouged at Hale's armor and snapped like bullets in a firefight as he crashed into the trees. A branch as thick as a telephone pole reared up in front of him and Hale crunched into a fetal position. He hit the thick branch and shattered it, dry rot saving him from serious injury.

Hale jerked to a stop, his feet dangling in the air. Twigs and sap clung to his armor. He did his best to pat himself down, seeking any injury masked by adrenaline and shock. His parachute was ripped and torn, tangled in an abattoir of branches. He would have looked a lot like his parachute had it not been for his battle armor.

Around him was thick fog, cloaking the ground and sky. He was lost in a sea of gray, thorny branches holding him aloft, and he wasn't even sure how high off the ground he was.

"OK ... remember your training," Hale said. He checked the display on the back of his forearm. The atmosphere was a little less than sea level on Earth; the mix of oxygen, nitrogen and carbon dioxide skewed toward oxygen, but it was breathable. Hale pushed a button behind his ear and his visor slid aside.

Hot, humid air flooded over his face. The sound of chittering insects surrounded him. The smell of rot and sawdust permeated every breath. This planet reminded him of the Florida wetlands, but only more miserable.

He looked down again, into the gray abyss beneath his feet. He could be ten feet in the air, or a hundred. Hale took a battery pack off his belt and let it go, counting until he heard it splash into water. Two seconds, which meant he was about sixty-five feet in the air. Airborne training taught him how to minimize injury from hitting the ground from fifteen feet in the air. Falling four times that far onto terrain he couldn't see was going to hurt.

He pushed his visor back down, grateful for the cool, filtered air his suit provided. The trunk of the tree holding him aloft was thick as a Pacific Northwest old-growth redwood tree, surrounded by thorny vines that writhed against each other. The idea of swinging toward the trunk didn't fill him with confidence.

"Well … let's think," Hale said.

His parachute slipped from a branch and dropped him five feet. The riders connecting him to the canopy groaned as the fabric stretched and tore like cooked flesh beneath a knife and fork.

"Shit."

His risers broke loose and he fell free. Hale pulled his feet and knees together and braced himself.

He hit water and his boots sank into wet silt, embedding him up to his knees in mud. Hale fell back and muddy water covered his face. He flailed, trying to find any kind of purchase as his hands and arms splashed over the surface of the water. One arm slapped into mud behind his back and the other grasped through air.

Hale stopped, still drawing breath from his armor, then sat up. Water the color of milk chocolate sloshed off him. He wiped a hand over his visor then looked around. He'd been lying in two feet of water, held fast by his boots. There was nothing around him but fog and tree trunks, melding into the gray distance.

His boots came loose after shifting from side to side and lifting his legs enough to extricate them a few inches at a time. He splashed out of the knee-deep water and unholstered his gauss rifle from his back. Mud and water came off with a few shakes and it charged to life.

The battery pack he'd dropped was lost to the muck.

Something tugged at his arm. He looked down and saw a vine creeping round his wrist. He yanked his arm free and backed away from the tree that still held his parachute. Protocol demanded he at least bury his parachute, but it was lost to the fog. Hale shrugged off his harness and wrapped it into a tight ball, glancing at the vines that made a few halfhearted attempts to reach out to him. Hale tossed the harness into the pond and tried to find his bearings.

Anthalas' star rose in the east and set in the west, same as Earth, but was lost in the fog. The beacon from the IR buoys couldn't reach through all the moisture between him and the satellite. Hale took an old-fashioned compass from his belt and opened it. The needle wavered between directions, seemingly indecisive until it settled on magnetic north. Depending where one stood on Earth, its magnetic poles could be anywhere from ten to fifty degrees off true north or south. Hale didn't know what the magnetic declination of Anthalas' magnetic field was, or if it had flipped itself like Earth's magnetic field was wont to do every couple million years or so.

Hale knew there was a mountain range to the east of the landing zone, so he found west and started walking. Dark bat-like shapes swooped through the fog over his head. He stopped and swung his rifle toward sudden splashes in the water around him, but nothing ever came out of the fog.

"I don't like this planet. At all," he said and kept walking.

****

The surface of Anthalas' moon was little different than Luna's. Gray dust and jagged rocks blasted from the surface by asteroid impacts over millions of years covered the surface. The Iron Hearts and Lafayette stood in the basin of a shallow crater, looking up at the interlinked cubes directly above them.

The armor bore variable vector jet packs on their backs. The dual anti-gravity repulsors had enough thrust to get them in and out of the moon's gravity well and maneuver through space at a slow speed. The fuel-burning jets had more oomph to them, but their enormous heat signature could have attracted Xaros attention.

Lafayette, wearing a smaller jet pack and an armored space suit of Karigole design, scanned the cube ships through an optic box atop his rifle.

"Well, professor?" Elias asked.

"There are three hundred and twelve cubes linked together ... but no engines," Lafayette said.

"What about these? I saw them on the planet-facing edge," Bodel said. He sent image captures of blackened wire frames attached to several cubes to the rest of the team through their local IR net.

"Ah, sharp eyes, Mr. Bodel," Lafayette said. "Yes, they could be engine mounts. But that begs the question of where those engines went, doesn't it?"

"Maybe the Shanishol version of Cortez led them all here," Elias said.

"What is a Cortez?" Lafayette asked.

"Not a *what*, a *who*. He was a Spanish military leader that burned his ships so his men knew there was no going back if they failed to conquer the native peoples and enslave them," Elias said.

"He sounds like a horrible person. Is he a venerated leader in human history?"

"He gets mixed reviews. All depends on who you ask. You find a place for us to start looking or should we throw a dart and go to whichever one it hits?" Elias asked.

"Look at that," Kallen said. She pointed her

arm with gauss cannons mounted on the forearms at the other side of the crater. She took long strides across the moon, each step aided by a quick boost from her jet pack.

She stopped near the edge and held up a fist to keep the rest of the team from going past her.

There, pressed into the dust, was a footprint. Whoever, or whatever, set foot on this moon had a four-toed foot larger than a manhole cover. Treads of the space boot ran beneath each toe splayed out like a bird's. There were slight divots at the end of each toe; whatever had been there had claws.

"There's more over the edge, lots more," Kallen said.

"Maybe the Shanishol sent someone down to have a look around," Bodel said.

"Shanishol had feet like humans, not like this. Look familiar to you, Lafayette?" Elias asked. The Karigole stared at the footprints, his gloved hand on the hilt of a knife sheathed against his thigh. "Lafayette?"

The alien look startled, and took his hand

away.

"Yes, sorry. There are many species with feet like that. Given that this moon lacks anything in the way of weather or geologic activity, these footprints could be millions of years old. They may be from the original inhabitants of Anthalas," Lafayette said.

"I went and saw Neil Armstrong's footprints on Luna, the originals from 1969," Bodel said. "They'd still be there if the Chinese hadn't 'accidentally' erased them when they took the colonies over."

"But that footprint could be a few hours old too, couldn't it?" Elias asked.

"That's correct, but there's no evidence anyone else is in system with us," Lafayette said. He raised his rifle back toward the cubes. "Best we hurry."

Elias looked at Anthalas. The bands of Xaros rings around the planet brought back memories of standing on the *Breitenfeld*'s hull during the battle for the Crucible. Inside the armored womb of his armor, Elias felt his heart beating faster as his withering body dumped adrenaline and stress hormones into his bloodstream. There was no battle—his mind knew it—but his body still had fight-or-flight instincts. Elias focused on the bio feedback from his armor, the press of the moon against his armor's feet, the sensation of heat from the enormous red star at the center of the system.

He hated the almost atavistic demands of his flesh-and-blood body—the constant feedings, physical therapy and cleaning. Nothing his body required aided him inside his armor. But there was no way out of his armor, never again. He'd pushed his mind over the limit to save the ship from a Xaros attack, damaging his nervous system to the point where it couldn't function without external input from his armor. So long as the plugs into his brain were connected to his suit, he could function. Without the armor, he was nothing. *Maybe Stacey will come back from wherever she is with something that will get rid of my body forever,* he thought.

He had no choice but to live in his armor. But his fellow Iron Heart Kallen took every chance she had to armor up. A paraplegic, being connected to her armor was the only way she could move, even if the limbs were mechanical and designed for combat.

"Let's start with one of the cubes that had an engine mounted to it," Lafayette said. "There may be a power source. Cube number thirty-seven?" A beacon point appeared on a cube through Elias' visual feed.

"Fair enough." Elias squatted, then launched himself into the air. The servos in his knees and hips sent him nearly ten yards high, then his anti-grav thrusters came to life with a flare of blue light.

The thrusters shook his armor as he accelerated. He cut them off once he'd achieved escape velocity from the moon and let his momentum take him the rest of the way to the ship. The charge in the thrusters was finite, and they still had to get back to the *Breitenfeld.*

As they neared, details of the cube's surface

came into focus. Each side was a jigsaw puzzle of metal plates welded together, none identical. There were no windows or airlocks.

Elias swung his legs around and reoriented his armor so it was flying toward the cube feetfirst. He pulsed his thrusters, losing speed with each tap of anti-gravity. He slowed to almost nothing a few yards above the surface and activated the magnetic liners in his boots to pull him the rest of the way down.

The soles and heels of his boots snapped against the cube's hull, and he felt vibrations as the rest of his team landed around him. They stood against the underside of the ship; an observer on the moon's surface would see them as if they were standing on a ceiling.

"Why are the stars twinkling?" Bodel asked. Stars seen between the cube ship and the moon were as expected—steady—as there was no shifting atmosphere to bend the light. But starlight seen between the cubes wavered and was slightly diffuse, like seeing them through a thin fog.

"It's only around the space and sun-facing sides of the ship," Lafayette said. "Why don't we get on another cube facing and investigate?"

"We aren't here for a science expedition. We need to hurry up and find the Shanishols' Omnium and get the hell out of here," Elias said.

"Agreed, but do you see a door around here?" Lafayette said, motioning to the flat expanse of welded plates.

Kallen slid across the surface, adjusting the pull on her magnetic linings so she skated over the surface like it was ice. She went horizontal as she came to the edge and fell into space. She swung her feet back to the other cube face and arced back to the ship with a touch of her thrusters.

No matter how much more time Elias spent in the armor than Kallen, she always managed to be more graceful in her movements than either Elias or Bodel. Elias would admit to a bit of jealousy to himself and no one else.

The other side of the cube was little different than the last. As they approached the edge, a gossamer wall appeared, stretching across the entire cube ship. The Iron Hearts stood at the edge of the cube, looking through the slightly opaque barrier.

Lafayette leaned close and tapped a finger against the wall. The wall stuck to his fingertip and pulled back with an elastic snap.

"Curious, there are micrometeorites embedded within the … film," Lafayette said.

"Like putting a cover over a car you're not going to drive for a while," Bodel said. "Keeps space from eating away at the cubes one tiny tick at a time."

"Why not have this all the way around the ship?" Kallen asked.

"The moon is between the open underside and the rest of space. Whoever put this on was either lazy or efficient," Elias said.

Lafayette scraped residue from his fingertip into a specimen tube. He held the sample up in front of his eyes and shook it.

"Fascinating, isn't it?" he asked.

Elias skated into the middle of the cube and

knelt. He raised a hand into the air and slapped it against the cube hard enough to leave an imprint in the metal. He felt a slight vibration through his armor from the strike.

"There's a strut beneath me," he said. "Find a thin point in the hull so we can get in," Elias said. Kallen and Bodel skated over the surface, stopping to kick their heels against the hull.

"Why don't we check for an access point along the passageways connecting the cubes?" Lafayette asked.

"Because this is a smash and grab, professor, not an excavation." Elias scooted over and slapped the hull again.

"Why do you keep calling me that? I have the Karigole educational equivalent of an associate's degree," Lafayette said.

"Because you keep yammering like you should be wearing tweed!" Elias flicked a fingertip against the hull, then again a few feet over. "Got a thin part."

He raised his arm into the air and punched

his fingertips through the welds of a hull panel. There was no rush of air from around the breach, so he squeezed his hand around the hole and peeled the hull of the ship aside. He stood and dragged a piece away like he was rolling up a throw carpet. He stopped when the hull panel was at the far edge; he might have to fold it back later and didn't want to send it floating into the void.

"Inelegant, but effective," Lafayette said.

The entrance was big enough for the Iron Hearts, and there was nothing but darkness to greet them.

"Who wants to go first?" Bodel asked.

****

The swamp morphed into tall, thin trees that reminded Hale of ash trees, but with thick bushy tops that looked like roots in the shape of a dandelion head. The fog thinned enough that Hale could see the great red disk of the system's primary in the golden sky. His IR couldn't find a buoy to connect to, and he had no idea if he'd gotten closer to or farther from the landing zone.

His Marines would wait at the landing zone for an hour, then continue the mission with or without him, which was five minutes from now. A gust of wind thinned the fog out and Hale saw a clearing beyond the thin trees. He made his way toward the clearing, boots crunching on tree bark that had shed from the thin trees like scales off a fish.

He got to the edge of the clearing and saw a flicker of movement on the other side. His fingertips drummed against the edge of his forearm display. Suit-to-suit IR wouldn't stretch through the fog. Mimicking a bird call on an alien world was about as useful as screaming "There's something weird right here!" to anything that wasn't from Earth. If there was a good way to tell friend from foe out there, it wasn't coming to him.

There was a whoosh of air and powerful arms grabbed him from behind. His rifle was knocked from his hands and his arms pinned to his side. A knife glinted in the weak light and he felt it press against his throat through his armor.

"Look up. Always look up," Steuben hissed into his ear.

Hale squirmed in the Karigole's powerful grasp and he slammed his head back. The edge of his helmet struck Steuben's face and Hale heard a grunt of pain. Steuben shoved Hale away and the Marine scooped up his rifle and swung it around at Steuben.

Steuben rubbed his jaw and slid his knife into a scabbard running along his forearm.

"Good reaction," Steuben said, "but you are still lacking in tactical awareness."

"Damn it, Steuben! I could have shot you," Hale said.

"If I've grown so sloppy then I deserve to be shot."

"Where's everyone else?"

Steuben pointed his clawed fingers toward the north end of the clearing. "There. We were preparing to leave when I heard you tromping through the undergrowth like a lost child. What happened to you?" Steuben reached over his shoulder and unsnapped his gauss rifle from his back armor. The Karigole used the same technology as their human allies for small arms, but his rifle packed almost as big a punch as a single shot from Orozco's Gustav.

"I got blown into an electrical storm and landed in a tree that tried to eat me. Other than that I'm fine," Hale said.

Steuben grunted and led Hale through the woods. They came to a knot of Marines and Lowenn, all huddled around a small IR radio antenna.

"Sir!" Standish waved to Hale. "Guess who's the first human being to ever set foot on an alien planet?" He poked both thumbs at his own chest. "This guy. Armstrong on the moon. Chang on Mars. Standish on Anthalas. We'll take some photos later so school kids know what to draw with their crayons and stuff."

"This mission is classified, you twit," Torni said, shaking her head as she tapped a button on the

IR radio. The antenna swiveled from side to side slowly. "School kids will never know about this."

"What?" Standish's shoulders slumped. "Sir, we've got to tell everyone about this when we get back."

"No, Standish. You're going to have to do something else to be famous," Hale said. "We have comms to the buoys?"

"Negative, sir. Atmosphere is playing hell with comms. I've got nothing from the *Breitenfeld*, nothing from the Rangers," Torni said.

"No loss of equipment on the drop," Cortaro said. "We've got food, water and batteries to last five days."

Hale looked up and saw white haze stretched across the golden skies. A few blood-red clouds marred the sky like scabs. Their mission wouldn't wait for perfect weather.

"All right," Hale said. "We've still got our mission. We move north to the capital, wait for the weather to clear then reestablish contact. Form up into your fire teams. We're moving in echelon formation. Ms. Lowenn, with me please."

Lowenn, who'd been sitting with her back to a tree, used her rifle like a walking stick to get herself to her feet. Hale wanted to snap at her for using her weapon like a tool, but she wasn't a Marine.

Lowenn at least kept her finger off the trigger as she fell in beside Hale. They walked behind the rest of the Marines, with only Steuben behind them.

"Lowenn, what do you think of this place?" Hale asked.

"You mean as a vacation destination? I'll pass."

"No, from your anthropologist background."

Lowenn shrugged. "There are a couple things that don't fit what we know about the Xaros, or even this planet. If the Shanishol did come here at the invitation of some advanced civilization, why don't we see more signs of it? One glance at Earth from orbit and you'd know it was inhabited. The Great Wall of China, the Suez and Panama canals, lights from cities and the hyperloops. All this before the Xaros wiped it away, of course.

"So where is all that? The Shanishol had decades on the planet before the Xaros showed up. If they had the wherewithal to cross interstellar distances, why not do some sort of infrastructure improvements? They didn't even build roads from the cities."

"Maybe the Xaros erased everything but the population centers," Hale said.

"The Alliance has sent probes to a couple planets the Xaros have preserved. There's one I remember, a red desert world the Alliance doesn't have a name for. The hypothesis is that the locals heard radio transmissions of a neighboring civilization being wiped out by the Xaros and decided to cease their reproductive cycles. Commit very slow species-wide suicide before the Xaros could get to them. The Xaros showed up and didn't erase a single thing. They left a few caretaker drones in the system and the murmuration of a few hundred million drones went on to the next species," she said.

"Other times, species have tried to play possum. Bury a few sentients deep underground or in a gas giant and hope to ride out the storm. The Xaros find the survivors every time, and every time they wipe out every trace of that civilization, even if they left the remnants intact to begin with."

"So this planet is exactly the way the Xaros found it?"

"That's right. Fascinating, isn't it?"

"Or horrifying, depends which side of annihilation you're on. How's the armor?"

Lowenn rolled her shoulders and tried to hike up her leg armor. "The atmosphere controls are fine, better than breathing this hundred percent humidity, hundred-degree air. The augmetics make it feel like I'm not wearing fifty pounds of armor and make carrying this thing," she raised her rifle slightly, "not that bad. The suit chafes. Is there some way to scratch my back?"

"The suit will fit you better the more you wear it, and there's no way to scratch your back."

"Damn lowest bidders," Lowenn said.

****

Elias slammed into the deck, his weapon-bearing arms up and ready. Floodlights flipped up from his shoulders and the top of his armored helm. Light poured forth, illuminating a wide passageway just tall enough that Elias could walk upright. Pipes marked with loops and swirls ran along the ceiling next to a wide air vent.

Elias took three steps away from his landing point, the magnetic linings keeping him secure against the deck. Bodel landed behind him, the light from his suit adding to the glow around them. Kallen and the Karigole weren't far behind.

"No gravity, no air or temperature regulation," Kallen said.

"Hard vacuum is an effective preservation medium—for nonorganic material, that is," Lafayette said.

"You saying this ship is in mothballs?" Bodel asked.

"That would appear to be the case. Now … let me read the signs," Lafayette pushed off from the deck and floated toward the ceiling. He ran has metal fingertips over a brass panel stamped against a pipe.

"Water, air … and power. How odd, I've never seen construction with the three so close together. The second and third order effects of a rupture in any of these lines … it just isn't safe." He tugged at the corner of a label plate and it came free. "I don't know if it's age, but this construction is shoddy. The pipes look cast, not additive manufacturing like from a 3D printing facility."

"You said 'power.' We can follow that back to an engine room?" Elias asked.

"I believe so." Lafayette pointed down the passageway. "That way."

The armor's footsteps were heavy as they had to lock against the deck with each step. Lafayette preferred to float along, pushing against the bulkheads or grabbing a handhold along the pipes to propel him along.

Kallen stepped around an intersection and her gauss cannon arm snapped up.

"Got a body," she said.

A Shanishol bobbed against the ceiling, its bare skin desiccated and shriveled like a dry corn husk. Its bare hands, feet and head—once neon blue—had faded to gray. The ratty jumpsuit it wore looked too small for the Shanishol wearing it, with torn patches and portions ground threadbare from friction.

Elias grabbed the body with two fingers and tossed it toward the deck. A stiff arm snapped at the forearm as it bounced off.

"Oops," Elias said.

Lafayette put a boot against the corpse chest and pushed it gently to the ground.

"Well?" Bodel asked.

"He's dead," Lafayette said.

"So glad we brought you. Who knows where we'd be right now without your powerful skills of observation," Kallen quipped.

"Have you considered *why* he died and who

left him in here?" Lafayette asked. "Based on what the Alliance's probes picked up on this civilization before the Xaros found them, the Shanishol took great care of their dead. Leaving a body out like this is uncharacteristic ... and he isn't decomposed beyond moisture loss. He could have died from vacuum exposure."

"Maybe there's a hull breach we don't know about," Kallen said.

"Anyone else starting to get a bad feeling about this?" Bodel asked.

"What's the matter, Hans? Iron heart but lily liver?" Kallen gave Bodel a little shove.

"Piss off, you know I don't like ghost ships," Bodel knocked Kallen's hand away.

"Ooo," Kallen's voice rose, "look everyone, the ten-foot-tall killing machine is afraid of ghost cooties."

"Piss. Off!"

"Hey!" Elias stomped a heel against the deck. "Quit acting like Marines. Focus. Both of you."

"The engineering section is ahead," Lafayette said. He lifted the Shanishol body up and pushed it away.

The passageway ended, opening up into a wide platform. Elias focused his lamps into tight beams of light and swept them across the platform. The light ran over a round hatchway twice as tall as any of the Iron Hearts. Lengths of metal bars had been jammed into hinges on the doorframe and welded over the seals.

"Looks like a barricade," Bodel said. "That should be one of the connecting passageways to the other cubes."

"Found engineering," Kallen said.

Elias brought his beams around to line up with hers. There was a double set of doors, a brass panel bearing golden Shanishol script across the top. But there was more, something else that sent a chill down Elias's spine. A swath of red paint passed through the spotlights and over the side of the doors. Elias lifted his lights and opened them wider.

Giant Shanishol letters in the same red covered a wall several stories tall and almost as wide as a destroyer.

"Put your spotlights to the upper left and bring them across," Lafayette said. "So I can read it."

The Iron Hearts did as asked.

"'The ... prophet … is … false.' How odd," Lafayette said.

"They wanted everyone to know it, too," Elias said. He walked over to the doors and dug his fingertips into the metal and shoved it aside. "Come on."

Elias ducked beneath the doorframe and swept a light mounted next to his gauss cannons over the floor. A walkway led into darkness.

"Sure, why not?" he muttered. He traced his light down the walkway and found a silver frame in the shape of a globe, spars of sparkling metal running up and around it like lines of latitude and longitude.

Tremors went through the walkway as Elias walked toward the globe. He stopped and looked back at the entrance. Kallen was on his side of the door, looking at a bank of dead control panels with Lafayette.

"This isn't that sturdy," Elias said. "Bodel, stay on the other side and keep an eye out."

"No problem," Bodel said.

The globe shimmered where Elias's light touched it, seeming to pull light into it as he ran his spotlights up toward a ceiling that his lights couldn't uncover.

Lafayette flew over and set down next to Elias. He took a data wand from his armor and touched it to the metal.

"Omnium?" Elias asked.

"It is indeed. The control panels around the wall are fried out. Perhaps there's something in the base of this lattice we might find useful," he said.

Lafayette bent over and gray hands reached through the darkness toward him.

Elias swung over Lafayette's body and smashed aside something that crumbled beneath his blow.

"Contact!" Elias set his lights to full power and wide angles and lit all the space around him. A Shanishol corpse, spinning like a top from Elias's strike, bumped into another floating body. And another. And another.

"Sweet mother of God," Kallen said.

Elias looked up and saw hundreds of bodies floating around them. Men, women and children Shanishol, all ashen faced, their mouths locked open in a final gasp for breath. Elias felt a stab of fear in his guts and hated the reminder of the inherent weakness of his body.

"A revolt, perhaps?" Lafayette said. He opened a panel in the floor and swept a small light over the wires he found. "This cube broke off from the rest of the ship. The captain decided to suffocate them all instead of shoot his way in and risk damaging an engine. Reasonable."

"You're awful calm," Elias said. He pushed away another body that rose up from beneath the walkway.

"You've been a soldier for a while. You

haven't seen worse?"

"You ever seen a pleasant battlefield?"

"No." Lafayette fished out a tag from within the open panel and tapped a finger against his face plate. "This electrical work is primitive, lacking several engineering advancements we normally see. They aren't even using fiber optics. But I wonder …."

The Karigole pushed off into the air and grabbed a wrung at the top of a safety fence and swung beneath the platform.

"Eureka! That's the word humans use for discovery, correct?" Lafayette said. "I always thought the 'that's funny' were the most important in science, but I guess humans have different standards."

Elias keyed his jump pack to get him in the air then used thrusters on his forearms to push him down. Below the walkway and underneath the platform holding the giant globe was a machine that looked like a rotten fang, the tip pointing away from the globe. The fang, much too large to get through the doors into the engine room or the passageway to the other cubes, was made of the same metal as the globe, but patterns swirled across the surface, just like the carapace on a Xaros drone.

Elias raised his weapons and a hand retracted into the forearm housing, a spike snapping out to replace the hand. His feet hit a deck plate and locked against it.

"This is what we're here for," Lafayette said.

"What is it? Sleeping Xaros?" Elias asked.

"No, don't be ridiculous. It's an Omnium reactor. The lattice above must be a containment field." Lafayette flit between control stations around the edge of the room surrounding the reactor.

"How do you know that?" Elias asked.

"Because this," Lafayette said, reaching out and tapping his fingers against a control station covered in buttons and levers, "is labeled 'Reactor Control' in Shanishol."

"You just … read it?"

"Not everything has to be difficult. But what

will be difficult is getting the reactor out of here. The cube was built around the reactor—the reactor wasn't installed into the cube," Lafayette said.

"You're asking the wrong guy, Lafayette. I'm a fighter, not an engineer."

"I know what we'll need. But we need support from the *Breitenfeld*. Do you know an engineer skilled with explosives who has something of a death wish?" Lafayette asked.

"Let's get out of this cube and get a line of sight on the buoys. As for your engineer, I have someone in mind."

****

Hours later, the Marines stopped in a patch of boulders not far from rising hills at the base of the mountains. Hale ordered a rest break, sending Cortaro and Yarrow scouting ahead.

Hale took a food pouch from his pack and raised his visor. The heat hit his exposed skin and he winced as his pores went into overdrive, starting to sweat. He opened the food pouch and shook out the tube of paste that constituted the main meal. Tiny black letters on the dark green label promised tuna with noodle flavor. Field rations were a combination of ultra-dense nutrients and carbohydrates mixed with appetite suppressors. One tube the size of two of his fingers would, theoretically, get him through a day under combat conditions.

"Ugh, what is this, spackle?" Lowenn asked as she sniffed at her tube.

"Chicken cacciatore," Standish said, his mouth half-full of paste. "You want my beef stew?"

"No, I want food that won't look the same going out as it does on the way in," she said.

Bailey spat out a mouthful of water and laughed. "Sir, I like this one. Can we keep her?"

Hale, his appetite lessened by Lowenn's metaphor but still hungry, sucked on the tube and swallowed the bland paste that had the consistency of applesauce.

Steuben, who'd volunteered to keep watch, was perched against one of the boulders, his head rotating nearly one hundred and eighty degrees on his neck as he scanned their perimeter.

"Hey, Steuben," Bailey said, "what're you going to eat?"

"We do not eat while in battle. My body maintains everything I need for several weeks of sustained—" The alien moved like lightning, his hand shooting toward Bailey, a glint of metal caught in the air.

Bailey rolled to the side and fumbled with her gauss carbine.

"Oye! What the hell are you playing at?"

"Forgive me." Steuben leapt from the boulder and landed with the grace of a cat near where Bailey had been sitting. He reached into the tall grass and picked up his knife. An insect that looked like a nightmare version of a caterpillar the size of Hale's forearm writhed on the tip of the knife. Blue blood seeped down the blade.

Marines scrambled to their feet and kicked at the grass around them.

"It was trying to drink the water you'd spat

out," Steuben said. He brought the insect close to his nose and sniffed at it. Steuben opened his mouth, and his forked tongue licked away a bit of blood.

"Steuben," Hale said "I'm not sure if you should—"

The Karigole's jaws distended and a maw of fanged teeth bit the insect in half. Dark blood spurted from the carcass and a smell like wet garbage filled the air. Marines groaned and protested. Lowenn dry heaved.

Steuben chewed, his mouth muffling the sound of cracking chitin. He held the blade that still impaled the squirming remnants out to Hale.

"It's fresh. Not bad," Steuben said.

Hale looked away and shook his head.

"Why, Steuben? Why would you eat that?" Orozco asked.

"You're the one eating extruded plant matter full of pharmaceuticals and designed to remain edible after being buried for a century, but I'm the one who must explain myself?" Steuben wrapped his lips around the insect and sucked it into his mouth.

"Sir!" Gunney Cortaro ran into the boulder field, Yarrow right behind him. "Sir, you'll want to see this. Looks like …Steuben, what the hell is in your mouth?"

Steuben's jaw crunched down on the insect, which cracked like he was eating a whole snow crab.

"Show me," Hale finished the last of his paste and stuck the empty tube in his pack. They'd leave no trash for anyone, or anything, to find later.

****

It looked like a corral, one meant for livestock two or three times the size of cattle. Wooden posts every few feet were strung with thin brass-colored wires. Wooden beams ran across the top of the corral, and the same brass wire was looped over the top in swirls that swung gently in the breeze. Within, the dried-out remnants of a creek that had once ran through the corral cut a slight depression through the enclosure.

"Don't touch anything," Cortaro said to the Marines as they approached.

The posts were sunk into something that looked like dried concrete. Tiny craters covered the surface like air had bubbled and leaked up while the material was still being poured. The area within the corral was almost the size of a football field, the ground nothing but a sea of grayish mud.

Hale stopped a little beyond arm's distance and looked at the ground. Grass and ferns stopped several inches from the corral; a neat line ran around the perimeter that no grass had encroached beyond. He looked up at the fence, which towered almost three times his height.

"Standish," Hale said, "you grew up on ranch, right? This look familiar?"

"Well, sir, thing about getting cows in and out of pens, you got to have a gate. I don't see one here," Standish said.

"Looks like the concentration camps the Chinese set up after they captured Darwin," Bailey

said.

"It's too tall," Lowenn said. "The gravity here is almost Earth standard. Local animals bred for food or labor shouldn't be able to jump over anything even half as high."

"There's a lot to this planet we haven't seen yet," Hale said.

"Great," Standish said. "Giant cow-sized rabbits that want to eat my face."

"The little one is right," Steuben said. He picked up a rotting log and tossed it at the fence. The brass wires cut through the log without effort, frictionless. Lumps of wood plopped into the mud. "Only intelligent species, those that knew the danger of those wires, would be dissuaded from pressing against it."

"I said no touching!" Cortaro yelled. "If there's an alarm, we are done. Don't you get that?"

"My apologies. I keep forgetting how useless your noses are. I can smell the remnants of birds and insects along the wires. Animals strike this fence regularly. If I was monitoring this place, I wouldn't care to investigate every single disturbance," Steuben said.

"How about you let us know before you do something like that?" Hale asked.

Steuben clicked his teeth together twice, Karigole body language for OK.

Lowenn tapped at the side of her visor, taking pictures with her armor's camera. "I don't understand why the Shanishol would need something like this. Or …." She leaned close to one of the posts. "This is wood, local wood by the looks of it. It doesn't look treated or refined at all, and it's sunk in concrete that looks almost primitive."

"What's your point?" Torni asked.

"The Xaros arrived here thousands of years ago. This structure must predate that. How can this wood *not* have rotted away?"

Wind whistled over the wires, moaning like a long-lost ghost.

"Not the answers we're here for," Hale said. A raindrop hit his gauss rifle with a smack. He looked up, and a red drop spattered against his visor. Red rain sprinkled around them, coating their armor with a pink film.

"Yarrow, tell me this isn't blood," Standish said.

"Nope," Yarrow pressed the tip of a data wand attached to his forearm rig into a drop of rain. "It's plain old water. Must be some dirt or something in the droplet that's giving it the coloration."

"Let's go. We'll skirt around the enclosure. Mark the location. We could use this as an extraction site in an emergency," Hale said.

The Marines moved on. Moments after they left, the remnants of the log Steuben threw into the corral rose from the mud and levitated a few inches in the air. The log floated through the fence, hovered at the edge of the grass line, and then were flung back into the surrounding forest.

****

Lieutenant Bartlett leapt over a fallen tree trunk and splashed through ankle-deep water. He slammed into a tree, fighting for breath. The Ranger raised his rifle and fired wild shots into the jungle behind him. A squeal rose through the fog.

Bartlett cursed and shrugged off the vines that tugged at his armor. They were still on him. The squeal cut off suddenly and Bartlett took off running.

"Hale! *Breitenfeld*!" Bartlett kept his IR transmitter open as he ran, praying someone could hear him. "We were ambushed by—" His foot hooked a root beneath the water and tripped him up. He twisted as he went down and landed with his back in the water. He fired off wild shots at loping shapes in the mist and got back to his feet.

The ground rumbled as something big ran toward him. Thumps through fog sounded like a herd of Clydesdales stampeding at him.

Bartlett set his rifle to high power. If a shot from this could take out a Xaros, it might put a dent in whatever he'd seen rip his soldiers to pieces.

"Come on," Bartlett braced himself against the ground and fired into the mist. The high-powered shot twisted the fog with its passing vortex. The recoil hit him like a hammer blow, rocking him back. The rumbling grew closer.

A green light on his rifle flashed—ready for a second shot.

He readied his next shot, determined to see the creature before he killed it.

The rumbling died away. Bartlett glanced around, but the jungle was still.

There was a hiss behind him, deeper than the warning from a rattlesnake. Bartlett spun around and saw an enormous clawed hand an instant before it enveloped his face.

The blow knocked him horizontal. He squeezed the trigger on his weapon out of shock, sending the high-powered shot straight into the sky.

His world went black.

****

The Xaros drone orbiting beyond Anthalas' atmosphere was one of many caretaker drones monitoring the planet. A net of drones had been in orbit since its fleet passed through this system thousands of years ago, all selected at random to oversee the planet's realignment and gate construction and to maintain the vigil over the world.

In the thousand years that the drone had held its watch, there had been two incidents of note. The first, a rogue radio transmission detected from deep space that turned out to be nothing more than a primitive exploration probe sent by a species that conveniently included a celestial map leading back to their location. The drones replicated a force sufficient to overwhelm the planet and reported the annihilation through the jump gate—all as per their programming.

The second incident was the routine removal of a comet that would have impacted with Anthalas in 9,007 years. Again, as per their programming.

The drone compiled reports from the rest of the net, noted no discrepancies, and continued monitoring the planet's surface. A routine check for emergent intelligent species was scheduled in exactly three hundred years. Its programming allowed for no deviation.

The drone's infrared sensors registered a detection, a small object breaching the atmosphere. All small heat traces going down the planet's gravity well were ignored. Meteorites fell into the atmosphere regularly and were of no consequence. But when an object burned through the air from the ground up, that was no random act of nature.

The drone traced the trajectory of Bartlett's final shot back to the surface and awoke the rest of the drones around the planet. The drone sent an alert to the jump gate, where the message would be passed to an intelligence much higher than its own.

The black oblong shape orientated toward the planet's surface and accelerated in that direction. The detection would be investigated and the full force of the Xaros around the planet would converge to aid in the search and annihilation mission. As per their programming.

CHAPTER 7

Bartlett fell to the ground, unable to see through his cracked visor. He tasted blood and his face ached from fractures along his jaw and around his right eye. His hands were bound beneath his knees and his armor had been stripped away. The sound of hissing snakes and guttural barks surrounded him.

"Bartlett? That you?" a familiar voice asked.

"Crenshaw?" Bartlett struggled to say the word through his swollen face.

"Yeah, I ... I'm pretty sure the rest are dead. The little ones ripped them apart before that big one got to me," the Ranger said.

"Don't say a word about anything. Anyone. Understand?"

"Got it. We … oh, what the hell is that?" Crenshaw asked.

Bartlett heard the sound of hydraulics, growing louder with each mechanical whirr.

"*Qabu*," the word boomed, trailed by a static hiss. "*Lu qabu. Alaksu qabu!*"

Crenshaw screamed, first from fear—a sound Bartlett knew from many battlefields. His scream then rose into a tortured wail, Bartlett's protest drowned out by his soldier's death cry.

Bartlett heard a body hit the ground. A mechanical claw grabbed him by the arm and sat him up. Something squeezed the sides of his helmet and yanked it from his shoulders.

There was a tank. Orange water bubbled within like it was boiling.

"Speak … meat." The words came from the bottom of the tank. He looked down and saw mechanical legs propping the tank into the air.

"False mind. Shallow mind. Wrong, wrong,

wrong," came from the speakers. An arm unfolded from beneath the tank, and a spike covered in red blood poked Bartlett in the chest. "Wrong. How? *How!*"

"Go to hell," Bartlett said.

"Taste. More taste. Yes."

Mechanical arms snatched Bartlett by the shoulders and lifted him into the air. The bubbles within the tank lessened, and Bartlett saw what was inside.

His screams echoed through the jungle far longer than Crenshaw's.

****

Three Mule drop ships and four Eagle fighters floated above Elias and Lafayette. A Mule lowered to the surface and dropped its rear ramp. A sailor in an armored space suit tried to walk down the ramp, carefully testing each step like a drunk trying to negotiate stairs.

"Oye! To hell with you, you big metal son of a bitch!" MacDougall shouted through the IR.

"I'd break my foot off in your ass if I could kick through solid steel. Bring me out of my nice and snug *Breitenfeld* to go spelunking through some alien Rubik's Cube." His Scottish brogue loaned a certain air of poetry to his rant.

"I don't understand what he's saying," Lafayette said.

"Neither do I, half the time," Elias said.

"What're you waiting for? Christmas? Come get these explosives out of the back of this Mule." MacDougall pointed at a pallet load of plastic explosives and pre-molded shaped charges strapped into the Mule.

"Armor, this is flight leader Gall. I'm taking the ships to the moon side of the cube, the side you *aren't* going to blow up, and latch on," Durand said.

"Roger, Gall," Elias said. "You'll know when we're done. Have the net ready so we can get the hell out of here."

"That's the plan," Durand said.

Elias slid the pallet of explosives out of the Mule and carried them to the cube's opening he'd torn open.

"You have the schematics I asked for?" Lafayette and MacDougall broke off into a technical discussion that Elias had neither the patience nor vocabulary to appreciate. Lafayette jumped over the opening and sent himself down with a burst from his maneuver thrusters, but MacDougall hesitated at the edge.

"Eh, wee bit dark in there," the sailor said.

"Jump or be pushed," Elias said.

"Just because you can crush me skull doesn't mean I'll let you bully me," MacDougall said. Elias reached for the engineer. "OK! OK! You can bully me, but I won't like it." He took a hesitant step over the hole and lost his balance. He floated over the opening, his arms pinwheeling.

"Ah, shit!"

Elias reached out and put the palm of his hand against MacDougall's helmet and pushed him down.

Once they were all inside, they made their way to the engine room with only a minimal amount of complaining from MacDougall.

"We'll need to set the shaped charges at these structure points," Lafayette said, pointing to an Ubi slate. "I've got the other two soldiers already exposing—what is that?" The Karigole looked up at the air vent nestled into the corner of the passageway.

"What's what?" MacDougall asked.

"There's a vibration. You can't feel it? In the air vent ... and it's coming this way," Lafayette said. He pointed down the passageway.

"Get behind me," Elias said. He felt the vibration that Lafayette spoke of and saw the air vent rattling as something moved through it toward them.

"I knew it," MacDougall whispered. "Told Standish just as much. Soon as I ever set foot off the *Breitenfeld* something would try and eat my face. Now I'll never get that last bottle of Glenfiddich."

The rattling grew closer and Elias slammed his fist through the air duct. He punched his other arm through the thin metal and yanked a section of air duct holding whatever was in it from the wall. Elias pinned the section against the wall with his hip and peeled the metal open.

Inside was a creature in a flimsy space suit that looked like a gecko with an alligator's uneven teeth. It clawed at Elias and convulsed, like a rat trying to wriggle out of a trap that failed to kill it.

"Toth!" Lafayette spat. He pulled his knife out and set the point against the creature's throat. It froze, bulbous eyes locked on the knife blade.

Lafayette leaned forward, his lips pulled apart, revealing his own sharp teeth. The Karigole put his visor glass against the creature's helmet and spoke. Sibilant words exchanged between the two of them, passing through where their helmets met.

"Kek kek kek," came from the creature and into Lafayette's IR. The creature made the same sounds, and Elias thought it was laughing.

Lafayette leaned back, raised the knife over his head and slashed the creature's space suit. Air and yellow blood burst into the vacuum. The creature thrashed uselessly then went limp.

"Jesus Christ, Lafayette!" MacDougall shouted as he wiped at his visor frantically, trying to remove the drops of blood that hit it.

Elias flipped the metal air duct back over the creature and pinched the ends tight into a makeshift coffin. Blood seeped through the torn metal.

"Care to explain?" Elias asked.

"Toth. The Toth are here. I am such a fool. We never even considered that the gravity tides would open stable wormholes for them too. The math was there but I didn't see it," Lafayette said.

"Why did you kill it? Are there more? Did you just piss them all off too?" Elias asked.

"The menials are never alone. It must have come from one of the other cubes." Lafayette knocked the blade against his thigh and slid it into the scabbard.

"You didn't answer my questions," Elias said.

"Lord have mercy, I shouldn't be able to smell it but I swear that I do," MacDougall said.

"The Toth are my enemy. The Karigole's

enemy. They will attack the moment they know you're here, no diplomacy or discussion. Now, we need to hurry before the rest arrive," Lafayette kicked the Toth's body and hurried down the passageway.

****

A footpath cut through the mountains, wide enough for three Marines to walk abreast. Hale and his team stopped at an altered hill, half of it cut away. Slag of shattered rock lay strewn alongside the path, the limestone pattern of the detritus matching the striations visible within the bare rock within the exposed hill.

Cortaro stepped off the path and kicked at a rock. "Hey sir, check this out."

Hale scanned the sky for Xaros before he stepped off the path, then came to where Cortaro stood, his feet straddling two boulders nearly a yard high and around. Cortaro pointed his muzzle at a circular hole in the rock.

"Looks like a Xaros disintegration hole,"

Hale said.

"Except that it's not," Cortaro said. "You see those striations on the side? Those were made by a drill bit. Whoever made this path blew out the side of that hill with explosives, dynamite or something. My grandfather used to work the mines in Mexico. He used to take me to the old shafts, show me how they did the work. I've seen this exact thing on Earth."

"You saying humans did this?" Hale asked.

"No, sir. The laws of physics are the same everywhere, right? Anyone does mining, eventually they'll use explosives to blow rock up. Better than knocking away at it with a pick axe, right?"

"Lowenn," Hale said to her through the IR. The air had cleared as their elevation increased. They still couldn't raise the *Breitenfeld* or the IR buoys, but they could talk to each other over a few dozen yards like they were right next to each other. "Lowenn, assuming the Shanishol did this, why would a civilization that can cross the stars still use tech from our twentieth century?"

"Maybe they left it all behind on those cubes. Decided to live at a lower technological level on their path to eternal life like the message promised," she said. "I know we run a risk of an equivalence fallacy by judging them to our cultural norms, but we don't know enough about their base behavior patterns to make any informed comparisons."

"I have no idea what she just said," Standish said over the open net.

"She means the Shanishol ain't us. Don't think that they're going to act like bluer, uglier human beings," Yarrow said.

"Steuben, any of this make sense to you?" Hale asked. "You've been on Xaros worlds before."

"I've been on one such world, uncivilized, and most of that mission was spent fleeing the drones once our presence was compromised," the Karigole said. "There were a number of theories discussed on Bastion before our arrival on Earth. None fit the evidence I've seen."

"Keep moving," Hale said. "We should see

the capital once we get to that next rise."

"Face-first, as always," Standish said.

"Standish!" Cortaro snapped. "You're on talking profile. Don't say another word unless you see something that can kill us."

The lance corporal nodded vigorously under his new constraints.

****

One of the first places Stacey insisted on seeing after she arrived on Bastion was the cartography lab. As a naval astrogator and star watcher since before she could walk, delving into Bastion's ancient databanks and star charts was a dream come true.

This trip to the laboratory had a different purpose than just the sheer joy of learning—she was there to test a hypothesis.

A platform, nothing more than a railing around a thin floor that Stacey thought was too flimsy to support any weight, extended into a tube-shaped room larger than any planetarium she'd ever been to on Earth. Stacey cracked her knuckles and shook her hands out.

"Chuck, show me a galactic map with a frontline trace of known and projected Xaros positions," she said.

The station answered her request instantly. A red shadow spread over the spiral arms of the Milky Way, encroaching on the last part of the galaxy still free from the Xaros' touch.

"Show me known Crucible gate locations and Xaros invasion fleets." Hundreds of stars lit up as Bastion plotted where Alliance members had seen the interstellar gates built during the drones' long march across the galaxy. Invasion routes, blood-red arrows stabbing toward inhabited systems, represented groups of drones numbering in the hundreds of billions strong. There were fifteen known invasion fleets, including the one that had bulldozed over humanity decades ago.

"Zoom in on Earth." Earth remained an anomaly in the entire galaxy, the only place where a Crucible gate was within Alliance control, and the only known inhabited planet behind Xaros lines.

"What are you doing?" a young woman's voice asked.

Stacey glanced over her shoulder where she saw a woman in her early twenties with the dark complexion of someone from the Indian subcontinent standing at the edge of the platform, her hands folded over her waist.

"Thrag'shak'a'zont … no, it's Thak'hath'a … damn it."

"Darcy." The woman waved a hand dismissively. Without the conversion field, she looked like a well-muscled manatee with long fingers instead of flippers and feeder tentacles instead of a mouth. Her species would be nicknamed "the Cthulhu" within a few minutes of meeting humanity anywhere but Bastion.

"Darcy, hello. Testing a theory. Care to help?"

"Always." She walked up next to Stacey and put her hand to her chin. "What are we looking for?"

"A pattern and a reason," she said to Darcy. "Bastion, show me where we still have spy probes and their effective collection range." A few dozen points spread up from free space and around the galactic core toward the other end of the galaxy.

"The farther the probe, the older the data," Darcy said. Despite all the Alliance's advancements, it had yet to find a way to transmit data faster than the speed of light. The only way it could coordinate action from the member worlds was by sending ambassadors to and from Bastion back to their home worlds with information and instructions.

"Show me a chart on worlds with known Crucibles on a habitability scale," Stacey said. A bar graph appeared with almost all the data points massed into a single column; shorter bars were on either side of the tall column. A few gates were in each data point, some containing only one or two. "So, the Crucibles go up on worlds like Earth. Oxygen, nitrogen and carbon dioxide atmospheres, in the Goldilocks' Zone for liquid water. Bastion, remove data points for star systems where planetary realignment rings are in use."

The short graphs next to the tallest bar vanished.

"So," Stacey said, "they're realigning potentially habitable worlds to meet their ideal. Make more room for what's coming. Now, eliminate data points with species that went extinct prior to Xaros contact and outside the main habitable zone." All the other data points vanished.

"They won't put a gate up on a world they can't colonize, but they will have one around planets with ruins, doesn't matter what kind of world it was."

"So what?" Darcy's hand came away from her chin like it was tossing the words out.

"So the Xaros aren't hanging around any of these worlds, making babies and living there. They move with a purpose. Who's going to live on all these habitable worlds the drones are setting up for them? And why are they interested in extinct civilizations?" Stacey asked.

"The accepted theory is that there's a colonization fleet coming behind the Xaros," Darcy said.

"OK, but where are they? The Xaros have been in the galaxy for almost a hundred thousand years. There's a pretty significant buffer from where they were first seen and where they are today. If there's a colony fleet coming, what're they waiting for? Bastion, show me worlds with Crucibles and surface activity."

A buzzer sounded. "No known data entry."

"The data may be old," Stacey said, "but so far there's no one moving into all the prime real estate."

"They could be waiting until the entire galaxy is theirs—hard to assign motives to a phantom civilization. We can only infer," Darcy said.

"Bastion, at current rate of advance, how long until the Xaros overrun the entire galaxy?" Stacey asked.

"Three thousand nine hundred and twelve

years," the station replied.

"Let's assume," Stacey said, "that you're right and they won't get here until they own every star. Maybe they're about four thousand years away from the spot where they first arrived." Stacey raised her hands and grasped at the edge of the galaxy where the Xaros were first encountered and pulled it toward her. The galactic display zoomed in to the edge of the star field.

"Now, this math contains a lot of inference, but if there's a colony fleet coming and it'll arrive the exact day the galaxy is conquered …," Stacey said, tracing a line out from the edge of the galaxy and drawing a circle, "they should be somewhere around here."

"That's wonderful, Stacey, fine detective work," Darcy said and Stacey was impressed with how well Bastion put a sarcastic tone to her words. "Too bad we'll all be long dead before any light or anything on the electromagnetic spectrum from that place can even reach the spy probes or Bastion."

"We don't have to *see* it, Darcy. We just

have to detect it. They want lots of room—that's why they're rearranging planets. So whatever's coming should be big, real big, to fill those planets. Right?"

"I think I know where you're going with this. Gravitons?"

"Gravitons don't bother with the speed of light. We could do a survey of that part of space and see if there's a dip in the space-time continuum that would indicate there is a colony fleet coming." Stacey's face lit up with excitement.

"Bastion, conduct a—"

"Negative," the station said. "Resources and computation power for such a project require Qa'Resh approval. The previous eight requests similar to what you desire were denied."

"What?" Stacey asked. "You mean I'm not the first person to realize this?"

"Correct."

"Why didn't you say something?"

"You didn't ask."

Darcy's laugh only made Stacey feel more

foolish.

"Who made the previous requests?"

"All requests came from species designation: Toth," Bastion said.

Darcy's laugh cut off.

"What?" Stacey asked. "Who are the Toth?"

****

The Marines took cover in the boulders packed into the mountainside. Lowenn, not used to climbing mountains in armor, had to be helped the last few hundred yards up the steep footpath. She sat against a boulder with her visor open, gulping for air. Yarrow checked her over.

"Yarrow, she going to live?" Hale asked him on a private IR channel.

"She'll be fine in a few minutes. I've got her armor pumping electrolytes. Want me to hit her with a tranq, get her nerves under control?" Yarrow asked.

"No, she's held up better than I thought she

would. Keep an eye on her," Hale said and closed the channel. He tapped Bailey and Torni on their shoulders. "Let's get up on the ridge and take a look at what's over there."

"Finally. I've already got a perch picked out." Bailey moved along the mountainside and climbed around the white boulders. Hale and Torni followed behind her.

Bailey unslung her rifle and reassembled the rail gun in seconds. She gave the buttstock a quick pat then slithered up to a pair of boulders on the mountain crest. She tucked a battery pack against the side of the boulder and ran a cable into the weapon. She tucked the sniper rifle against her shoulder and looked into the scope.

The feed from her weapon went onto Hale's visor and he saw the capital. Four pairs of stepped pyramids, each cut with staircases leading to the flat apex, ran along a center line, two pairs on either side of a massive pyramid dead center of the city. The massive pyramid was alabaster white with milky hues covering the sides. Hale squeezed his eyes shut and looked again. He could have sworn he saw some of the colors changing from subtle shades of ivory and eggshell to marble and pearl.

The feed zoomed in to smaller buildings, two- and three-story stone structures laid out haphazardly on either side of the pyramids. There didn't seem to be any roads in the city other than the one on either side of the great white pyramid and between the stepped pyramids.

Bailey's head popped up from the scope, then went back down.

"What the hell was that?" she asked.

"I didn't see anything," Torni said. "Is it Xaros?"

"Ain't Xaros, that's for sure." Bailey said. Hale zoomed away from the stone building and tried to find what had Bailey's attention.

"Bailey, send it to me," Hale said.

His feed zoomed in on a gap between stone buildings. There, clinging to the side of a building, was what looked like a giant salamander. It was almost six feet long from stubby tail to the pointed end of its head. It wore a tight blue body glove that stopped midway down its calves and arms; bare scales over its six-fingered clawed hands and feet were a ruddy black. The feed zoomed in on its head; yellow eyes twitched independently of each other. A half mask covered its upper snout leaving its jaw free to snap at insects buzzing around it, and wire ran from the sides of the mask and into its body glove.

The creature climbed up the stone building, peeked its head over the roof, and then darted into an open window.

"Was that a local?" Bailey asked.

"It had a breathing mask on. Something native wouldn't need that," Torni said.

Bailey tensed. "Sir, this just got weirder. Look."

Hale's feed panned to the stairs on a stepped pyramid. A reptilian centaur walked up the long staircase, its clawed legs similar to the alien he saw on the stone house. Its upper torso hinged up from the front pair of legs, its arms little different from the legs carrying it up the stairs. The alien wore pale blue armor, which shifted of its own accord so as not to hinder the alien's movements. A long weapon that looked like vines twisted into the shape of a rifle was slung diagonally across its back. The head was larger than the other one, wider and crested with a bright red fan. It wore the same breathing mask as the others.

"Must be an officer, look at all that shiny," Bailey said.

Two of the smaller aliens scampered toward the larger one. With a wave of the larger alien's claws, the others bolted away.

Hale considered his options. Once, just once, he wished a mission would go as planned and as expected.

"Steuben, Lowenn, any idea what these things are?" Hale asked. He sent pics from his feed history to them both with a few swipes against his forearm display.

"Well," Lowenn said, "they're definitely not Shanishol. Given—"

Steuben sprang from his seat next to her and charged up the mountainside with more speed and determination than a human armor suit charging into battle. The Karigole bounded off boulders and stopped his advance just short of Bailey. He crawled next to the sniper, the claws on his fingertips distended more than double their normal length and dug into the earth.

Steuben spoke in his native tongue, guttural words Hale didn't understand.

"Steuben? Something you care to share?" Hale asked.

"They are the Toth. Betrayers, traitors and murderers." Steuben's hand gripped a rock and squeezed. The rock trembled then burst apart. "We should have known they'd come. A race of carrion feeders couldn't resist this."

"Something tells me they aren't going to help us find Omnium and how the Shanishol died," Hale said.

"The Toth." Steuben said the name with derision. "They were once the lynchpin to the entire

Alliance. With the Alliance's technology and their numbers they could have been the grand army that turned the Xaros back. But they turned on us all, tried to capture a Qa'Resh, and raided worlds that once depended on them for protection. All to feed their overlord's addictions. They ...." Steuben tapped a closed fist against his chest. "The Qa'Resh did something I don't understand—they kept them from using their stolen jump drives. There's been no contact with the Toth for a century. Now they are here."

"Are they hostile?" Hale asked.

"We must kill them. All of them," Steuben said.

"Steuben, I'm not going to start a war between Earth and these Toth if I don't have to."

The skin on Steuben's face rippled with color. "You don't understand, Hale. The Toth look at all other sentient species as fodder for their overlords. They will kill all of us without hesitation."

"Then we'll do our best to avoid them.

227

Remember why we're here. The codex. The Omnium. Not to pick a fight with every new civilization we come across."

"Hale, if they detect us …."

"I'm guessing they're here for the same reasons we are. They know the Xaros are here. I'm willing to bet they're doing their best to not be noticed too. If we have to shoot Toth in the face we will. We're Marines, Steuben, not sheep. Now let's get down there before that storm rolls in."

CHAPTER 8

From where she stood on the roof of the apartment building, the night skyline of Phoenix wasn't as Shannon Martel remembered it. She'd stood atop this same building many nights and looked out to see skyscrapers and the rolling dome of the Veteran's Memorial Coliseum, all lit against the desert sky. She used to count the delivery drone running lights as they ran from fulfillment centers or neighborhood 3D printing maker factories to the millions of homes in the city.

Now, what remained of the city stood against the night sky like tombstones, silent and cold. The Xaros vivisection had touched few of the city's skyscrapers, leaving empty buildings rotting away from exposure and neglect.

Every person in the Ibarra fleet that planned on settling the moons of Saturn found themselves rebuilding the city of Phoenix and living in and around the utility grid that survived around Euskal Tower, the center of Marc Ibarra's once vast financial empire and where he'd hidden humanity's one alien ally during the Xaros occupation.

Martel spotted a robot crew laying a new solar-collecting roadway to the empty city center, the forward edge of reclamation efforts. Most survivors lived in tent cities until the construction crews could renovate homes for a more permanent housing solution.

The irony didn't escape her. With all the room in the world to live, most of humanity still lived right on top of each other. The sanitation conditions were better than the mega-slums had been in Beijing and New Delhi, but the amount of personal space was about the same. The rehydrated extruded plant-matter meals weren't the best, but they'd have to make do until the robot farms along the Salt River were up and running.

Most of the company executives that were with the fleet had apartments around Euskal Tower, making it easier for Marc Ibarra to summon them at all hours of the day and night. These apartments were repaired and renovated first, which didn't sit well with the average would-have-been colonist, but the executives were putting in twenty-hour days to get the city back up and running, to build Titan station and to repair the space fleet. It wasn't as if they could spend many nights in their old rooms anyway. Martel was one such executive. She'd feigned exhaustion to get away from work for a few hours, but sleep wasn't part of her plans for the evening.

Martel glanced at her Ubi and kept waiting. She was early, like always. The clean desert air helped her focus, rationalize what she was asked to do. She thought the days of carrying out Marc Ibarra's dirty work had ended once the Xaros wiped out the vast majority of humanity, but he'd sent her a target packet a few hours ago with a termination order.

She'd killed for him before: The occasional corporate employee that tried to sell trade secrets to their rivals or foreign spies. Government officials that didn't have the courtesy to stay bought after Ibarra had paid the demanded bribes. Nothing she hadn't done for years when she'd worked for the American CIA.

Decades ago, Ibarra had found her in Baja California, disillusioned and drinking herself to death. He'd offered her a chance to put her skills to use protecting his dream for humanity. A humanity where science and technology and one's willingness to work hard and smart would determine success, not the lottery of birth or allegiance to the right political theory. He'd lied to her, hadn't told her that he was engineering humanity's survival from the impending Xaros invasion. After she'd returned to Phoenix after the Battle of the Crucible, she'd looked back and seen how her actions shaped that destiny.

Marc Ibarra, or whatever his intelligence inside that probe was now, had called her and tried to apologize for lying to her, but she'd forgiven him before he could finish explaining. She would have done the same thing in his position, and she had a long career of lying to subordinates for their own good while she'd been in the CIA.

Regardless, Martel thought her days of killing in service of Ibarra's plan were over, until a few hours ago.

A delivery drone flew up the side of the building and set a tote bag against the roof, then buzzed away. Inside the bag, Martel found a prescription bottle of pills with her target's name on it, a bottle of store-bought alcohol, an unlabeled hypospray and a gauss pistol. Everything she'd need.

She got into the elevator and hit the button for her target's floor. Living in the same building certainly made this mission easier, and Ibarra would take care of the camera footage as he always did.

Martel leaned close to the glass on the side

of the elevator, examining her face. Ever since she'd come back from the fleet, something seemed off. She'd had the best plastic surgery and rejuvenation treatments Ibarra could afford while she worked for him—a woman in her nineties couldn't run around assassinating people otherwise—but there was something different about her face. She still had the same half-Korean half-Caucasian features, exotic and hard to quantify, but her jawline was tighter, her nose a bit flatter than she remembered.

Must be something to do with the time jump, she thought. Not that anyone had mentioned the physiological effects of missing nearly three decades of time. She'd have it set just right once Phoenix had recovered to the point where elective plastic surgery was available again. She chuckled. She'd probably have natural wrinkles by then.

The display above the elevator door closed in on her target's floor. She reached into the bag and wrapped her hand around the gauss pistol's grip. She felt the weapon chamber a round as it responded to her palm print. The door opened and revealed an empty hallway.

"Lock all doors and freeze this elevator," Martel said. The building's automated controls were slaved to her voice, which would make this assignment easier than usual. No chance or worry of someone seeing her at this odd hour. She heard deadbolts click shut on apartment doors as she walked down the hallway.

"Kill the lights." Martel tapped at her left temple and the night-vision lenses within her eyes activated to compensate for the now dark hallway. It wouldn't do to have light spill into the target's apartment while she was sleeping. Martel stopped at apartment 437 and pulled out her pistol. She opened the door with her toe and waited, listening for any sound that her target was awake or moving around.

She heard nothing and went in, closing the door behind her, but not all the way. The click of a door latch had been enough to alert people in the past. The apartment was a one-bedroom affair meant for overworked and lonely executives. A few hundred square feet of upscale housing with an unused kitchen, a couch used more as a spot to leave jackets and briefcases than for relaxing in front of a television projection, a single bathroom and one bedroom with a closed door.

Martel tested the closed door and found it unlocked. She swung it open slowly, keeping her muzzle flush with the door.

Her target was in bed. The woman's breathing was deep and regular, exactly what Martel expected from a sleeper. Martel kept the pistol trained on her target as she crept toward her. She set the tote down and pulled out the hypospray. She pressed a button on the back of the nozzle and waited to hear a slight click telling her the deadly contents were active.

Martel reached her arm over the bed and hovered the hypospray over the woman's neck. The hypospray ticked, and Martel pressed it against the exposed flesh. There was a hiss, and Martel leaned back and dropped the hypospray into the bag. She took out the alcohol, unsnapped the lid and poured a little bit of the amber liquid on the floor and on the bed, then set it on the nightstand.

The bottle of pills came out and Martel stopped to read the name. She knew the woman and wondered exactly what she'd done to earn Ibarra's sanction. The coroner's examination, carried out by a pliant Ibarra Corporation medical service robot, would list the cause of death as suicide. All too easy.

A lamp snapped on.

Martel dropped the pills and aimed her pistol at the woman lying in bed, her hand on a lamp and her terrified face staring right at Martel.

"Don't," Martel said quietly and forcefully. "I've already killed you. You can stay quiet and go peacefully or make this difficult for both of us. You scream and you will go slow and painfully."

"Martel? No, this is impossible," Caruthers said.

"It is possible. It is happening and the feeling in your chest is your internal organs failing. Stay. Quiet."

"I saw you next to Ibarra when he addressed the fleet the last time. You were there. There's no way you could have made it to the fleet before the jump. How did you survive on Earth all that time?" Caruthers asked. She rubbed her jawline as the poison in her system made speaking more difficult.

"I don't know what you're talking about. I was on the fleet, same as you," Martel said.

"No … I have … pictures on my Ubi. You're there. You must have died," Caruthers' eyes lost focus as her pupils dilated. "You're one of Ibarra's abominations, aren't you? Grown in a tube … no soul." She coughed and slumped back against her pillows. Her hand fell from the light and knocked an Ubi on her nightstand to the floor.

"What the hell are you talking about?" Martel's voice rose to a hiss. She sidestepped around the bed, her pistol ready to end Caruthers's life a few seconds early if she made any sudden moves.

Tatiana Caruthers' breathing became shallow, irregular. She coughed twice then went

238

limp. Her head lolled to the side and white foam fell from the corner of her lips. Dead.

Martel picked up the Ubi and pressed her thumb against the screen, her print overriding Caruthers's lock, and the device came to life.

"Show me Ibarra's last address to the fleet," she said. The Ubi played a video—Marc Ibarra, elderly and leaning against a cane, reading from a prepared speech. Martel's face twisted in confusion. This was a major event. Why didn't she remember this? In the background, Martel saw a woman with dark hair behind the regular group of Ibarra flunkies he traveled with.

The video continued and Martel got a good look at the person behind the group.

"Freeze, zoom in on the third person from the left," Martel said. The Ubi did as requested, and Martel saw herself.

"This can't be right," she said. She looked at the video's time stamp, just tens of minutes before the false engines in the Saturn fleet took the entire fleet out of the space-time continuum and held them beyond the reach of the Xaros fleet for almost thirty years.

"No, I remember. I *remember* being on the fleet, you dead bitch," Martel said to Caruthers. She dropped the Ubi to the ground and bolted from the apartment. She ran to the elevator, her mind failing to reconcile what she remembered, what she knew, and what she'd just seen.

She got to the elevator and hit the button for her floor. Nothing happened.

"Reset!" The elevator doors closed once she removed her restrictions and the lift got moving.

Martel's hands opened and clenched, running over her face as her mind raced.

"Not right, not right at all," she muttered. She looked at her reflection, seeing a face that didn't match her memories.

The elevator opened and Martel sprinted down the hallway and into the security of her own apartment.

She ran into the bathroom and locked the door behind her. She reached beneath the sink and pulled out an Ubi.

"Marc? Marc, it's Martel."

Ibarra, his younger-looking hologram, filled the screen. "Hello, Martel. Mission accomplished?"

"It is done." Martel swallowed hard as panic crept up from her stomach and doused her heart with fear. She'd never reacted this way to a killing, her decades of composure in the face of stress and danger unraveling.

"Marc, she said something. Said I was dead. I saw the video, saw me. Me. Right next to you. Was I there? With you? Why don't I remember that? What the hell's happening to me?" Martel set the Ubi on the bathroom sink and looked in the mirror. She pulled at her face, trying to remake it as she remembered.

"I'm sorry, Martel," Ibarra said.

"What?"

"There's been an error in your memories. I thought we'd fixed this production flaw but it seems something slipped through the cracks," Ibarra said sadly.

Martel snatched the Ubi up and held it close to her face.

"She called me an abomination. Something without a soul. What the hell have you done to me?" She could see her wild-eyed reflection.

"I'm sorry, Shannon. This is my fault. I take no pleasure in this," Ibarra said.

A tiny capsule in the base of Martel's brain popped, disrupting just enough blood flow to kill her instantly. Martel collapsed against the sink, smashing her head against the edge. The Ubi clattered to the floor and shut off.

****

Ibarra's hologram stood in the Crucible control room. He put his hands on his hips and shook his head from side to side.

"That was unexpected," the probe said. Its silver light rose from the plinth in the center of the room.

"Shut the hell up," Ibarra said. "That was the second time I've killed her."

"Your brain patterns are erratic. Should I shut you down for a maintenance scan?"

"It's called grief. Grief, you stupid lump of electrons. Let me have it before you try and purge it as programming error." Ibarra swung back to the communications panel and his fingers swiped through contacts until he found who he needed and doubled-tapped the screen to make the call.

His hologram didn't actually touch the screen, but the computer system in the control room reacted accordingly. Ibarra's mental imprint rejected the notion of doing everything by mental command. It still wanted a tactile connection to the physical world and the probe gave Ibarra that illusion.

The call went through and Thorrson's very tired and bleary-eyed image came up.

"Boss? You know what time it is in Hawaii?" Thorsson murmured.

"I don't sleep anymore, Thorsson. It does wonders for productivity and I suggest you learn to do the same," Ibarra said.

"My report." Thorsson sat up and rubbed sleep from his eyes. "You want it now or can I get it to you once the next batch of tubes are online, like usual?"

"I need you to regrow and reload specimen thirty-seven immediately," Ibarra said.

"Thirty-seven … Martel? Why? You know iterating a specific body type and her recorded experiences put a real toll on the computers. I could have nine more proccies decanted and in the general population by the time another one of her is ready to go." Thorsson looked at amended production graphs on a screen and held up his Ubi so that Ibarra could see the impact of what he'd just requested.

"I'm well aware of what it'll do to our production timeline, Thorsson. I need her back. And I need her as soon as you can give her to me. We'll send over some amendments to her memory file and I want the face molding done in utero, not plastic surgery once she's regrown," Ibarra said.

"That'll add another day to her tube occupation," Thorsson said with a roll of his eyes.

"Get it done. I don't pay you to whine."

"Wait, are we getting paid again?"

"You know what I mean. I want updates on her twice a day. Make sure you encrypt and hide the report. The rest of the council can't know about this," Ibarra said.

"You're the boss, boss."

Ibarra ended the call with a flick of his hand.

"You exhibit the exact emotions and irrational behavior you're trying to prevent in the other humans," the probe said. "Why is your emotional attachment to the Martel specimen overriding the logic needed to rebuild the crews for the fleet? There will be eleven fewer Marines, pilots and crewmen available to fight the Xaros when they arrive. And for what?"

"Martel has skills we need," Ibarra said.

"We do not need an assassin."

"We did today. Caruthers was trying to contact bleeding hearts in the company and in the fleet. She opposed what we're doing—the only course of action we came up with that will beat the

Xaros when they return in fourteen years. I can't have our plans disrupted, same as when we were preparing the fleet for the Xaros' first arrival," Ibarra said.

"You think we will need Martel again?"

"I hope not, but it's possible."

"Your cognitive patterns remain distressed. You risk this same disruption by recreating, and thereby creating the chance of losing, Martel. Why not let her stay dead, so to speak. We can create an intelligence that will serve the same function."

"Because it won't be *her*, Jimmy. It won't be the same," Ibarra said. He found the file with his address to the fleet that Caruthers must have mentioned to Martel and purged Martel's image from it. He sent the probe a command to repeat that action on all known databanks and any that might be encountered in the future.

"This is illogical. You're taking an unnecessary risk to satisfy some legacy biological needs in your memory matrix." The probe's light wavered in annoyance.

"You're so eloquent when you're pissed off. Don't try to make sense of human beings, Jimmy. We've been trying to do it since we figured out how to speak to each other and we haven't made much progress," Ibarra said.

CHAPTER 9

There was a thin line around the edge of the city, a dark band the width of a thumb. Hale looked down at it from where he stood on the dusty plain that extended to the mountains. The city beyond the line was pristine, rough cobblestone streets without a speck of dirt or invading weeds growing between the seams of concrete and stone. Stone-and-mortar buildings with doorways built for something twice the size of a human looked like the occupants had left for lunch, ready to return at any moment.

"Lowenn," Hale said, "how long has this place been abandoned?"

"The Xaros arrived a thousand years ago.

The last invitation went out a few months before that," she said.

"Why is it so … clean?" Yarrow asked. "Phoenix, Tucson, St. George, they were all empty for about thirty years, and now they're falling apart. Anthalas has rain, lots of plant and animal life. But this looks like the Shanishol were here yesterday."

"Maybe they're all ghosts," Standish said.

"There's no such thing as ghosts, Standish," Hale said.

"Remember when you said there was no such thing as aliens? Yeah …."

"You're violating your talking profile," Cortaro said.

Standish raised his hands in mock surrender.

"I do not understand your trepidation," Steuben said. "The Toth are in the city without incident. What are we waiting for?"

Hale glanced down at the charge reading on his gauss rifle and flexed his fingers around the handle. He lifted his boot and set foot over the line. There was no reaction, no warning klaxons, no swarm of Xaros drones emerging from beneath the cobblestones. He took another step over the line and waved his Marines on to follow him.

"This is a recon mission," Hale said. "Avoid detection and don't fire unless our lives depend on it." He raised his rifle to his shoulder and kept the muzzle low. He jogged to the nearest building, three stories of rough stone and concrete with the same bubble-shaped imperfections they had seen at the corral.

He took cover against the wall and took a quick peek around the corner, seeing nothing but more crude buildings and silence.

"Sir, look at that," Torni said as she ran up beside him and pointed to the ground leading back to the edge of the city. Dust carried in by the Marines and knocked loose from their boots trembled on the cobblestones then blew through the air, carried by a strong breeze Hale couldn't feel. The dust flew off the edge of the city and over the black line.

"Let me try something." Orozco pulled a

pebbled from between the tread of his boots and tossed it in the air. The pebble froze in midair just above the cobblestones, then was swept from the city.

"That's … different," Bailey said.

Cortaro, standing beneath a window sill that was almost seven feet above the ground, jumped up and grabbed the edge. He pulled himself up and took a quick glance inside. "Sir, there's stuff inside this house. Open doorway on the other side," Cortaro said.

Hale nodded and led the Marines to the other side. There was no door in the entranceway, not even a frame or hinges to suggest one had ever been there. *The Shanishol weren't much on security or privacy*, he thought. He ran inside, scanning the room over his rifle sights. A staircase without a railing led up from the back wall. A high wooden table with clay bowls and metal knives sat against the wall to Hale's left. Two round wooden lids covered depressions on the floor next to the table. Mats made of thatched reeds were laid over the floor next to the far wall.

The rest of the Marines filed in behind Hale.

"Cortaro, clear the second floor," Hale said. The Marine and Standish ran up the too-tall stairs.

"Clear," Cortaro announced a moment later.

Lowenn, her weapon dangling from loose fingers, looked around the room. She picked up a knife from a table, the handle and blade meant for a much larger wielder.

"This isn't right," she said. "This is the home of a civilization that's pre-industrial. I don't see any evidence of electricity, do you? But this blade …." She took a sensor wand off her gauntlet and pressed it against the knife. A waveform coalesced on her display and she gingerly set the knife back on the table. "That's made from Omnium. The underlying energy signature is there."

Against Hale's protest, she turned and lifted a wooden lid from the recession. Lowenn stood still, balancing the wooden lid on its side. "Huh," she said.

Hale pointed his rifle at the depression and

walked up to it. Inside was a clay urn full of plastic pouches, the Shanishol dash and whirl writing printed on each one.

"What does it say?" he asked Lowenn. He put his hand on the lid; it felt new and full of sap as squeezed it, not a thousand years old.

Lowenn picked up a packet and her mouth moved as she tried to read the writing. She flipped the packet over then frowned. "'A gift from the prophet.' That's what they all say." Lowenn pulled at the edges and a corner ripped away, revealing a square of white chalky material. She wafted air from over the open package toward her nose and sniffed. "I think it's food."

"Steuben, you want a bite?" Torni asked.

The Karigole shook his head emphatically.

"Giant half-dead alien bugs, yes. Millennia-year-old field rations, no. Remind me to get you a can of *Surstromming* or anchovies," she said.

"Sir," Cortaro said from the top of the stairs, "this is …I don't know."

Hale plucked the food packet from

Lowenn's hand and tossed it back in the urn then set the wooden lid back down. "Show me."

There was a suit of armor on the second floor. A silver and gold breastplate with pearl-like inlays attached to shoulder pauldrons hung on a wooden crossbeam. Platinum chain-linked mail, so fine and intricate Hale mistook it for silk until he touched it, was attached to the underside of the breastplate and extended to the floor. The armor was twice the size of the combat armor Hale wore. A halberd made from the same gold and platinum hung on the wall, the shaft too large for Hale to wrap his hands around it.

"Then there's this," Cortaro said. A poster, the construction too cheap and flimsy to be a meaningful work of art, hung on the wall. A Shanishol, his arms held up to his side and wearing a white robe, basked in golden light. The worshiper had bright golden eyes and was flanked by Shanishol wearing the same armor as stored in the building.

"'Exaltation for all,'" Lowenn said, reading

the words on the poster from where she stood on the stairs.

"Sir, can I keep this?" Standish asked. He held a straw doll, wrapped in threadbare cloth, a blue pigment added to the hands, arms and face of the doll.

Of all the things he'd seen in this city, the doll set Hale's nerves on fire. His breathing quickened and fear's icy touch brushed over his heart. *Children*, he thought. *There were children here.*

"What did I tell you about touching? And talking?" Cortaro said. Standish laid the doll back on the floor, reverently.

"OK." Hale went back downstairs, wanting more than anything to just get away from that doll. "This obviously isn't what we're looking for. Let's keep moving toward the pyramids, keep our eyes open for anything useful."

The Marines moved through the city slowly, and with purpose. Half the team bounded from one house to another while the rest kept them in over watch, covering their movement. There was no deviation among the houses, other than a few three-story buildings. Every glance Hale made inside the homes revealed the same thing—a simple lifestyle. Some had open meal packets arrayed in a circle on the ground floor; others had wooden blocks and hand-carved figurines strewn about the floor.

Life had ended in this city suddenly, and the Xaros weren't to blame.

Cortaro's fire team ran past Hale and pressed against a wall. Yarrow glanced around the corner, then glanced again. He held up a fist to stop Hale and his team from moving up. Yarrow looked at Hale and tapped his index finger against his forehead, mimicking the lieutenant rank bar Hale wore when he wasn't in his armor.

Hale, alone, ran forward.

"Sir, not sure what this is," the young medic said. Yarrow held his rifle around the corner and the camera feed from the tip of his rifle showed Hale a road of wooden planks flush with the ground around it. The road looped around homes and led toward the distant pyramids.

"I thought it was a canal," Lowenn said over the IR. "I saw it on the pictures the *Breitenfeld* took from orbit. It runs beneath all the pyramids."

"It's boarded up. … I've got an idea," Hale said. "Bravo team, cover me and alpha. We're going to pry up one of those boards. If the canal is empty, we can take it straight to the pyramids without being exposed."

Hale made his way to the canal and knelt next to the edge. Deep-red wooden beams cut into rectangles extended from one concrete lip to the other. Hale looked closer—the wood was stained red, like its sap had bled through the wood when it was hewn. He tried to stuff his fingers into the gap between the wood and the concrete, but his armor was too thick to get any purchase.

Hale squeezed his right hand into a fist and cocked his hand to the side twice. A blade snapped from the gauntlet housing. He raised his arm then plunged the blade into the beam. He pressed his body weight against the blade, using the next beam over as a fulcrum. The beam raised a few inches in the air and Cortaro grabbed hold of it. He lifted the beam higher and Standish and Torni struggled to push it aside.

"Almost …," Standish grunted. "Got it!"

The beam tumbled over and Standish slipped. He fell face-first into the gap and Hale heard a dry snap as he yanked his blade free from the beam.

Standish let out a wail and flopped away from the gap, backing away on his hands and knees as fast as he could. Cortaro and Torni crossed themselves.

"What is it?" Hale looked into the gap.

Skulls. Dozens and dozens of Shanishol skulls were exposed, their bulbous craniums and bone spurs stained red and brown from dried blood, mouths agape in eternal screams. More bones lay beneath the skulls, filling the entire canal to the brim. The skulls ranged from adult sized down to ones so small they must have belonged to Shanishol children.

"Put it back. Put the beam back," Hale said quietly.

"Jesus, Mary and Joseph, sir," Standish gasped, on the verge of hyperventilating. "What the hell happened to them?"

"You think I know? You think any of this makes sense to me?" Hale set a foot against the beam and shoved it toward the gap. He kept his head turned from the charnel house beneath the beams. "This happened a long, long time ago. There's not a damn thing we can do about it so get off your ass and get this covered up so we can keep moving!"

Torni and Cortaro got the beam put back in place. Standish looked down and when saw he was still sitting on the beams, he scampered off like he suddenly realized he was on a hot plate.

Hale's hands squeezed his rifle again and again. He felt his heartbeat pounding in his ears as he tried to focus on what to do next. He'd led his Marines into a crypt, and he didn't know how to get them out.

A peal of thunder cut across the sky. He looked up and a drop of red rain hit his visor. The sky darkened as sheets of rain poured from magenta clouds. The rain fell harder, but it didn't make a sound as it fell around Hale.

Just when it can't get any worse, he thought.

"Whoa," Yarrow said.

Hale looked at the medic, who was backing into a Shanishol house. Raindrops were suspended in the air around the medic's ankles, each new drop coming to a halt just above the ground, never touching the cobblestones.

Around the Marines, rainfall formed a carpet of drops, quivering and glistening in the sun light.

"I hate this planet. Hate it, hate it, hate it," Standish muttered.

The raindrops started moving, running together and forming a stream of red water as thick as Hale's arm. The new stream, which never touched the ground, ran over the canal and toward the pyramids. Newly fallen raindrops wavered over the ground, then traveled over to join the stream.

Raindrops never touched the buildings either. Water ran down invisible drains from the roofs and walls and into the ever-growing stream.

"There's no delta on the city's edges," Lowenn said. "No place where all this water's being dumped. If it's been like this for a thousand years, all this water must be going into a sewer system of some kind."

"We get beneath the city, maybe we'll find a way into the pyramids," Steuben said.

Hale was about to answer when a golden mote of light zipped past his face.

"Did anyone else see that?" Hale asked.

"Sir, look up," Cortaro said.

Golden motes streaked through the sky, bending like magnetic waves toward terminal points along the boulevard that ran through the center of the city.

Hale held his arm out. Motes passed through his body without sensation or effect to him or the motes.

"It's the energy field that keeps the city

pristine," Yarrow said. "There's an access point where the fields converge."

"Marine, how the hell do you know that?" Cortaro asked.

"Know what, gunney?"

"About energy fields and this city. What you just said."

"I didn't say anything, gunney," Yarrow tapped the base of his palm against the side of his helmet.

"How much longer will we stand in this rain?" Steuben asked.

"We're going to the source of the energy fields," Hale said. "The source of what keeps this place looking like new should be more important than where they flush the toilet. Anyone have a better idea?" No one spoke up. "Let's move out before the rain stops."

****

A Toth menial in a space suit floated through space, adjusting its course with a handheld vector gun that shot compressed air.

It could see the human buoy, matte black but just visible against the dead gray of the moon's surface. The menial shot off most of its vector fuel to bring it to a dead stop just above the buoy. The creature took a ruby-colored lens from a pouch and placed it over the IR receiver/transmitter node.

The menial's face twitched as it waited. Its tongue lashed over an eye to clear away a mote of dust. A double beep came through the suit's IR system; its mission was accomplished. The Toth had a wiretap on the humans' communication system. The information the overlord pulled from the fragmented and incomplete human minds hinted at an IR relay system. Finding it hadn't proved difficult.

The Toth underling fired off the last of its vector fuel and went tumbling end over end into space. Its mission didn't include recovery.

CHAPTER 10

The motes flowed into a tower that stood fifty feet over the boulevard, which was nothing but packed earth as wide as a football field. The tower was a square with a single door and two windows at the very top through which motes converged.

The rain had faded away, but not before it coated the Marines with a sticky film of red mud. Their armor looked like it was as bloodstained as the planks over the canal of the dead. Golden rays of sunlight stabbed through the passing storm clouds and flowed across the pyramids.

Hale ran into the tower, which held nothing but a dirt floor. He looked up and saw a few stray motes of light come and go, but there was nothing else to see. As he wandered into the middle of the room, his foot hit something. He jabbed his toe into the dirt and found a thick metal ring attached to the floor.

"Let's lift it up," Hale said.

"Move." Steuben waved Hale away and grabbed the ring. He pulled and lifted a metal hatch into the air, dirt billowing through the enclosure as Hale wondered just how long it had been since anyone—or anything—had disturbed this place. A ladder with wrought-iron rungs descended into the darkness.

A hot wave of air blew out of the hole and Hale felt the heat seep through his armor like it was a breath from the devil.

"You first, sir?" Torni asked. "Like always?"

If ever there was a time to reconsider his lead from the front ethos, this wasn't it. Hale snapped his rifle against the magnetic locks on his back and turned on his visor's night-vision filter. He could see the next couple rungs, but not the bottom of the ladder. He grabbed the first rung and lowered himself down.

The wide-spaced ladder demanded caution; the biomechanics of the Shanishol weren't easily compatible with his smaller frame. He counted nineteen rungs before his foot hit the ground. His Marines followed. Bailey, the shortest Marine, complaining bitterly and with an amazing assortment of expletives as she struggled down the ladder.

His filter didn't pick up anything past more than a few yards. Hale touched his temple and an IR light illuminated the cave around him. The walls were bare stone, rough angles and slick with moisture.

"Going to have to use the lamps," Hale said. "Go vocal. The IR suit-to-suit will get washed out." His Marines knew the drill, but it never failed that one person would forget what to do and end up talking to themselves the entire time they were down here, wondering why everyone was ignoring him or her.

The tunnel extended away from the ladder, a pathway just big enough for a Shanishol but with plenty of overhead clearance for Hale's team. Hale set his gauss rifle to SCATTER. His cobalt-coated tungsten bullets would fire as several small-shot rounds when he pulled the trigger. He desperately wanted *not* to get into a firefight down here; it would be as quick and deadly as a knife fight in a closet.

After a few dozen yards, Hale saw a pale green light at the end of the tunnel. The tunnel opened up into a larger tunnel shaped like a half cylinder. Individually cut blocks, each a jagged starburst, fit against each other as they stretched across the ceiling. Raised walkways ran along the sides. Frescos of Shanishol following and worshiping the white-cloaked Shanishol with the glowing eyes decorated the walls. The loop-and-whirls script bordered the top and bottom of the frescos. Hot air ran across the top of the new tunnel, moved along quickly by an unseen force.

"It's like the subways in Washington, DC,"

Yarrow said, "but alien and without any rats or that pee smell."

"What's that writing say?" Hale asked Lowenn.

"'Follow the path to exaltation' over and over again," she said.

The wide tunnel led to their right and left. Hale tossed a rock toward the roof and the airstream pulled it to the right.

"That way," Hale said.

"Anyone else notice that the prophet-looking guy is the only one with the glowing eyes in all the murals?" Bailey asked.

"It's probably a religious observance. Catholic and Christian Orthodox medieval art put golden halos around the heads of saints," Lowenn said.

"But he had glowing eyes in that weirdo invitation he sent out to the whole galaxy, didn't he?" Bailey asked.

"That is an astute observation," Lowenn said. She stopped to peer closely at one of the murals. She drew her analysis wand and pressed it against the golden eyes of the prophet on the mural.

"Omnium," she said and snapped the wand back into her armor.

"That guy sure loves the stuff," Orozco said.

They came to a cross section where a stone circle lay in the middle of two tunnels showing Shanishol script and a carving of a Shanishol arm pointing to each direction.

Lowenn walked around the circle and looked over her shoulder toward each direction.

"Well?" Hale asked.

"We came from 'The Waiting Place of Souls,' which translates roughly to purgatory. To the left is 'Servants to the Prophet' and to the right is 'The Long Death.' Hell? Maybe. Straight ahead is … um …." She put her hands on her hips and turned around to read the script from another direction.

"Lowenn, we brought you down here for precisely this reason," Hale said.

"It's not Shanishol! It's some sort of

phonetic transcription but there are a few honorific marks denoting high status," she said.

"I vote any direction but hell," Standish said. "Anyone else?" Bailey raised her hand.

"Straight," Hale said.

"I see a wall straight ahead," Steuben said. "My eyes are a bit better than yours down here."

The wall Steuben saw was a mural the size of the entire tunnel. The same prophet stood at the top of the central pyramid, his feet floating just above the stairway, arms held open and light emanating from his eyes and mouth. Guards wearing the gold and silver armor led a naked Shanishol up the stairs to a huge sphere, depicted with the same swirling fractals Hale and his Marines had seen on the bodies of Xaros drones.

"'Exaltation,'" Lowenn said.

"This part wasn't in the video," Bailey said.

"How much you want to bet the next scene in this little church drama ends with that naked Shanishol dead and in that ditch we uncovered?" Orozco asked.

Hale heard the clatter of claws on stone from the tunnel leading off from the mural, like the sound of a gigantic rat in a ceiling. Hale swung his weapon toward the sound and his Marines did the same.

"I know that sound—a Toth menial," Steuben said.

"Did it see us?" Hale asked.

"Their vision is poor. Their hearing is even worse. Doubtful we were detected, but if a menial is here, so are the warriors." Steuben said.

"You mean the big ones with six arms aren't the overlords?" Bailey asked.

"Correct. The overlords won't come down here until they're certain there's no risk to themselves. I suggest we hurry," Steuben said.

"Sir," Cortaro said, "why don't we get up on those walkways? It leads all the way down the tunnel and those damn big Toth can't fit up there."

"Good idea, help me up there," Hale said. Cortaro laced his fingers together and hoisted Hale to the upper walkway, the pseudo muscle layer in the gunnery sergeant's armor straining to lift Hale's armored bulk. Hale's fingertips gripped the edge and he pulled himself onto the walkway.

Hale's feet hit corrugated metal, surprising him. Everything else about the tunnel was cut stone and harkened back to some historical period in the Shanishol past. The metal was an anachronism.

The Shanishol walking the hallway wouldn't see this, no need to keep up whatever show the prophet had going, he thought.

Hale helped the rest of his squad onto the walkway and they continued on.

A light appeared in the distance, undulating as whatever carried it ran through the corridor. The Marines sank against the side of the walkway and held still. The *click-clack* of Toth claws against stone passed beneath them and the light vanished down a different corridor.

"We need to follow them," Steuben said. "They reek of command pheromones. A warrior wants his menials to return to him. He must have found something."

"Maybe they found nothing and they're leaving," Orozco said.

"No, they'd smell of failure and fear if that was the case."

"Follow them," Hale said. He stood and traced the menial's path.

"Steuben," Lowenn said, "how do you know the Toth so well? I thought they betrayed everyone centuries ago."

"The Karigole and the Toth had formed a joint-species fleet to defeat a Xaros invasion of my home world. We trained with the Toth for a time before our cohort went on a reconnaissance mission to a different star system. We weren't there when the Toth turned against us," Steuben said.

"Wait, how old are you? In human years?" Lowenn asked.

"I am … four hundred and twelve," the Karigole said.

Hale stopped and looked back at Steuben. "That can't be right."

"It is correct. My species is very long-lived.

That made us irresistible to the Toth. We should have seen their betrayal as inevitable."

"I don't follow," Lowenn said.

"I have had enough of your incessant pestering, she-ape," Steuben said. He raked his thumb claw against the other clawed fingertips. Hale took the gesture as Karigole body language for "drop it."

A faint glow from around a distant corner grew brighter as they approached. More packs of menials ran toward the glow from connecting tunnels. Hale turned his suit-to-suit IR on and looked over his shoulder. He tapped a knuckle to the mouthpiece on his visor, sending the team the hand signal to kill their IR lamps and go back to their secure—and quiet—communication channels.

"Toth ahead. Let's sneak up and get a look," Hale said. He secured his rifle against his back and went to his hands and knees. The team followed suit, Steuben's wide shoulders scraping against the side of the walkway.

As they crossed in front of the lit hallway,

Hale heard the Toth speaking to each other in hisses and purrs. The clang and whirl of heavy equipment drowned out any noise the Marines made as they crept forward. Hale didn't stop until every Marine was stretched across the open hallway. If they were about to get into a firefight, he wanted every rifle in action at the same time.

The lieutenant slowly raised his rifle, sending the camera feed to the rest of his team. The camera edged over the lip of walkway, and they saw the Toth.

There were nearly two dozen menials swarming around a standing drill pointed at a silver wall that stretched beyond the edge of the tunnel. Round symbols full of squares and circles were embossed over the silver wall. Two large warriors shouted commands to the smaller menials, emphasizing their orders with strikes to any menial that got too close to them.

One of the warriors had human armor plates attached to a belt around its waist—rank plates and bits of gear that Rangers never would have parted with while they were still alive. There was no doubt in Hale's mind now that the Toth were hostile.

"Lowenn, what is that place?" Hale asked.

"I have no idea, but it's definitely not Shanishol."

"I'm so glad we brought you this far. You have as little idea of what's going on as the rest of us," Torni said.

"Stow it," Hale hissed.

The Toth drill whirled to life. The tip blurred as it revved faster, then touched against the silver wall. Sparks flew from the contact and the reek of ozone filled the air. The drill came to a halt with a crunch.

One of the warriors shouted and grabbed a menial by the leg. The warrior slung the menial in the air then slammed it into the ground. The crack of bones echoed through the corridor. The injured menial struggled to crawl away, its futile move ending when the warrior hurled it across the corridor and into a mural. Yellow blood splattered against the wall and the menial fell to the ground, its limbs twitching.

The rest of the menials looked at their dead comrade for a moment, then scrambled back to work.

"Remember that the next time you think I'm being too hard on you," Cortaro said.

A pair of menials pulled the drill bit back. The cone-shaped depression morphed, then returned to its original state.

"Not sure how we're going to get in there, sir," Cortaro said.

"They're making progress, I think. Let's wait and see if they can ...." Hale cocked an ear up as he heard the sound of claws against metal. A light appeared at the end of walkway. The menial carrying it ran down the walkway straight at Hale.

Hale reached up for his rifle, then reconsidered. He extended the combat knife from his gauntlet and pulled his arm back.

"Bad eyesight, right?" Hale asked. He hoped the menial's reflexes were just as poor.

"Hale, you must—" Steuben's warning was

lost as the menial sprinted toward Hale. It saw the armored Marine and tried to slow down, but its momentum carried it forward like a dog sliding over a waxed floor.

Hale slammed his blade beneath the menial's jaw, the tip exiting the back of its skull. Any creature on Earth would have been killed instantly from the blow. The menial, yellow blood gushing from the entry and exit wounds, started squealing.

It reared up on its back feet, yanking Hale to his feet. The squealing grew louder, then the Toth went limp.

Hale looked to the side. Every single Toth was staring right at him and the dead menial impaled on his blade.

One of the warriors pointed at Hale and bellowed an ululating war cry.

"Light 'em up!" Cortaro shouted. He stood up and blasted his rifle at the Toth, his rounds ripping through the unarmored menials. The rest of their Marines added to the fusillade moments later.

Hale struggled to remove his blade from the menial's skull. He slammed the corpse to the ground, braced his foot against the body and finally got the blade free with a sickening crunch. He reached for his rifle and saw one of the warriors fire its weapon.

A blue laser blast cut through the walkway between Hale and Torni. The walkway heaved, then collapsed, sending Marines and chunks of rock and metal falling to the ground. Hale landed on his feet, but stumbled when a rock struck the back of his shoulder.

A menial tackled him, its claws scraping and prying at his visor. Hale tried to shove it away, but its bottom legs were wrapped against his waist tighter than a vice. The menial bit at his helmet, shaking its jaws like a hunting dog with a rat in its teeth.

Hale grabbed the menial's upper and lower jaws, the teeth useless against his armor, and used the augmented muscles to rip its head apart. It finally fell off him and he grabbed his gauss rifle from the rubble.

He switched the rifle to LOW POWER and aimed at a warrior at the edge of the melee between the Marines and the menials. He squeezed the trigger and sent a burst of rounds into the warrior. One round severed the warrior's arm holding its weapon. It snarled in pain, then used one of its clawed feet to pick up the weapon and aim it toward Hale.

The *bam bam bam* of Orozco's Gustav tore the warrior to shreds. One of the heavy gauss cannon's rounds blew through the warrior's forearm and smacked into the silver wall. The round, stained yellow with viscera and blood, stopped a finger's breadth from the door, then fell to the ground.

"Ghul'thul'ghul!" Steuben ripped a menial off him then launched himself at the remaining warrior, leaping into the air. The Karigole unsheathed the blade carried on the small of his back and slashed it across the warrior's chest as he landed. Blood spurted from the cut and Steuben brought the blade across its stomach with his reverse strike.

The warrior collapsed against itself and Steuben hacked at the dead Toth's head. Again. And again. Steuben shouted in his own language as he hacked the Toth into pieces.

The Marines had finished off the menials and watched as Steuben beat at the Toth with a berserk fury.

"Steuben!" Hale yelled to get the alien's attention. "Steuben, stop!"

The Karigole, his chest heaving, let his blade fall to his side. He turned to Hale, his face, chest and arms covered in yellow blood. His forked tongue whipped out and licked blood from his face.

"What?" Steuben asked.

"You ... you OK?" Hale asked.

"Fine. That felt good. Let's go find more." Steuben knocked the flat of his blade against his thigh to rid it of Toth blood and slid it back into its scabbard.

"Lowenn? Anyone seen Lowenn?" Orozco kicked over a dead menial and looked around.

The sound of muffled cries came from beneath a pile of rubble. Orozco set his Gustav down and shoved lumps of rock off a pile. The rest of the squad rushed to help. Torni lifted a section of a grate, revealing Lowenn's helmet.

"Help!" Lowenn squeaked. Torni and Orozco knocked rubble away and hauled her out by her shoulders.

"Are you alright?" Orozco asked her, wiping dust off her visor.

"Some giant alien lizard just shot at me with a blue lightning bolt and if you hadn't dug me out I would be some future archaeologist's amazing discovery. No. I am not alright!" Lowenn shook free from Torni and brushed herself off.

"She's fine," Torni said. "Still, let's get the medic to check you over. Yarrow?"

Yarrow wasn't with the rest of the Marines. He was standing next to the silver wall, his head cocked up, his body swaying from side to side.

"Yarrow!" Cortaro shouted. "What the hell are you doing?"

Yarrow's head shook, like he'd just been woken from a nap.

"Huh? What're you all doing over there?" the medic asked.

"Yarrow. Come here," Hale said. The medic stood between the wall and his commanding officer.

"Don't you want me to open it?" Yarrow asked.

"Son, you don't know how to do that," Cortaro said.

"Sure I do." The medic turned around and tapped the symbols embossed on the wall. The symbols lit up as he touched them, glowing with a pale green light. A black line ran up from the floor and traced out a doorway. The wall slid down without a sound.

Yarrow waved to the squad and went inside.

"Not this shit again," Standish said and the squad ran after him.

Beyond the doorway was a wide metal boulevard leading deep into a cavern. The pathway stopped at a dark hole in the cavern, an open circle so wide three Mule drop ships could have flown into it with room to spare.

In the middle of the opening hung a sphere, its surface undulating with fractals and swirls like the body of a Xaros drone. A stone platform hung beneath the sphere, Shanishol writing glowing from computer screens around the platform.

Yarrow walked toward the sphere, dropping his weapon and stumbling forward like a toddler that was just learning how to walk. He looked determined to walk right off the edge and into the dark abyss beneath the sphere.

Hale ran up to Yarrow and grabbed him by the carry handle on the back of his armor.

"Yarrow! Snap out of it!" Hale jerked Yarrow back and put himself between the medic and the sphere. Yarrow stopped, then looked at Hale like he'd never seen him before.

"Sir? What's going on?"

"You're acting like a damn weirdo, that's what's happening," Cortaro said as he picked up Yarrow's weapon and sat the Marine down. "Don't move. You'll get your weapon back when this is over."

"Finally, some electronics." Lowenn stopped at the edge of the open pit and looked down. There was nothing but darkness below. Hale and Standish joined her, both craning their necks over the side.

"Well, none of us can fly," Hale said. The gap between the sphere and the edge of the pit was at least twenty-five feet.

Standish lifted his visor and spat over the side. The drop fell flush with the edge of the pit and spattered to a stop midair, looking like it had hit an invisible floor.

"That's funny," Standish said. He knelt slightly and jabbed at the air around where his spit had stopped. The muzzle thumped against something solid, and a ring of coherent matter rippled away from the contact like waves over a still pond. The first two steps of a stairway leading to the sphere appeared, then faded away.

"No. No way." Standish backed away from

the pit.

"Yes, you're the lowest-ranking Marine," Cortaro said. "You go first, just like when we test for chemical warfare."

"New guy! What about new guy? I outrank him and I bet he'd love to do this," Standish said.

"Yarrow's down. You're it. Go." Cortaro pointed a hand toward the pit.

"This is horseshit, Gunney. I'll write my congressman ... when we have those again," Standish said.

"I'll do it." Lowenn grabbed Hale's hand and stepped over the edge. A stairway appeared as she pressed her foot down, and more steps came into being as she set more and more weight on the staircase. "There. See?"

She took two cautious steps up, looked around, and took two more. The step attached to the edge of the pit faded away, but Lowenn's staircase remained steady. Her hands went out to steady herself, and she quickly moved up the stairway as it appeared for her. She got to the platform and turned around. She mimicked a courtesy for the Marines and ran her hand over the computer banks.

Hale swallowed hard and followed Lowenn up the on-demand stairwell.

The sphere glowed from an internal light, the striated lines shifting without rhyme or reason, like a time lapse of Jupiter's atmosphere. Hale's weak reflection on the sphere roiled with the surface. He pulled back from the sphere just as he saw the reflection blink of its own accord. Hale adjusted his visor, his stress and nerves getting to him.

"Well?" he asked Lowenn.

"It's Omnium, that's for sure. Not in the form the Xaros keep it but it's the real deal. The controls …." She walked around to the other side of the platform. "This platform is mobile. Yeah, right here," she said, pointing to a pair of knobs. She looked up. The cavern grew into an apex far above them. "I think we're beneath the main pyramid."

"Makes sense. The star of the show would have the biggest stage," Hale said. "How does this interface with the sphere? We need to bring back more than pictures and a crazy story."

"You're asking me to figure out an alien computer operating system in two minutes. Give me a little time," she said.

A Toth war cry echoed through the cavern.

"You're asking the wrong person for time. Make it fast," Hale said. He looked around for another exit, but the door through the silver wall was the only way in and out.

Torni aimed her rifle through the doorway and let off a burst of shots. The sound of a squealing menial joined the war cry. A last bolt sizzled over Torni's shoulder and impacted against the stairway, sending ripples racing around the platform. With the hit, Hale could see the entire stairway, a series of stepped disks, one atop another.

"I think … yeah! I can get us to the top of the pyramid," Lowenn said.

A warrior tried to squeeze through the doorway, his armor caught against the entrance, pinning him in place. Steuben and Standish pounded the warrior with gauss shots before it went slack.

"Everyone! Get up here!" Hale shouted.

Marines kept firing as they backed to the pit, threading rounds over the dead warrior's bulk and into Toth that Hale couldn't see from the platform. Cortaro, one hand on Yarrow's carry handle, struggled to keep the eager Marine from running up the stairway while firing into the doorway.

The Toth yanked the body of the warrior away and a dozen menials boiled through the doorway.

Hale fired as fast as he could, tearing through the charging menials with each shot. The Toth menials kept coming, heedless of casualties and the force of fire the Marines sent to meet them.

Orozco and Bailey were the last two Marines to make it up to the platform, their carbines firing on full auto as they backed up the stairs.

The tide of menials ceased, and a warrior burst through the doorway, charging forward on all six arms and legs, far faster than anything that size should have been able to move. It crushed wounded menials underfoot and let loose a war cry that rattled Hale's visor.

Hale connected with a burst of gauss rounds, but the warrior didn't seem to notice or care about the hunk of flesh blown away from its tail.

"Lowenn!" Hale reloaded as the rest of his Marines kept firing at the charging warrior.

"Maybe … this one?" Lowenn hit a button then twisted a knob as hard as she could. The platform bobbled, then raised into the air far too slowly for Hale's liking.

Menials ran forward and leapt after the platform. They fell short, and instead of a staircase materializing for them, they plummeted into the abyss below. Menials behind them struggled to stop, some tumbling over the edge while others were pushed in as they fought against their momentum.

The warrior sprang from the pit edge and reached for the platform, claws glinting in the light from the sphere. One hand caught the edge. The claws tore paths through the rock as the hand slipped back, and then vanished over the side.

"It's beautiful," Yarrow reached out to touch the sphere.

"No you don't, Marine." Cortaro yanked him back to the edge of the platform. "You're not going to—" A warrior's claw arced over the edge of the platform and stabbed through Cortaro's calf, pinning him to the stone. Cortaro stifled a cry of pain and pushed Yarrow away.

"Gunney!" Hale shouted. The Toth warrior's head rose over the edge of the platform, hissing at the Marines. Cortaro looked down at his stricken leg, then back at Hale in disbelief.

The warrior's other six clawed hand slammed into the platform and its thick arms came over the edge.

Steuben swung his rifle around...and aimed it at Cortaro. Steuben fired a single shot and blew the Marine's leg off. The warrior's grip on the platform slipped as its hand disintegrated along with Cortaro's leg. Steuben blasted the lip of the platform, shooting away the Toth's remaining handhold. The Toth fell away, its scream of rage fading.

Cortaro fell to the ground, his hands pawing at the bloody mess just beneath his knee. Hale ran to Cortaro, the Marine's teeth grit in agony.

"Medic!" Hale called out. He pushed Cortaro's hands away and found a knot for the bodysuit's integrated tourniquet. Blood pulsed from the ruined meat of the leg, spreading over Hale's armor with each of Cortaro's weakening heartbeats.

"Do it, sir," Cortaro said.

Hale grabbed the knot in his fist and yanked it. A ring of pseudo-muscles just beneath Cortaro's knee tightened mercilessly, earning a sharp scream from Cortaro and cutting the loss of blood to a trickle.

Golden light poured over them as the platform slowed to a stop and the Marines found themselves at the apex of the white pyramid. Anthalas stretched out before them, haze filling jungles and worn mountains.

"Yarrow? Gunney needs you," Hale said. Cortaro rolled to his back and raised what remained of his leg into the air, rags of flesh and a jagged chunk of bone dripped blood down his thigh.

"Yarrow! Get your ass over here," Hale glanced over his shoulder to the rest of the Marines and saw the medic. He had a glove off and touched his bare fingertips to the sphere. The sphere darkened at the touch, its entire surface blackening like burnt flesh. Red cracks ran over the surface and the sphere jerked from side to side, like something inside was trying to punch its way out.

The medic backed away from the sphere, confusion writ on his face.

The sphere shrank inward, then formed into a javelin shape, pointed straight at Yarrow.

"Sir?" Yarrow sidestepped, but the tip followed him. "Help!"

Hale grabbed Yarrow and spun the medic behind him. A hum filled the air and the javelin sprung from the platform. It shot straight into Hale's chest … and passed through without sensation. Hale looked down and saw nothing amiss. He whirled around.

Yarrow, his mouth agape, choked on something, then golden light rose from his eyes and mouth. The medic collapsed to the ground. Hale knelt next to him, hesitant to touch him. Yarrow's chest rose and fell, breathing hard.

"Yarrow?" Hale shook him, but there was no reaction.

"Sir? What do we do?" Torni asked.

"Check Gunney, make sure he's stable. Steuben," the Karigole knelt next to Cortaro, wrapping the Marine's injuries with bandages taken from the field packs attached to Cortaro's belt. Cortaro had a rosary in his hand and mumbled prayers in Spanish as the alien tended to the wounds he inflicted. "Steuben what were you thinking?"

"I didn't have a straight shot on the Toth. Freeing Cortaro from the Toth was the only way I could save him," Steuben said.

"You couldn't have aimed a little higher?" Cortaro asked, his words tinged with pain.

"Toth claws are poisoned, you would have lost the leg anyway. Do you require pain killers?"

"Yes, you asshole, I need pain killers!" Cortaro draped his forearm over his eyes, not wanting to look at the bloody bandages covering his leg.

"I've got something," Orozco pawed through Yarrow's medic bag, spilling compresses and rolls of tubing as he found a hypo spray. Orozco thumbed through the drug settings. "What's the difference between an opioid and an analgesic?"

"You think I give a shit right now?" Cortaro asked.

"Opioid it is," Orozco pulled Cortaro's collar down and pressed the hypo spray against his bare flesh. Cortaro groaned for several more seconds, then the tension in his face soothed as the drugs took hold.

"Where's Lowenn?" Hale asked.

"Here," she said from behind the control panels. Hale found her half in, half out of the control panels. She grunted and the screens went blank. She wormed her way out and held up a silver box, severed wires dangling from it. "I figured there was a computer core somewhere. This should teach us something."

"That's … something. Sure. Put it away and—"

"Sir! We've got company," Bailey said. She pointed to the boulevard leading away from the silver pyramid. Toth menials scurried from one of the step pyramids like ants out of a disturbed nest.

"Kill the warrior," Steuben said. "It'll slow them down."

"I don't know if we can make that shot, Steuben," Hale said. A warrior finally joined the mass of menials and they swarmed toward the Marines.

From behind Hale came the click of Bailey's rail rifle fitting together. Bailey lay on the platform and slid a round into the breach.

"Oh ye of little faith," she said. She snuggled against the butt stock and exhaled.

The rail rifle snapped. A line of burning air

roiled briefly then disappeared. The warrior was nothing but a yellow smear in the dirt. The menials ceased their charge, the entire mass looking at what remained of their leader.

Hale felt a thrum in the air, like the growl of a great cat. He hadn't felt something like that since he'd been on the Crucible.

"Xaros!" Standish raised his rifle straight into the air and fired a Q-shell at the lone drone plunging toward them, stalks out and burning with amber light from the tips. The Q-shell burst and coherent energy lashed the drone. The drone's descent continued straight down. Steuben pulled Bailey from her sniper's perch an instant before the disabled drone slammed into it, sending rock shrapnel bouncing off the Marine's armor. The drone tumbled forward and down the long staircase, crushing stairs with each hit.

Another Toth warrior emerged from a stepped pyramid, just in time to see the Xaros tumble away from the base of the pyramid and through the menials, killing dozens. The drone came to a stop, stalks twitching.

"That's his problem now." Hale looked down the other side of the pyramid. Another stairway led into the jungle. Through the jungle, Hale spotted a distant clearing. "Let's go."

Steuben and Torni lifted Cortaro off the ground and slung his arms over their shoulders. They were slow going down the pyramid, drops of blood dripped free with each step. Orozco lifted Yarrow over his shoulder and followed the rest of the Marines down the stairway.

"Weren't you supposed to be looking up?" Standish asked Steuben.

"Yes, you did very well," the Karigole said. "Now shut up."

****

Durand looked at the clock on her heads-up display and exhaled loudly. She and the rest of her ships had been attached to the hull of the cube for hours, waiting for the demolitions work to announce its completion with an impressive fireworks display.

The hours-long wait when she and her squadron had ridden a luxury liner into the Battle of the Crucible had been longer, but at least she knew when that was scheduled to end.

"So, Filly, how's shipboard life treating you?" she asked her wingman.

"Most of the crew is friendly. Some are still angry about the series of political disagreements between China and the rest of the world, even though none of them matter anymore," Choi Ma said.

"You mean the 'political disagreements' where China invaded most of East Asia and occupied half of Australia?"

"Yes."

"You mean the 'political disagreements' that led to me shooting you in the leg on the flight deck?"

"I have forgiven you for that. If the situation had been reversed, my aim would have been better. Once we changed our uniforms to the Atlantic Union blue, the crew was much less overtly hostile.

America had enough of an Asian population that no one seems surprised to see us. But then we open our mouths and suddenly we become 'one of them' again," Ma said.

"There are no more countries anymore, Ma. All we've got now is Phoenix."

"Yes, and the next jerk that asks me when I'm going to open an authentic restaurant will get dick punched," Ma said.

Durand laughed. "I think you'll fit right in with the crew. Don't worry about … that's not right." Durand leaned against her canopy and peered at the Crucible hanging below Anthalas. The thorns were moving.

"Filly, look at that Crucible and tell me I'm not seeing things," Durand said.

"It is moving. Have you seen that before?" Ma asked.

"The Crucible around Ceres moved around right before the Karigole jumped through, and … it was moving right before we jumped through to get here. Son of a bitch. Something is coming through,"

Durand said.

A white portal of light spread within the center of the Crucible. Strands of light pulled away from the portal like rain falling up from a pond.

Durand moved a gun camera toward the Crucible and zoomed in. Dark dots emerged from the plane and flew into a growing swarm.

"Xaros are here," Durand said. There were already dozens, more than the *Breitenfeld* could handle if caught unaware.

"*Breitenfeld*, this is Gall. We've got Xaros arriving in force through the Crucible," Durand sent through the buoy network. There was no answer.

"*Breitenfeld?*" Still nothing.

She was the squadron commander and the only one who could make a command decision. The success or failure of the entire mission to Anthalas could depend on what she chose to do next.

"All ships, detach!" she ordered. Her Eagle floated from the cube face with the flip of a switch and she charged up her anti-grav thrusters. "Filly, Mule One and Two, you're with me. We're going to the surface and we're going to find the ground teams. Mule Three, you deploy your recovery net and get prepped to recover whatever the armor is going to bring out. Then get them and you back to the *Breitenfeld* as soon as you can. You know Xaros speeds. Don't stay so long that you can't get back to warn the ship. Let's go."

Her four-ship formation rocketed toward the surface.

"Everyone, switch from anti-grav to your burners. The Xaros know something's up, doesn't make much sense to try to get in on the sly anymore. *De l'audace, encore de l'audace et toujours de l'audace,*" Durand said, quoting her favorite French revolutionary.

"Loud ass?" Ma asked.

"No—just shut up and fly!"

They cut into the upper atmosphere, on course to the pyramid city where the Marines and Rangers were supposed to be. Durand pulled a lever on the side of her seat and held her breath as her fighter shifted from void to atmosphere flight mode.

Wings swept out from the sides of the fighter and twin rudders unfolded along the tail. Void flying required thrusters to maneuver. Surrounded by Anthalas' air and wind, older methods of flight were required. She wasn't as nimble in atmosphere, but feeling her wings groan against the air felt better to Durand.

"Filly, your variables deploy correctly?" Durand asked.

"I'm not corkscrewing toward the dirt like a dead bird, so yes they came out just fine," Ma said. If any part of the transition failed, a rudder stuck halfway or a wing sweep out, the aerodynamics of the fighters would become impossible and Ma's metaphor would prove apt.

"Good, keep your eyes peeled for …," a glint of silver shown on the horizon, "bogies. Eleven o'clock and closing." A blocky craft with down-swept wings rose in the air, up and away from Durand and her formation. Flanking it were two blade-like escorts, two sets of stubby razor-blade wings along its edge.

"They don't seem interested in us," Ma said.

"What the hell are they? Can't be Xaros," Durand said, her neck craning to watch the unknown craft fly higher into the air. Durand shook her head. She had other things to worry about.

"I sure hope they're listening," Durand said. She keyed open the radio transmitter and started broadcasting.

CHAPTER 11

Carrying wounded through the jungle kept the Marines at a pace that felt glacial to Hale. He stopped and looked back at the great pyramid. Flashes from Toth weapons sparred with red energy beams from Xaros reinforcements. He'd counted only a handful of new drones, which proved to be enough to keep the Toth off the Marines' heels.

The old saying about mutual enemies aside, Hale hoped the Toth and Xaros kept right on killing each other.

Steuben tromped past Hale, Yarrow slung over his shoulder like a felled deer. The medic had been unresponsive but for a few moans and intermittent babbling as they made their way through the swamp. Bailey and Orozco did their best to keep up while carrying Cortaro.

Torni, carrying a handheld satellite dish, stopped and held the dish to the sky. Wherever she could find a line-of-sight shot to Anthalas' moon, she tried to raise the *Breitenfeld*. No luck thus far.

"Anything?" Hale asked Torni.

"I can't even pick up the buoys. I don't know if it's the atmosphere … or if the whole network is gone," she said. If the latter were true, Hale and his Marines would be on Anthalas for a very long time. "Should we risk radio?"

"The Xaros would pick it up and swarm us. So would the Toth. Keep trying the IR until we get to the clearing," Hale said. He looked up at the thick thorn vines and spiked branches. Even if a Mule could get to them here there was no way it could land.

Steuben stopped, sniffed twice, then set Yarrow against a tree.

"Toth," the alien said.

Hale and the Marines looked around, and up, but saw nothing in the fog.

"Form a perimeter around Yarrow and Cortaro, hurry," Hale said.

He grabbed Lowenn by the shoulder and tried to push her toward where Yarrow and Cortaro were propped against each other, back to back, inside the protective circle formed by the rest of the team. She shrugged him off and joined the circle. She raised her gauss rifle level with her face and switched the weapon off SAFE.

"I know how to use this," she said.

Hale felt a rumble through his boots, the once-still ponds around them shivering as something large ran through the jungle.

"Shoot the big ones first," Hale said.

Orozco slammed his rear foot into the ground, the pneumatics struggling to secure a foothold in the loose muck beneath him.

Steuben unsheathed his blade and twirled it, the razor-sharp edge hissing in the air.

"Shoot, Steuben, shoot," Hale said.

Steuben broke from the circle as the rumble grew stronger. He set a foot on a fallen log, then jumped against a thick tree. He pushed off and flipped over, just as a warrior broke through the fog, its red eyes glinting with malice as it bore down on the Marines. Steuben's blade flashed and cut through the warrior's spine just below the base of its skull.

The Toth went limp and crumpled against the ground. Its hindquarters reared over its front shoulders and almost bent the alien in half, then it fell on its side, motionless.

Steuben sheathed his sword with one hand, flipped his rifle off his back with the other and backed into the circle. The sound of clattering claws and hissed commands echoed through the fog.

"Standish. Now would be a good time to pray to the Flying Spaghetti Monster," Steuben said.

"Yeah, about that …," Standish said, "I'm not sure if anyone briefed you on the concept of human irony but—"

"Incoming!" Hale shouted as he glimpsed a menial charging through the fog. He fired a burst of magnetically accelerated rounds into the fog, the bullets leaving converging whirls of fog in their wake.

The rest of the Marines let loose, the snap of their gauss rifles mingling with squeals of dying menials. Orozco's Gustav spoke like thunder, the heavy-caliber bullets cutting through trees and blowing menials into pulp as he swept his cannon through its arc of fire. The grav and anti-grav rings around the barrel glowed as they fought to tamp down the recoil.

A half-dozen menials charged straight at Hale. He switched his weapon to shotgun mode and blasted the menials. Two went down as a third tumbled end over end and splashed into a puddle. The fourth took a full blast to the shoulder, the rounds blowing away an arm and leg. The last two leaped at Hale. He ducked down and shot one as it sailed overhead. The last menial hit Hale like a linebacker, knocking his rifle out of his hand.

Hale smashed his fist against the menial's head, but the creature's hold pinning his other arm between them didn't give.

A shotgun blast turned the menial's head into yellow mist. Lowenn, her muzzle smoking, kicked the dead menial off Hale. She swung the butt of her rifle into a menial, knocking it off balance, then finished it off with a close-range blast.

Hale saw his weapon in a puddle. He grabbed it by the handle and shook it to clear away mud and water. Looking up, he saw a warrior at the edge of the fog, its weapon aimed right at him. Time seemed to slow down as Hale raised his weapon, certain that he couldn't get a shot off before the Toth blew him apart.

The warrior backed away, then vanished into the fog. Firing around Hale slowed.

He glanced over his shoulder. All the Marines but Yarrow were still on their feet, their rifles smoking hot.

"Everyone OK?" Hale asked.

Nods and curt replies came back.

Dead Toth littered the ground around them, their yellow blood seeping into the mud, adding a neon tinge to the swamp water. The smell of cut grass and bile bled through Hale's rebreather.

"Ugh, that smell won't be easy to get out, will it?" Standish asked.

"Steuben," Hale's combat high rang in his ears as he kept searching for the warrior that was still out there. "Steuben, one of the warriors had me. Could have pulled the trigger but didn't, why?"

"We have something they want," Steuben said. "It doesn't do much good to fire lasers at something you need whole."

"They just charged us with all those little ones because they don't want to shoot us?" Bailey asked.

"Correct. The Toth have no regard for the lives of their menials. The warriors will sacrifice themselves for the overlords without hesitation," Steuben said.

"The fog is getting thinner," Torni said. "How about we keep moving?"

"I am pleased," Yarrow said. His head rose from his chest and he breathed in deeply, as if relishing the smell of death around them. His voice was several octaves lower than usual.

"Yarrow? Can you hear me?" Hale knelt in front of the medic and put his hands on his shoulders.

"Bring me …." Yarrow's eyes opened, the whites of his eyes now gold. "More. Bring me more." Yarrow blinked, his eyes returned to normal, and he fell against Hale's arms, unconscious.

"Ohhh … kay," Bailey said, backing away from Yarrow.

"Standish, pick him up. Your turn to carry him," Hale said.

"Sir, maybe we should—"

"Now, Marine!" Torni shouted. As the highest-ranking Marine after Cortaro, she'd stepped into his role without having to be asked.

Standish got Yarrow over his shoulders in a fireman's carry, his face ashen behind his visor.

"I can smell your soul, Standish," Yarrow

said.

"Sir! New guy is seriously weirding me out right now," Standish said, his voice reedy with panic. "No? Nothing? Fine, I'll just carry the evil alien thing. It breaks loose and eats our faces you know who's going to laugh and say I told you so? No one, because we won't have lips anymore."

"Shut up, Standish!" more than one Marine said.

Steuben and Torni got Cortaro back up and the Marines moved on. Hale stepped around Toth bodies, their flesh blackening and pulling away from their skeletons. Hale didn't know if that was a peculiar feature of their anatomy, or if something on this planet had accelerated their decomposition. Steuben might know, but Hale found bliss in his ignorance.

Whatever was inside Yarrow scared Hale worse than the Xaros, but he wouldn't leave the Marine behind. What happened after he got Yarrow back to the *Breitenfeld*, and Earth, was a problem beyond his station.

"—der six. I repeat, Raider six, please respond," the voice came through Hale's helmet, an icon showing a live radio transmission. He recognized the voice immediately but hesitated to open a radio channel.

If she was calling him, the situation must have gone straight to hell. He pressed and held a button on his forearm display to reply.

"Gall? This is Raider six," Hale said.

"Thank God, do you know how long we've been looking for you?" Durand asked. "Something kicked the Xaros hornets' nest and this whole mission is about to shit the bed. Where are you?"

"I've got wounded and precious cargo with me. Can you extract us at …?" Hale swiped a map over, trying to find the coordinates for the clearing, which wasn't on the map. "We're heading for a clearing, maybe five miles north of the big pyramid. We'll send up a flare when we get there."

"I see it," Durand said.

A Toth ululation broke through the fog.

"Looks like they're not done with us," Torni

314

said.

"Move out, hurry," Hale said to the Marines. They picked up their pace to run as fast as they could through the swamp. "Gall, hostiles are closing in on us. Can you provide some close air support?"

"You mean whatever's flying those silver fighters?" Durand asked.

"Did you see a giant six-foot lizard at the controls?"

"A giant *lizard*? Ken, what the hell is going on down there?"

"I don't know where to start. Just shoot anything that's not human, OK?"

Steuben's head snapped around, his face contorted in what was either the Karigole equivalent of betrayal or anger.

"Not you, Steuben," Hale said.

They came to the edge of the clearing. Fog had burned away to a slight haze, diffusing sunlight over dark green grass. Hale pulled a signal flare off his belt and slapped his hand into the bottom of it. Red star clusters arced into the sky.

"Gall, did you see that?"

"Roger, I've got two Mules with me. They'll set down on the opposite side. What the …? Raider, you've got movement to your south. Lots of it," Durand said.

Hale heard the whine of approaching aircraft in the air.

"I wasn't kidding about that air support," Hale said.

"Get to the far end of the clearing. You're danger close for my guns," Durand said.

"Run! Run!" Hale waved his Marines onward. He remained behind the slowest Marines, short-legged Bailey and the overburdened Standish. A Toth war cry from multiple warriors came from the jungle behind them.

"Starting our attack run," Durand said.

Brrrrrrrrrrt!

The Gatling gun on Durand's Eagle shot the same bullets as Orozco's heavy cannon, but at 4,200 rounds per second. The sound of the rounds firing melded into one continuous tone. Durand's bullets tore through the jungle, kicking up mud and Toth bodies like the hand of an angry god tearing up an imperfect creation.

Brrrrrrrrrrt!

The next fusillade hit the tree line, shattering giant trees into kindling and sending gouts of soil into the air. A dozen Toth menials followed by a warrior made it into the clearing. Hale aimed his rifle at the warrior.

A Mule roared overhead, the blast from its engines staggering Hale and sending his shot wide.

Brrrrrrrrrrt!

The Toth vanished as dozens of small explosions ripped through their advance.

"Damn, I love that sound," Orozco said.

"You're all clear!" Durand yelled. Two Eagles zoomed over the clearing and pulled into a steep climb.

Hale spun around and saw two Mules idling in the clearing, their ramps opening far too slowly for Hale's taste.

"Torni. I want you, Standish, Cortaro,

Bailey and Yarrow in the port Mule. Everyone else on starboard," Hale said. "Man the turrets and let's get the hell out of here!"

Hale waited until the last of the Marines had boarded, then he ran up a Mule's ramp. Orozco was already climbing into the bottom gunner's turret.

"Button up!" Hale turned his suit IR to broadcast, hoping the pilots heard him. He slammed his fist against the bulkhead and the ramp rose from the ground. The pilot didn't wait for it to close before taking the drop ship into the air.

Hale grabbed a handhold and looked back to Anthalas. He saw the white pyramid just before the ramp clanged shut.

"If you don't strap in you're going to have a really rough ride," the pilot said over the IR.

Hale snapped out of his reverie and grabbed a seat strap just as the Mule banked hard.

"Steuben, man a turret. I need to call the *Breitenfeld*."

Steuben looked up at the cramped space within the turret, then down at his considerable bulk.

"Should I take your ridiculous notion as an insult to my current relevance or as a compliment to my perceived skill?" the alien asked.

"What? Oh …." Hale stumbled toward the middle of the drop ship and pointed to the dorsal turret. "Lift me up."

Steuben grabbed Hale by the waist and hoisted him into the air. Hale slid the turret door aside and pulled himself up and into the gunner's chair. He strapped himself in and tested the controls.

The twin gauss cannons could cover almost the entire upper half of the drop ship as he spun the ball turret to and fro. The cannon automatically swung over the tail fins and upturned wing tips—it wouldn't do for the gunner to blow off parts of the ship he was in. Full ammo cans and two reloads were ready for him. He slapped a button on the side of the seat and the turret door sealed shut.

The only video game allowed on the *Breitenfeld* was a VR turret simulator, and Hale held the second-highest score on the ship. He was positive Standish had found some way to cheat, but Hale hadn't caught him in the act … yet.

Anthalas' golden skies thinned as the Mule ascended, giving way to darkness. Lightning cracked through distant, towering thunderheads, their tops ripped aside by trade winds. It always surprised Hale how peaceful a world could look from orbit.

"Sir?" Orozco said through the ship's IR.

"Go."

"You good up there?" Orozco asked.

"Field of fire checks out. Guns read green."

"That's not what I mean. That was the worst I've ever been in, ever even heard of. You kept it together real good for us. You ever need to charge hell with a bucket brigade and I'll carry your water."

"Thanks, Orozco. But we're not home free just yet," Hale said.

"Hale, this is Captain Valdar. We're secure over IR. What's your status?" the *Breitenfeld*'s master asked him.

"Sir, we've got one wounded. I don't know how to classify his injuries but he'll need to be quarantined once we're back. The entire Ranger squad is Missing In Action, but presumed dead," Hale said.

"I'm sorry to hear that, Ken," Valdar said. "What about the Omnium? Did you find anything?"

"Roger, sir. We've got a computer core that should have something on it. The Xaros are—" A wave of static filled his helmet and Hale shut off the entire IR net, his ears ringing from the assault. He switched channels to the ship's network, testing to see if it was malfunctioning too.

"Pilot, what was that?" Hale asked.

"Don't know. Transmissions along the buoys went down. We've got local IR and that's it. I'm not going to open radio comms and have Xaros jump down our throats," the pilot said.

"Bogies inbound!" Durand said. "Looks like three of those silver fighters we saw earlier. Coming in off our three o'clock."

Hale swung his turret to the right and saw a glint of sunlight off an approaching fighter.

"Those are Toth ships," Steuben said. "They are much faster than your Eagles."

"I don't think they're coming over to say hi," Durand said. "Mules, you haul ass back to the *Breitenfeld*. We'll cover you."

The Mule's engines flared and Hale felt the push of acceleration against his body. Durand's Eagle winged over Hale's turret. He looked up and found her gaze as she passed. Most of her face was covered by her helmet, but he could see the concern and worry in her eyes.

He nodded slightly and tapped two fingers against his temple. Durand and Ma's Eagles fell away beneath the Mule's wings. With a new threat bearing down on them, he wasn't sure if she was right or wrong to end their relationship. He set the holographic crosshairs of his cannons ahead of the Toth fighters and pressed his thumbs against the triggers. No matter what feelings he still had for her, it had no effect on just how much he wanted to kill the Toth.

Hale aimed for the center Toth fighter and pressed hard against both triggers. The turret shook as the gauss cannons flashed, the only sound the cycling ammo canisters rattling like old typewriters.

His first shots fell behind the Toth as they approached, their speed varying and fouling his shots. Orozco joined the fray, sweeping rounds across the Toth's path. The three silver ships broke apart and weaved against each other before flying apart in a maneuver Hale could only imagine from an airshow.

The vibration from Orozco's shots rumbled through the ship.

"Where'd they go? Call out targets!" Hale said. He swung the turret around and a Toth ship sliced through space just meters above him. He ducked out of reflex and tried to follow the fighter, his turret moving like a tortoise in comparison.

"Human," a modulated voice came over his IR. "Human meat will stop. Meat will submit."

Steuben got on the channel and spoke in the

Toth language, vehemence and malice behind every sibilant word.

"What he said," Hale said, closing the IR channel. He looked over his shoulder and saw a Toth fighter orient toward his ship.

Hale swung the turret over, nearly inverting himself, and opened fire. His cannon rounds crossed paths with blue laser blasts. Lasers annihilated his first burst of rounds and slashed over his turret, so bright they left an afterglow on his eyes.

The Toth fighter banked away, atmosphere and debris venting from it. The craft slowed down just enough for Hale to lead it with confidence, and he stitched rounds down its back. The fighter exploded in a blaze of blue light.

"Good shooting, sir," Orozco said.

Hale's euphoria was short-lived. Laser blasts shot up and past the engines. A bolt connected with the port engine, blowing it clear of its housing. The remaining engine spun the drop ship around so hard the centripetal force pinned Hale against the back of his seat, unable to reach the control sticks.

The starboard engine cut out and Hale could move again. A Toth fighter blurred past the damaged Mule and flipped over. Its engines flared with red light and shifted its momentum toward Hale.

Hale twisted the control sticks … and nothing happened. He tried again, but there was no power. The Toth ship drew closer.

"Pilot! Reset the power! Reset the power!" Hale struggled against the dead controls.

Tracer rounds streaked past the Toth fighter. It banked over on its side then wobbled as it came closer and closer. The fighter lost speed and coasted past the Mule, riven with bullet holes. An Eagle streaked past it.

Two down.

"Pilot?"

"—working on auxiliary batteries until we can reboot the core," the pilot's voice finally returned to the IR.

"How long until you're mobile?" Durand asked.

"Five minutes," the pilot said, "even then we'll be slow."

"We don't have that much time until the rest of the Toth get here," Durand said.

"What? Bring me up to speed." Hale searched the sky and saw distant glimmers of Toth fighters. Dozens of them. There was no chance his ship could outrun them, or the two Eagles could outfight so many. They'd come to Anthalas on a mission, a mission too many had died for. And the result of that mission wasn't on Hale's Mule.

"Durand, I want you to escort the other Mule back to the *Breitenfeld*. Leave us behind," Hale said.

"What? No way!" Durand shouted.

"The precious cargo is on the other Mule. It's all that matters," Hale said.

"Nag, get the other Mule back. I'll cover the other one until it's mobile," Durand said over the IR.

"Gall, we've got new contacts coming in fast," Choi Ma said. "On intercept to the Toth wing."

"Fine, more Toth to the party. You have your orders," Durand said.

"I'm pretty sure they're Xaros," Ma said.

"Well … *merde*," Durand said.

****

Durand saw the mass of Xaros coming up from the planet, spiked oblong drones, their stalks already burning with energy.

"Nag, you moving out?" she asked.

"Yes, ma'am. I don't like it but I'm doing it," Choi said.

Durand watched as all but two of the Toth fighters broke away and dove toward the Xaros. "That's more like it," she said.

She checked a clock on her control panel. At least four more minutes until the stricken Mule was operational, and that was if the system rebooted as designed. The likelihood it would start moving again depended on how well the lowest bidder decided to do their job on the day the ship was assembled.

"Come on, you bastards." Durand hit her afterburners and flew to the oncoming Toth. Laser blasts streaked past her. She jinked her Eagle around the line of fire and put a hand on the emergency release for her rocket pods.

Durand inverted and jerked the handle. A bolt snapped inside her ship and flung the rockets into space, ejecting from their mount like a dandelion's blossom. The rockets became caltrops to the advancing Toth, and one flew right into one of the tumbling munitions. The rocket exploded on impact and the Toth ship tumbled end over end through space, flinging damaged parts and hull plating into the void.

Durand pulled into a tight loop, g-forces graying out her vision as she searched for the other Toth. She glanced over her shoulder, then swung her fighter over into a barrel roll. Laser bolts singed her cockpit and left black scars down her fuselage.

She hit her retro-thrusters and the Toth flew ahead. She squeezed her trigger and a hail of bullets slashed through space. The Toth's engines died and it hung limp in space, like a drowned rat.

"Splash four! Mule, what's your status?" Durand brought speed back to her fighter and flew toward the drop ship.

"We're about two—"

A black metal plug thumped against Durand's hull. She frowned at it, then went pale. She looked back at the Toth fighter she'd just take out, but it was gone. *The Toth know how to play dead*, she thought.

Electricity arced from the plug. Discharge crackled through her controls and crept up her arms, stinging her so badly she gasped in pain. Electricity stabbed through her suit and she convulsed against her restraints. The last thing she saw before losing consciousness was a Toth fighter approaching her ship.

****

MacDougall wrapped a strand of explosives around a metal beam and pressed a remote control detonator into the clay-like substance. He triple-checked that he put the correct amount of explosive against the correct spot and annotated the diagram on his Ubi.

"How much longer?" Elias asked.

"Do not rush me. Never rush explosives!" MacDougall shot back.

There was a thump against the barred passageway. And another. A divot formed where a blow bent the metal into the engineering compartment.

"Tell that to them," Elias said. "Bodel, go topside. Kallen, flank the door. Lafayette, you ready to blow this joint?"

"To what the what?" Lafayette asked. The Karigole was beneath the walkway, extracting the reactor's control panel from the ship.

"You done yet?" Elias asked. Bodel attached himself to the wall above the doorway and Kallen took up her assigned position. They'd have whoever broke through that door in a three-way cross fire.

"Yes, there's a significant delta in the tech

used for the Omnium and the rest of the ship. Thankfully the interface between the two is easy to find and uncouple," Lafayette said. "Need I remind you that this cube is full of very sensitive equipment that won't react well to gunfire?"

"And explosives!" MacDougall added.

"Fine, you know how to say 'Don't shoot' in Toth?" Elias asked.

The door broke off one of the hinges and another blow sent it tumbling toward Elias. Flashes burst from Bodel's and Kallen's gauss cannons. Elias's first instinct was to dive out of the way from the multi-ton door flying toward him, but it would have smashed into the Omnium reactor and that would have complicated matters.

Elias held his arms out and slapped against the lip of the door as it spun toward him. He caught a glimpse of dead menials and a larger creature behind them. He stopped the door flat against him and its momentum pushed him back a yard.

Elias shoved with all the power his shoulder and elbow actuators could muster and sent the door flying back.

It impacted against the wall, crushing several menials like olives in a press. Yellow blood spurt from around the door.

Elias, with a straight shot down the passageway, unloaded with his gauss cannon at full auto. The mass reactive rounds, designed to penetrate Xaros armor and explode within, tore through the charging Toth. One of the larger warriors managed to make it over the threshold using menial bodies as a shield. It barely got the length of its body through the tunnel before Kallen and Bodel cut it down from their open fields of fire.

Elias sent single aimed shots into the menials hesitating in the passageway leading to another cube.

"Lafayette, you didn't mention anything about there being bigger ones," Elias said.

"Damn things don't feel pain, do they?" Kallen asked as an ammo canister popped off her back and a fresh magazine loaded into her guns. "How can we—behind!"

Elias ducked as the forward arms of a warrior passed overhead. The middle arms of the charging warrior wrapped around Elias, pinning them against his sides. The impact snapped Elias from his magnetic lock and the two went spinning through vacuum.

Damage icons flashed against his display as the face of the Toth warrior pressed into his helmet camera, red eyes glowing with what must have been hate. They hit the bulkhead, Elias taking the brunt of the impact beneath the warrior's bulk.

The warrior's fore and rear arms slashed at Elias, tearing away the ammo feed to his Q-shell launcher on his left arm.

Elias shunted more power to his shoulder actuators and broke from the Toth's grip. His hands dug into the warrior's space suit. Elias ripped its suit open, exposing wide swaths of scaly flesh that bubbled and popped as the blood within boiled into the vacuum. The warrior stabbed its claws into Elias's chest plate, embedding two inches into the armor.

Elias slammed his fist into the Toth's arm, breaking it badly enough that a jagged spike of bone tore through its suit. He grabbed the Toth by the chest, shoved it almost arm's distance away, then jerked the Toth toward him. The Toth's helmet impacted with Elias's armored helm and shattered.

He flung the dying warrior away and found Kallen and Bodel sniping at menials scrambling along the walls.

"Where did they come from?" Elias asked.

"There are two other passageways connecting this cube to others," Lafayette said. "The probability of either is—"

"Are you done yet?" Kallen shot at the Karigole.

"I suppose now is as good a time as any. Shall I detonate?"

"Yes!" the Iron Hearts said in unison.

"Fire in the hole!" MacDougall shouted.

Demolitions work in a vacuum had a number of inherent advantages. With no oxygen, there was no risk of fire. With no atmosphere, blast waves were of little concern. The charges set up around the Omnium reactor blew with white flashes of light, rippling up and around the struts holding it in place.

The flash overloaded Elias' cameras, shutting them down as a failsafe to save Elias' brain from red lining. Elias opened the view port on his chest plate and saw that the reactor was gone. Struts that had held it place burned white hot from where charges had sliced through them like a red-hot scalpel. He ran to the edge of what remained of the platform and looked down to see a massive hole in the cube's side open to space. The reactor spun end over end into the void.

"Did you see that? Bloody glorious!" MacDougall said from the ruined edge of the cube's hull.

"Let's get out of here. We need …." Elias twisted his body to look around. "Where's Lafayette?"

"I am on the reactor," the Karigole said.

Elias' cameras came back online and he

zoomed in on the ever-more distant reactor. "You're where?

"We were in a hurry, and it seemed prudent to remain with the reactor and the control stations. Excellent. I see the recovery Mule on approach with the net already deployed. I'm going to stop the rotation with my jet pack. One moment."

Elias saw flares from Lafayette's jet pack push against the spinning reactor, slowing it.

"Out, everyone out," Elias said. He activated his jet pack and flew toward MacDougall. He scooped the sailor up in his arms and landed on the cube's surface.

"Gall, this is Armor. Ready for pick up," Elias said into the IR net. He could see one of the Mules stopped next to the reactor, IR-guided thrusters wrapping a carbon fiber–and-graphite net around the alien technology.

"Armor, this is Mule three. Gall took the rest of the flight planet-side to get the ground pounders soon as the shit storm started," the Mule pilot said.

"How did you know about the Toth in the

cube? We were out of IR contact," Elias said.

"The what? Look at the Crucible. We've got to get the hell out of here," the pilot said.

Elias found the Crucible beneath the planet's south pole. Light burned from its center. He zoomed in and saw dozens of black dots emerging through the light. Xaros drones. Hundreds more by the minute.

"Mule three, you have the precious cargo secured?" Elias asked.

"Roger. That cyborg friend of yours just jumped on our cargo bay."

"Burn back to the *Breitenfeld* now. We'll get back on our own," Elias said.

"You don't have to tell me twice. Good luck down there." The pilot cut the transmission and Elias saw its afterburners flare against the void.

"Oye, how the hell am I supposed to get back?" MacDougall asked.

Elias looked down at the sailor, who stood at his feet, arms on his hips. "Oops."

"'Oops?' 'Oops!' Are you a tin man in need

of a brain instead of a heart?" MacDougall took a wrench off his belt and hurled it at Elias' head. It bounced off his forehead and tumbled into space.

"Did you forget about him?" Kallen asked on a private channel.

"A little," Elias sent back.

"Need I remind ye that I've got six hours of rad exposure left in this suit until I start pissing neon for the rest of my shortened lifespan?"

"Hold on," Elias said to the angry mechanic. "*Breitenfeld*, this is Armor. Mission accomplished. Can you send a pickup for our specialist?" The only answer was a hiss of static.

"Kallen, report in. My IR to the buoys might be down." Elias ran a diagnostic on his comms system, which came back optimal.

"I've got nothing," she said.

"But we could talk to the Mule," Bodel said.

"We had line of sight on that." Elias tapped at the side of his transmitter. "We're on the buoy net. It's almost like we're being jammed."

"While you're trying to call tech support,

my nuts are shriveling away," MacDougall said.

"Take your mag liners off your boots and put them on your forearm mounts. I'll attach you to my chest and you'll have to hang on like a remora," Elias said.

MacDougall grumbled and put his right foot across his left thigh.

"'Join the navy,' they said. 'It'll be fun,' they said." He unlatched the lining from his heel and held up an admonishing finger toward Elias. "And one more thing ... bloody hell—what is that?"

Elias looked up and saw a massive spaceship wavering in and out of existence. Its pearlescent hull looked like it had been fashioned from the inside of a sea conch. Windows and open hangars dotted the side. Elias made out jagged weapon mounts and a focusing crystal the size of a Mule on a laser cannon slung beneath the ship's prow.

"So that's where the Toth came from," Bodel said.

"Looks like there's a dogfight in atmo,"

Kallen said. She pointed to flashes of red Xaros disintegration beams flitting against blue flashes of energy from Toth fighters.

Elias zoomed in and a glimpse of a Mule and Eagle crossed the bottom of his vision. He scanned around until he found them again and saw the energy of a green tractor beam connecting them to a Toth fighter on course to the ship. A gunner was slumped over in the Mule's upper turret ball.

"They've got prisoners," Elias said. He watched as the tractor beams from the Toth spaceship grabbed the human planes and brought them into the maw of a hangar.

CHAPTER 12

Hale snapped awake, struggling to breathe. His lungs refused to inhale and he gawped like a fish as he tried to move his hands. A breath finally came to him, the smell of heavy oil permeating every breath. He tried to look around, but everything was a blur.

His arms were held up and away from him, his legs at wide angles, turning his body in to a giant X.

"Anybody?" he said. The last thing he remembered was the Toth fighter coming at his ship, Durand's Eagle behind it with a blazing white tractor beam. There'd been a flash from the Toth, then an electrical storm. He wondered if that was what it was like to be hit by a Q-shell. He felt like every college hangover he'd ever had compressed into one miserable experience.

"Sir? That you?" Hale heard Orozco's voice.

"Yes. Who else is here?"

"I can't see too good, and I feel like hammered shit."

Hale pulled at his restraints, but whatever was wrapped around his hands was solid. He heard a woman's groan, Durand.

His vision stayed blurred. He couldn't make out anything but his own body and an outline of someone trussed up like he was across from him.

"You remember what happened?" Hale asked.

"I was locked in my turret. Saying a Hail Mary when the ship's electrical tried to fry me."

"I don't think it was the Mule. We're not on the *Breitenfeld*. Xaros don't take prisoners. We must be on the Toth ship," Hale said.

"If we're prisoners of war, guess I should

stop calling you 'sir,' eh?" During wars on Earth, captured officers were more often subject to torture and separated from the men and women they were supposed to lead. Hale had a feeling he'd find out how the Toth treated prisoners pretty soon.

"Ken?" Durand asked meekly. He heard her spit. "Ken, what have I got myself into?"

A door slid open and hot, fetid air blew into the room. A tall shape came in, deep orange in color. The door closed and Hale's vision improved.

He blinked hard and saw a cylindrical tank supported by six mechanical legs. Slowly, what was in the tank came into focus. It was a misshapen brain, and a thick spinal column dotted with bone spurs ran down the tank. Long nerves floated in the tank like columns of seaweed buffeted by tide. *This must be a Toth overlord,* Hale thought.

"Meat, language zero," a modulated voice came from the tank. The tank crab walked over to the person bound across from Hale, one of the pilots from his Mule. A mechanical arm extended from beneath the tank, a thick red-stained needle attached to it. The needle split open, revealing dirty filaments. "Language, one."

The arm lifted over the pilot's head and the filaments crept through the pilot's hair.

"What're you doing? Stop!" Hale struggled against his restraints.

The filaments went rigid and plunged into the pilot's skull. The pilot jerked his head up as his eyes opened and rolled back in his head. The filaments gloved like hot electric wires. The pilot collapsed and the wires extracted, leaving behind blood spots on his skull.

The nervous system in the tank shuddered, nerves lashing against the edge of the tank like it was in the throes of sexual pleasure.

"Exquisite," came from the tank, the voice matching the pilot's. "But ... not the taste I was expecting. That was fuller, natural. I thought you all would be false minds. You ...." One of the tank's mechanical arms jabbed at Hale. "That meat remembers you as an officer. Hero of ... Crucible. You have a Xaros gate, how fascinating. Tell me why the meat on the planet had false minds but his was true."

The nervous system in the tank formed into the outline of a six-legged Toth warrior as it spoke to him. A face leaned toward Hale.

Hale didn't answer—out of spite and because he had no idea what the overlord was talking about.

"Strange, strange yes. Some motivation, perhaps?" the overlord said. The restraints holding the dead pilot lifted the corpse away and a panel on the wall flipped around. The Mule's co-pilot, a blond woman Hale remembered seeing in the ship's gym, floated toward the overlord.

The co-pilot screamed when she saw the overlord and tried to pull an arm from the cap over her hand.

"Yes, scream. The fear changes the taste," the overlord said. "Hale-meat, explain how your species creates false minds. Does your ship have the technology aboard?"

The co-pilot babbled in German, thrashing

against her restraints.

"Tell me, or I will drink from this one to learn more." The overlord's needle arm touched the co-pilot's thigh and ran up her body.

"I don't know what you're talking about. What do you mean by false minds?" Hale asked.

"The minds I drank on Anthalas, they were shallow. A false front over nothingness." A Toth word came through the speakers. "Perhaps I lack the words. Let's see if she has them for me."

The co-pilot's screams cut off as the tendrils jabbed through her skull. Her body went stiff then as limp as a cloth doll.

"No, she doesn't know either." The overlord extracted the needle and returned it beneath his tank. "Such a monumental achievement, yet they both knew nothing. I will ask you again, Hale-meat. How does your species create the false minds and the weed hosts? The Toth will trade for this knowledge, give you everything the Alliance and the Qa'Resh are withholding from you. We would even stand beside you when the Xaros return to your system."

Hale spat on the tank.

"A curious gesture. Let's consult another." The overlord's outline reached out and touched an unseen control. A panel on the ceiling swung around, and a bound and gagged Steuben floated down to take the co-pilot's place. The caps around Steuben's hands and arms were twice the size of Hale's, but they still gave way as Steuben struggled.

"A Karigole in the wild, what a treat. I could sell this one on my world for a billion slaves. The supply has been dry for so long since we overindulged ourselves. Not all of us had the wisdom to prolong what this meat could give us. Such a shame, but that is the price of excess." The restraint on Steuben's mouth parted and Steuben growled at the overlord, hate burning in his eyes.

"Tell me, Karigole, how are the humans creating false minds? Or don't tell me. Give me an excuse to drink from you. It might be worth the loss in trade for the pleasure—and what I could learn."

Steuben breathed heavily, his teeth bared.

"Eh?" The overlord's outline looked up, then the outline broke away as the nerves went loose. "Seems it's time to negotiate with someone a bit more senior." The door opened and the overlord left.

"Steuben, what the hell was that? What does it want from us?" Hale asked.

"The Toth are broken. At some point in their past, they meddled too deeply with their genetic code to try to preserve their lives indefinitely. They found a way to keep their nervous systems going, but they had to feed off the other sentient lives to do it. The process was addictive, drove the ones rich enough to afford the conversion mad with cravings. They learned that an older, more developed mind gave them a bigger high when they 'drank' from it.

"The overlords consumed their own species to the edge of extinction, then they began cloning the ones that remained. The system was imperfect, and they grew weaker with every generation. Then the Alliance found them." Steuben shook his head. "They helped the Toth get off their world, stabilized the decline in cloning and helped them grow stronger. The Qa'Resh thought the Toth would become the army for the Alliance.

"The Karigole used to ostracize addicts, for they could never truly be trusted. The Toth came to our world to incorporate us into their war machine. We are longed-lived; many of our elders were over a thousand human years old. We were a temptation too great for the Toth to ever resist. I and the rest of the cohort were off world when they finally turned against the planet. I don't think they meant to … consume all of us. They must have lost control, binged on my species."

"How many of you are left?" Hale asked.

"We never settled other worlds, and my all-male cohort was the only group to survive. There are four of us left, Lieutenant. Four, where once we were hundreds of millions. Four. You asked me what g*hul'thul'ghul* means. It means, 'I will not be the last.'"

****

Captain Valdar tapped at the control panels on his armrest, counting down the seconds until the extraction Mules were scheduled to clear the moon and report that they had the Marines and Rangers he'd sent to the planet's surface.

He wanted to get up and pace, but under combat conditions the captain's place was strapped into his command chair.

"Spotters? Anything?" he asked.

"Negative, sir. Still have thirty seconds to go," Ericsson said.

Valdar swiped down a contact list and called Lafayette.

"Is that giant lump of alien tech going to blow us up when we hit the wormhole?" he asked the Karigole, his icon showing him on the flight deck next to the Omnium reactor.

"No, Captain. The engines project a pocket of real space around the ship. The jump will be just as safe as we are right now," Lafayette said.

"We haven't had the best of luck when it comes to strange new engines on this ship. Now lock that reactor down tighter than Fort Knox and get off the flight deck. We've got birds coming in," Valdar said.

"The birds will not loosen Fort Knix," Lafayette said.

"Sir! Contact, one Eagle, one Mule inbound," Utrecht said.

"One of each? Open a channel." The communications officer sent him a thumbs-up. "This is *Breitenfeld* actual. Where is the rest of your flight?"

"This is Mule 1. Mule 2 was damaged. Gall stayed back to cover them. We lost contact a few minutes ago," Choi Ma said.

Valdar's hands clenched into fists. Who was on the incoming Mule? Who had he lost now?

"*Breitenfeld*, we've got a serious Xaros problem. The Crucible is open and they are pouring through," Ma said.

"How many?"

"All of them!"

"Get back here at best speed." Valdar cut the

transmission and pointed to the engineering officer.

"I know where your missing planes are," came over the IR. "Want to see them?"

Valdar looked at the communications officer, who shrugged her shoulders.

"It's coming in through our buoys, sir," she said.

"Valdar. Captain. *Breitenfeld*. Your name was prominent in their minds. You are who I can deal with," the Toth overlord said.

"Who is this?" Valdar asked. He scrawled out a message on his forearm computer ordering the ship around the moon once the remaining Eagle and Mule had landed and sent it to the astronavigation ensign.

"You will not have my name. Meat does not learn Toth names. Meat cannot bargain with Toth, but the Xaros are here and they are getting closer. Meat can exchange with Toth and leave," the overlord said. "A good bargain for meat."

"Do you have my people?" Valdar asked.

"Some live. Some don't," the overlord said.

Valdar heard a tapping sound come through with his transmission. "Their meat helps us speak. Fair. Fair. You will give us the engine. You will give us the meat with the high mind. You will give us the secret to your meat with false minds and weed bodies."

Valdar sent a text message to the communications officer, telling her to check the Toth's transmission for Morse code. The tapping was too fast and controlled to be transmission static.

The *Breitenfeld* lurched as the engines fired.

"How about you return my people unharmed and I won't blow you out of space?" Valdar asked.

A savage growl filled the speakers.

"Meat will give us the false minds and weed bodies. Now. Or I will taste your mind, Valdar, know what you will not bargain," the overlord said.

The communications officer rolled her hand forward several times, wanting Valdar to keep him talking.

"Toth, we may have a different term for the 'false minds and weed bodies.' Can you explain it better?"

"Minds of lies. False images over shallow souls. Bodies not born of females. Bartlett was false mind and weed body. Crenshaw was false mind and weed body. False minds! Weed bodies! You will give this to me now. Now!"

"Enemy contact, dead ahead!" the gunner officer announced.

Valdar looked through the portals and saw the Toth ship as it came around the moon. Its bulbous hull was pearlescent and refracted light into waves along its hull. Valdar was mesmerized by its beauty, like it was some ancient sea creature come to life in the void.

A pen bounced off his visor. He looked over in the direction it came from and saw his comms officer gesturing madly at his forearm screen.

Valdar looked down and read "FIRE Q-SHELLS? RESCUE? IH" Valdar chewed at his lip, unsure if the Q-shells would even work on the Toth.

"Toth if you want to bargain. We need to—"

A bolt of blue light lanced out of the Toth ship and flashed over the *Breitenfeld's* hull.

"Damage report! Anti-aircraft turret two not responding," the XO said.

At the prow of the ship, a burning mass of metal marked where one of the many gauss cannon batteries used to be. Five sailors crewed that station.

"Meat. We are done with bargains. Give me the false minds," the overlord said.

"Toth, if we gave that to you, we'd have to have iron hearts and *fire* in our bellies," Valdar said, hoping the Iron Hearts would pick up on his hint before the Toth fired again.

****

Elias raised his rail gun over his shoulder and fired it up. Deep purple energy pulsed up and down the twin spikes like a Jacob's ladder.

"Find a strut to stake," Elias said. He turned around to the three jet packs that were mag locked together and to MacDougal, his magnetic liners now attached to his forearms and stuck against the sides of two jetpacks.

"Elias, this isn't funny. What're you doing?"

MacDougall asked.

"You're crunchy. I do this because I care." Elias grabbed the jet packs—with MacDougall still attached to them—and tossed them up into the void, well away from the line of fire to the Toth ship. "Don't let go."

MacDougall lct out a stream of profanity that would have made sailors of yore blush.

Elias skated across the cube's face and found a spot over a strut. He raised his right foot off the surface, and a yard-long stake shot out of his heel. It glowed red with heat and he slammed his foot into the cube, securing himself to it.

"We've only got one Q-shell each," Kallen said. "Let's hope their point defense is asleep."

"Aim for the base of the laser with the crystal," Elias said. "Should be something delicate there. Fire on my mark. Three … two … one … mark!" The Iron Hearts' rail cannons twisted magnetic fields into an acceleration vortex and fired quadrium shells the size of a man's forearm at the Toth ship.

The recoil from the triple shots snapped the struts beneath the cube face and left a divot against its side like a giant fist had hit it.

The rounds burst against the starship's hull, launching bolts of electricity that walked over the ship like a spider born of lightning. Lights within the ship winked out and the engines taking it toward the *Breitenfeld* cut out. The Toth ship listed in space.

"Get our packs and let's get on that ship," Elias said. He broke his heel free from the stake, leaving a human artifact in the ship to puzzle would-be explorers—if any ever dared violate Xaros space like mankind and the Toth had done.

He jumped from the cube and activated his anti-gravity thrusters to catch up with MacDougall. He got a hand against the spinning mass of jet packs and the still-cursing sailor.

"You all right?" Elias asked.

"Someone pissed in me suit," MacDougall said. "I did not join the navy for this."

"Recruiter lied to you too?" Bodel asked,

357

coming to a stop near Elias.

Elias pushed a button on the side of a jet pack to unlock it and tossed it to Bodel, who attached it to Kallen's back. She returned the favor and put the last pack on Elias.

Elias pressed MacDougall's forearms against his own chest and looked into the face of a sweaty, stressed-out man.

"Are we going home now?" MacDougall asked.

"No, we're going to get our people back. Hang on."

"Sure, why not. This day won't get any easier, will it?"

Elias activated his jet pack and soared toward the Toth ship.

****

Elias landed on the Toth hull and skated toward the edge of the hangar he had seen the Mule and Eagle enter. He detached MacDougall and slid into space, swooping through a weak force field and landing on the hangar deck.

The Eagle lay in pieces, surrounded by dead menials who'd been on the deck when it lost atmosphere during the Q-shell overload. One menial was in the cockpit, its tongue stuck to the canopy.

The Mule's turrets had been cut away to get to the humans held within. A menial lay dead across the top of the Mule, dangling from rents that ran down the hull where the alien had held on as the venting atmosphere tried to suck it in to space.

Kallen and Bodel landed next to Elias, their weapons primed and ready.

"Clear," Elias said. The other soldiers echoed him.

Elias grabbed the dead menial hanging from the ship and tossed it aside like a dead rat. It flopped against the deck, boneless.

"Gravity's back," Kallen said.

"MacDougall, get in here," Elias said.

"Coming." MacDougall grabbed the top edge of the hangar and swung himself feetfirst inside. He floated down slowly, then came down much faster.

"Gravity, careful!" Elias shouted.

MacDougall accelerated to the deck, hit hard and tumbled up the Mule's ramp.

"You all right?" Kallen asked.

"Bloody giants and your god damn fancy suits." There was a crash of tools and ammo canisters within the Mule. "What did these lizards do to my lovely Mule?"

"He's all right," Elias said. "Cover him and get that thing space worthy. I'm going to go find the prisoners."

"How're you going to do that?" Bodel asked.

"I'm going to make as much noise as I possibly can and hope Hale has the common sense to run toward the sound of gunfire," Elias said. He slammed fingertips into the seal between the doors of the hangar. The doors groaned as they gave way to the strength in his metal arms.

He stepped into the corridor and pistol shots

from a swarm of menials bounced off his armor. He fired back with much larger bullets and charged into them.

They tried to run. The sight of a ten-foot-tall biped covered in claw marks and dried Toth blood firing bullets that either tore through their ranks like they weren't even there or exploding with enough force to kill not only the menial it hit but the two next to it was more than their obedience could handle.

Elias stomped one to death as he overtook their dwindling force. He punched one hard enough to send it through the bulkhead and tumbling into a cavernous space beyond. He looked through the hole and saw fires raging through the dark ship, skittering shadows of menials racing between infernos, some carrying tanks that sprayed retardant foam into the flames.

A growl rumbled behind him. He whirled around and saw nothing. He looked up at the ceiling and found a Toth warrior, covered head to tail in crystalline armor.

"You come here to dance or just look pretty?" Elias fired off a burst that tore through the ceiling, just missing the warrior as it leapt to the deck and pounced at Elias. Elias swung an uppercut into the warrior that hit just beneath its throat, driving the Toth into—and off—the ceiling.

The warrior's tail snapped over its body and embedded into Elias' chest. A dent appeared against the inside of his armored womb that Elias saw with his true eye. Elias snatched the armored tip out of his chest and plucked it from the warrior's armor. It came away with a gout of yellow blood. The warrior reared back on its hind legs and let out an ululation that echoed through the hallways.

"What? You mad now?" Elias tackled the warrior.

****

The ship shuddered and groaned. The lights flickered, then faded out. Red emergency lighting along the edge of the ceiling came on. The restraints holding Hale and the rest of the prisoners in the air went loose. Hale fell to the ground as the heavy caps split apart and tumbled across the floor. He rubbed his wrists and looked around. Orozco, Durand and Steuben were all free as well.

The bodies of the pilot and co-pilot lay in a heap against the wall. Hale went to them and pulled dog tags from beneath their flight suits. He slid them into a small compartment on his armor.

"Hale, we should go," Steuben said.

"I'm all for that, but where?" Durand asked.

The staccato rhythm of gunfire echoed through the brig.

"I thought they used energy weapons," Hale said.

"That's a dual gauss blaster if I've ever heard one," Orozco said. "Only armor carries that weapon."

"Could it be the Iron Hearts?" Durand asked.

"Let's find out," Hale said. "I don't want to be big ugly's next fix." Hale cocked his hand and his forearm blade snapped out. Orozco did the same.

"I'll just stand behind the two of you," Durand said.

Steuben slammed his hands into the side of the door, digging his claws into the metal and heaving the door aside. Two menials, who had their backs to the door, turned around and saw one very angry Karigole towering over them. Steuben swept his arms down and bashed the two menials together, crushing their skulls.

He took a small pistol from each of the menials and tossed them to Durand.

"Five shots each, don't waste it," Steuben said.

The corridor was large and octagonal, meant to allow the much larger warriors easy passage. Hand rungs ran along each side of the corridor, and open hatchways dotted the sides with no discernable pattern Hale could recognize. He saw small shadows of menials racing along the walls.

"Oh boy," Durand said. "Steuben, I hope you know where you're going because I've got nothing right now."

"I've been on ships of this class before. The Toth will restructure the ship based on the wealth of the overlords traveling within it. The richest will be the farthest from their engines, which have a habit of leaking radiation." Steuben looked up and tapped a claw against his teeth. "Based on the runes and corporate markings I see on that passageway—"

Gauss rounds tore through one of the walls and passed through the other side.

"That way!" Steuben pointed to the new battle damage.

An explosion tore through the side of the passageway. Smoke and fire rose to the ceiling as an armor suit charged through debris, struggling with a Toth warrior. The armor fell on top of the warrior and pounded a fist against the Toth's carapace. The second blow cracked the carapace and the warrior wiggled free from the armor and then jumped against the slanted wall and sprang back toward the armor.

The armor's hand retracted into its forearm

housing and a Xaros breaker spike snapped out. The warrior impaled itself against the spike, still hissing and grasping at the armor as it struggled to get free. The armor slammed the warrior to the ground, stomped a foot against its lower half then ripped the spike up.

Most of the warrior was ripped away, although some stayed beneath the armor's heel. The armor flicked the warrior's corpse away. It hit the ground with a wet thump and oozed yellow blood over the floor.

"Elias?" Hale waved to the armor.

"Hale!" Elias' armor megaphones boomed through the hallway. "Are there any others?"

"No, you have a way out of here?" Hale asked.

"We might. Follow me." Elias led them back through the destruction, heedless of the smoke and fire around him.

"I'm not complaining, but how the hell did you get here?" Hale asked.

Elias knocked aside a flaming crossbeam

and fired a burst of rounds down an adjacent hallway.

"We were waiting for evac off the cube ships when this cruiser de-cloaked," Elias said. "Valdar got a message to us about prisoners, so we hit it with our Q-shells and made our own way in. Seemed like a good idea at the time."

"How're we getting off this ship?" Durand asked.

"Same way you got on," Elias said. "Your Mule. I left a trail of bullet holes for us to follow. ... Damn it." The helm on top of his armored shoulders cocked to the side, a psychosomatic mirroring gesture of the man inside the armor. "We've got a problem. Hurry." Elias ran down the hallways. Because they were large enough for the Toth warriors, they were large enough for him. Lights snapped back on up and down the hallways, and clouds of gas blew from nozzles embedded in walls at burning fires. The ship was coming back online.

"Power? How is power a problem?" Durand asked, struggling to keep up with Elias and the

Marines.

A red beam cut through the hallway. The smell of burnt hair and smoke blew past them with a wave of superheated air. Hale and the rest skidded to a halt. Black tendrils grasped through the hole in the bulkhead and a Xaros drone, morphed into a long, wormlike shape, squeezed into the corridor.

Hale looked at the small-caliber weapon in his hand, its effectiveness against the drone on par with harsh language.

Elias aimed his forearm-mounted gauss cannons at the drone and pelted it with shots. One round penetrated the Xaros' shell and the variable mass fuse exploded. A section of carapace blew away and ricocheted off Elias' chest. A red and gold fractal mass within the drone shimmered with energy, then the drone disintegrated, burning away from an internal fire.

Air blew into the Xaros hole, tracing back to the vacuum of space where the Xaros had burned its way in through the outer hull.

"Button up," Hale said. He pulled an

emergency hood from his armor and unfolded it. His suit's air tanks were dangerously low, but if they didn't find a way off the Toth ship in the twenty minutes of air he had left, asphyxiation probably wouldn't be much of a problem.

They ran toward a T-intersection.

"There's a drop into the hangar level just ahead," Elias said. A torrent of blue Toth energy blasts filled the intersection, then crisscrossed with Xaros disintegration beams. A pack of menials charged across the hallway and were erased by the Xaros beams. The firefight continued.

"Guess we're not going that way," Hale said.

"Step back. I've got an idea." Elias pointed the gauss cannons on his forearms at the deck.

Hale slapped Orozco on the arm and pointed at Durand. The two armored Marines forced her to her knees and shielded her from what came next.

Elias' cannons pounded the deck, blowing through grates and pipes carrying everything from water to data and power cables. Chunks of metal and shell fragments careened off Hale and Orozco. Elias stood in a circle of destruction, then raised his right foot. The spike meant to anchor him for a rail cannon shot from his heel and he slammed it into the deck. The plating gave way and Elias fell through the access way of his own making.

Hale ran to the edge of the hole. Sparks showered from a burst pipe and mixed with brackish water that almost certainly came from a sewer line. Elias was twenty feet below, firing his gauss cannons.

"Get down here," Elias said, glancing up at Hale and as he kept firing.

Orozco pulled a jagged hunk of metal from where it had embedded against the back of a leg and tossed it aside.

"Damn you, Elias!" Durand shouted through the IR. "Not everyone is a walking tank, you know. I could have been killed by your little stunt."

"I am not a tank. I am armor. And you're welcome." Elias ejected spent ammo cans off his upper arms. Fresh ammo cycled into the belt feeds.

"Use your anti-grav linings," Hale said to Orozco. He grabbed Durand by one arm and Orozco got the other.

"What're you two—" The Marines stepped into the gap and took Durand down with them. The free fall lasted for half a second before they activated their boots, slowing their fall just enough to avoid injury.

Hale slipped in the pooling sewage and fell on his face. He pushed himself out of the muck and saw a Mule, Kallen and Bodel standing next to it. The cockpit was shattered and both turrets had been ripped out. Dead Toth littered the ground around the drop ship.

They were in a small hangar. Blade-like Toth fighters were stacked atop each other in container slips just big enough to hold the silver ships. A large mechanical arm was anchored against the ceiling next to Elias' hole.

A sailor in a void suit ran from behind the Mule and waved to the new arrivals.

"Oye!" MacDougall yelled at them. "Get

your lollygagging arses over here before this hunk of shyte falls apart for good."

Kallen's arms snapped against her side then rotated over her chest. Her legs pulled together and treads unfolded from her calves and the backs of her legs. Now in travel formation, Bodel pushed Kallen into the back of the Mule.

"Strap her in," Bodel said to Orozco as he ran up the Mule's ramp. "I'm next."

"Hale, I need you in the cockpit with me," Durand said.

"I don't know how to—"

"Just shut up and follow my instructions. Cockpit. Go! Go!"

Hale ran through the drop ship and into the cockpit. He grasped the frame around the top seat and pulled himself up.

"Bottom seat! Are you going to pilot this?" Durand pulled down and vaulted into the pilot's seat.

The co-pilot's seat was far too narrow for him and his armor. He reached beneath his breastplate and found the quick-release handle. With one tug, the armor plates loosened and fell away, leaving him in his body glove and bio-augmentation layer. He got into the co-pilot's seat and strapped himself in.

The control panel was a myriad of switches, dials and blank view screens.

"What now?"

"MacDougall, fire it up!" Durand shouted. A hum of power shuddered through the ship. "Hale, reset the anti-grav regulators to factory default. I think the gravity in this ship is a little lighter than Earth standard."

"Umm …."

"Hit the red switch by your left elbow and push the yellow button next to it when it flashes!"

Elias shot a burst of rounds at a menial that tried to peek into the hangar.

"Move faster," Elias said, backpedaling away from the hangar door and toward the rear of the Mule.

"There's only two tie-down spots for the

armor. What'll we do about the Elias?" Orozco asked over the IR.

"I'll do a mag lock once you're in the void," Elias said. He hefted Bodel into the ship and slapped a metal hand against the back of the Mule.

"Raise the ramp," Durand said.

Hale could almost feel her roll her eyes as his hands floated over the controls, uncertain.

"Lever by your right knee, hold it up for two seconds," she said.

Elias's cannons barked again. He walked down the side of the corridor, blowing gaps through the bulkhead.

Hale's screens came to life and the drop ship shuddered as the anti-grav thrusters in the wings came to life.

"OK, let's get out of here. Is that force field down?" Durand asked.

"One second." Elias shot around the edge of the hangar until the force field flickered and fell away.

Atmosphere hurtled into the void with the

force of hurricane winds. Debris skipped across the deck and bounced off the Mule. A lump of pipe flew through the broken windshield and hit the side of Hale's seat frame with a muted clang as the atmosphere dissipated into nothing.

"I swear his answer for everything is to just shoot it," Durand muttered. The Mule rose in the air, then spun in place to face the void. "Time to go." She engaged the rear engine, and the Mule lurched to the side. Elias fell to the deck before the wing tip could take his armored head right off.

The Mule banked hard into the void of space and swung back around toward the blue and white hull of the Toth ship. Durand sent the ship into a dive and missed a collision by a few feet.

"What the hell?" she asked.

"We lost an engine earlier," Hale said.

"*Now* you tell me?"

Lights on Hale's control panel switched on and off as Durand reset the ship to compensate for the unbalanced engine.

Durand swung the drop ship around and

pulled it up to fly in front of the hangar.

Elias leapt into space and floated toward the Mule. Small thrusters spun him until his body was perpendicular with the ship. The suit of armor was coming in fast, way too fast for him to stop without ripping a hunk off the hull.

Elias pointed his forearm cannon in his direction of travel and fired off a round. The momentum exchange slowed him down slightly. More shots brought him to a relative stop over the Mule.

"Show off," Durand said.

Elias ran his forearm over the top of the Mule until the electromagnets within found an anchor point and he attached to the ship with a thump. He pounded an armored fist against the hull twice to signal he was good to go.

Durand sped the ship up slowly, not wanting to risk sheering Elias off the top.

"Elias, hold on tight," she said.

Durand flipped the Mule upside down and flew closer to the hull of the Toth ship.

"What're you doing?" Hale asked.

"Nap of the earth. I'm guessing the Toth have flak guns. Hard to hit us when we're this close," she said. The Mule zoomed over the rolling surface, banking around blown-out sections of the hull. As they sped past an angular Toth weapon the size of an Eagle fighter, the menial crew beneath the clear dome nearly snapped their necks watching the Mule dash across their field of view.

Hale looked up and saw the flash of red Xaros beams dueling with silver blasts from the Toth fighters. The wide path of stars making up the galactic center wavered, like a thin cloud passing beneath the moon. Stars winked in and out of view as dark objects blocked their light. He remembered the recording the *Breitenfeld*'s former wing commander left after the Earth was overrun by the Xaros, how he described a mass of drones so numerous it blocked out the stars.

The Xaros were on Anthalas in force.

"We really need to hurry," Hale said.

"We could lighten the load by ejecting you,"

Durand said. "Now pull some weight and adjust our starboard trim by ten percent z-axis. Purple knob third from the right, second row from the top."

The Mule crossed over the prow of the Toth ship, and they saw the *Breitenfeld* just beyond the orbit of the planet's moon.

"Mule zero-six, this is *Breitenfeld* actual, do you read?" Captain Valdar said over the IR.

"Sir, this is Raider six. There is a mass of Xaros right on our tail and closing fast," Hale said.

"Roger, Raider six, we see them. Need you to clear the line of fire on the Toth ship. We can buy just enough time to get out of here soon as you get the hell out of the way."

****

Valdar tapped his fingers against the target plot, counting down the seconds until the ship was clear of danger.

"Gunnery, ready the rail guns. Fire Q-shells on my mark," Valdar said.

"We'll hit the Toth ship as well," Ericsson

said. "Do we really want to do them any favors?"

"Every Xaros that slips by becomes a problem. We'll let the Toth deal with it," Valdar said.

"Sir, Mule zero-six is clear!" the gunnery officer announced.

"All batteries, fire!"

The *Breitenfeld*'s rail guns crackled with energy, then shunted quadrium shells down a magnetic vortex fast enough to bring the rounds within a few full percentage points of the speed of light. A shell burst deep within the Xaros swarm, roiling toward the Toth ship like a rogue wave. The Q-shell sent massive crooked spikes of energy into the swarm, arcing from drone to drone. A few were burnt out of existence while many more were knocked off-line, tumbling against each other like stones propelled along by an avalanche.

The second Q-shell blew through the leading edge of the Xaros murmuration. The third exploded short of the mass, taking out a few drones and sending a tendril of energy over the Toth hull.

Valdar watched as the mass of drones flew onward, ballistic and uncontrolled. The drones weren't beaten, but they were down for the count. He zoomed in on the Crucible beneath Anthalas' southern pole. A disk of white light appeared within the thorns and more drones emerged.

"Mule zero-six has docked," Ericsson said.

"Helm, full speed back to the gravity rift. Let's get out of here," Valdar said. He keyed a ship-wide address. "*Breitenfeld*, we didn't come here for a fight, but we got one. We came here for knowledge, and that mission is a success. Make ready for jump. We're going home. *Gott mit uns.*"

****

The dark energy engine in the *Breitenfeld's* hull awoke. It followed its standard programming and readied the quantum shunt that would take the ship through the rift and back to Earth. A protocol for action flagged in the engine's programming, and it scanned the ship as the protocol required.

An anomaly registered in the ship's brig.

The artificial intelligence within the engine awoke to examine the anomaly, determined that the detection was valid, and changed the quantum shunt fluctuation as its programming demanded. With the new course laid in, the AI went back on standby.

This ship wasn't going to Earth. Not yet.

CHAPTER 13

The blinding light faded away and Valdar opened one eye. Everyone and everything looked as expected. The blast shields remained up.

An ensign leaned against the side of his workstation and dry heaved.

"Joachim?" Valdar asked.

The lieutenant gave him a thumbs-up and sat back against his workstation.

"Comms, raise Titan station and the Crucible. Tell Ibarra and Admiral Garret that we're back and we'll need to offload whatever's in my brig," Valdar said.

"Sir, we don't seem to be in the solar

system," the navigation ensign said. "I'm not reading any pulsars or navigation beacons."

"Lower the blast shields," Valdar said.

The shields slid down. Beyond was an endless gray expanse, featureless but for a dark band in the distance.

Valdar got out of his command chair and walked down the bridge, the entire crew staring out the windows with him. The deep nothing beyond was unwavering in its stillness.

"What's on sensors?" Valdar asked quietly.

"Nothing, sir. It's like the universe just stops a few hundred yards from the ship. There's vacuum around us, but no gravity wells," Ericsson said.

"What about the wormhole we came through?"

"It's … gone, sir," the navigation ensign said.

"Engines? Can we move?"

"They're off-line," the engineer said.

Valdar looked into the gray expanse and shook his head.

"Stand down from combat conditions. Reintroduce atmosphere and bring our computers back online. Get Lafayette up here. Maybe he can explain this," Valdar said.

"Sir, Lafayette is in the brig. He wants you to see the … specimen. Says it's important," Ericsson said, reading from her forearm display.

"It had better be," Valdar said.

****

Valdar, Lafayette and Hale stood two yards—well beyond arm's distance—from the barred cell. A navy guard, standing next to the only door in and out, held a shock baton.

Yarrow sat on the bare metal bunk, his hands lying to his side with palms up. His head lolled from side to side, a string of drool glistening from the edge of his mouth. His eyes opened and closed at irregular intervals, and each time they opened the light glowing within was a little bit brighter.

"It's nearly awake," Lafayette said.

"Do you have any idea what it is?" Valdar asked.

"There are numerous species that are known to exert control over other animals," Lafayette said.

"Any with glowing eyes that claim to smell your soul?" Hale asked. He was still in his augmented musculature suit, his emergency helmet tucked beneath an arm.

"That is unique," Lafayette said.

Yarrow rose to his feet, then levitated into the air, his toes hanging loose just above the deck.

"Captain … Valdar," Yarrow said, his voice lower and resonant. "You are … decision maker. Leader. You can assist." Yarrow floated toward the bars and pressed against them.

The guard rushed forward, his baton crackling. Valdar held an arm up to stop him.

"What are you?" Valdar asked.

Yarrow floated back, like a balloon wandering across a room.

"I am your salvation. I am your exaltation. How many humans are there? Your souls are bright, stronger than the Shanishol. They could have given me enough to complete the journey, join those who left me behind. But they were too few, too weak. If I'd had more time … just a few more generations … they would have bred themselves to the numbers I needed. The Xaros spoiled my plans. I had to take what I could just to prolong myself."

"You massacred the Shanishol. We saw the bodies on Anthalas," Hale said.

"Most were willing to accept exaltation through me. Others … less so. Tell me, how many humans are there on Earth? This host remembers many and he remembers few."

"I think we're done speaking with you," Valdar said.

"Omnium. Yes, you want Omnium," Yarrow said. "A parlor trick, it's nothing compared to our capabilities. I will teach you the secret and much, much more. All you must do ... bring me to Earth. Let me show you the path to immortality. What good are the temporal concerns of power and life when your soul can exist forever? Only through me is this possible."

"There are others like you?" Lafayette asked.

"They moved on. All of them. They left me behind, said I was unworthy of their paradise. But I know the path. With enough strength I will find them, make them suffer for imprisoning me on that rock." Yarrow held a hand through the bars toward Valdar and pale yellow flames ignited in his palm. "Would you like a taste of what I offer? You can bring my message to your crew, then to the rest of your species."

"I'll pass," Valdar said.

"I was on the cube ships, read the inscriptions. Were you the prophet?" Lafayette asked.

"No. I heard the prophet's voice through space. Reached out to him on his home world and gave him the knowledge to bring his people to me. They were too slow and too few. They weren't enough by the time the Xaros arrived. Such a shame, most were so pliant."

The glowing eyes looked over Valdar and stopped at his belt buckle.

"*Gott mit uns*, indeed." Yarrow held a flaming hand toward Hale. "For so long you have claimed that God is with you. Now, one truly is." Hale backed away.

Valdar's forearm computer buzzed, three pulses in rapid succession for a priority message.

"We'll be back," Valdar said. The Man at Arms opened the door, a worried expression on his face. "Don't let him out and don't let anyone near him," Valdar said to the guard, who was growing paler by the moment. "In fact, why don't you wait outside and monitor him by cameras." The guard nodded so hard Valdar thought his neck would snap.

Once in the corridor, Valdar double-tapped his communicator pad.

"Valdar."

"Sir? Is that really you?" a familiar voice asked.

"Ensign Ibarra?"

"It's just Stacey now. Hard to juggle navy and ambassador duties. But you're here! Wow, this is *really* unusual," she said.

"Ens—Stacey, where the hell is the *Breitenfeld*?"

"You're at Bastion. The Qa'Resh are very security conscious after the Toth betrayal. The Toth, they're—"

"We've met. Why is my ship here? Wherever this is."

"You met them? How did …? Yes, I'm just about to get to that," she said to someone else. "Captain Valdar, are you aware of an … evil alien intelligence on your ship?" she asked hesitantly.

"Yes, I was just speaking with it."

"Oh, good. I mean bad, very bad. You speaking to it, I mean. Please don't do that anymore. We need to get it off your ship right away," Stacey said.

"Stacey," Hale said, "that thing is inside one of my Marines. How do we save him?"

"I'm not sure we can, Ken, but we're going

to try. Here's what I need you to do."

****

Torni and Hale, both in battle armor and carrying gauss rifles, stood next to a gurney holding an unconscious Yarrow. For all the strange behavior exhibited by the young medic and the entity inside him, it was still susceptible to human frailty, namely tranquilizer darts fired by the guards.

They waited at the edge of the flight deck, staring into the gray expanse. Crewmen and a platoon of Marines ready for combat watched from the wings.

"You don't have to come," Hale said to the Torni.

"And according to Stacey, neither do you," she said. "Yarrow is my Marine now, same as yours." Torni swallowed hard. "I can't replace Gunney Cortaro, but I will assume his duties until he's back in action."

"Thanks, Torni. You'll do him proud."

"Thank me after this is over, whatever it is,"

she said.

Hale shifted from side to side and glanced at Yarrow, who lay motionless, his breathing shallow and regular. He looked over the entire gray expanse beyond the force field. It was still, like a perfect movie frame set to pause.

"I kind of like it," he said. "It makes me feel calm."

"I thought of purgatory, where God sends souls to await judgment."

"Suddenly I don't feel so calm," Hale said.

"I regret nothing. That's the church's dogma."

"No, look at our two o'clock. Something's out there." Hale pointed to the abyss. Marines and crewmen murmured to each other. The sound of fresh batteries slapping into gauss rifles echoed from the walkways.

The small gunmetal gray line Hale had his eyes on grew larger. With no reference point, Hale couldn't tell how far away it was, or how fast it was moving. He tucked his rifle into his shoulder and set a thumb against the weapon's safety.

As the object approached, Hale made out a thin railing on the upper side. It sped toward the *Breitenfeld*'s hangar with no apparent deceleration. Crewmen shouted warnings and ran off the flight deck.

Hale and Torni stood shoulder to shoulder in front of Yarrow.

The object came to an impossibly fast stop just at the edge of the hangar force field. It was a flat rectangle, big enough to stand five or six Marines comfortably with a tube railing floating a yard above it.

The object floated into the hangar and came to a stop in front of the armored Marines. The section of the railing facing the Marines vanished, like it had never even been there.

"I guess this is our ride," Hale said.

"Mother always said never take a ride with a stranger. This is pretty damn strange, sir."

A tiny circle slid aside in the middle of the object and a sphere popped into the air. It floated at waist height then a hologram morphed around it. Stacey Ibarra, colored in shades of blue and white, stood before them wearing a simple jumpsuit.

"Wow," she said. "Love what you've done with the place. New armor looks great on you, Ken. Hi Torni, you're still … really tall. Good to see you!"

"Stacey," Hale said, pointing his thumb over his shoulder at the prone Yarrow, "can we deal with this situation?"

"Right, of course. Get him on our sled and we'll get going." Her hologram stepped aside to make room for Yarrow's gurney. The railing reappeared once the three were on the sled.

"Do we need to strap him down?" Hale asked.

"Nope!" Stacey waved her fingers in a swirl and the sled rose from the ground. Hale held his arms out to steady himself, but there was no sensation of movement at all. The sled shot out of the hangar and away from the *Breitenfeld.* Hale and Torni slammed their hands against the railing and held on for dear life.

As Hale looked back at the retreating *Breitenfeld*, there was no feeling of wind against his face or even the slightest sensation as the sled banked away and continued on into the gray expanse.

"Inertia-less drive," Stacey said. "Isn't it amazing? Don't even need the railings but I had to insist on them. Humans have a certain expectation when it comes to sensation and movement. Violate that expectation and the brain has trouble processing it."

Hale looked at Torni, her eyes squeezed shut and her lips mouthing a prayer.

"Where are you? Why didn't you come yourself?" Hale asked her.

"I'm not allowed on Qa'Resh'Ta—none of the ambassadors are. Thing is, I don't know why that rule is even in place. None of us are Toth," she said.

The *Breitenfeld* had vanished into the abyss, but the view ahead of them hadn't changed.

"What do they have to do with this?"

"When there was a Toth ambassador, they tried to kidnap one of the Qa'Resh and … ugh … you know what they do. Bastion was relocated, and now none of us know where the place really is." Stacey looked to the side and nodded. "Almost there. We're sorry about the null sphere around the *Breitenfeld*, but we're not willing to take a risk the ship might record something that will lead to our location."

"What's this *we* stuff? Aren't you still human?"

"Humanity is part of the war with the Xaros, whether we like it or not. We can survive together or die separately. I'm afraid you haven't had much of a chance to see the wider conflict, but what's inside Yarrow might be useful," she said.

"Marines and sailors died for 'might be useful'?"

"Hold on to the railing. This part is a little weird." Stacey's hands tapped at unseen controls.

Hale grabbed the railing, and the gray

expanse vanished. Bright white light stung Hale's eyes. He put a hand over his face and looked over the edge of the sled. A swirling mass of red and black clouds writhed far beneath him. Bands of multicolored clouds stretched so far into the distance Hale thought it was another sort of illusion.

Great pillars of nebulous clouds rose from the bands and towered hundreds of miles into the pale blue sky. Bolts of lightning rose and fell soundlessly within the pillars.

"This is Qa'Resh'Ta. To your left you'll see Bastion," Stacey said. The space station hung far above the gas giant, faded by the atmosphere between Hale and where Stacey actually was.

Hale saw the two stars at the center of the planet's star system, one large and blue, the other small and white.

"Sir, can I open my eyes now?" Torni asked.

"I think you'd better. You don't want to miss this."

Torni yelped and shut her eyes again. She relaxed a few moments later and looked around in wonder.

"Whoa," she said.

"Humanity could have sent a poet for a moment like this," Stacey said. "Instead we've got two Marines. But … I don't think there are many poets left on Earth. Ready for something special?"

The sled cut through a tuft of white cloud and banked around a cloud pillar. Sunlight glittered off something close to the roiling cloud layers. Hale looked over the edge of the sled. A city floated above the clouds, immense crystals the size of skyscrapers fused together, glowing from within. It looked like the entire island of Manhattan redone in crystal with skyscrapers fused together at the base, clutching against a solid mass of stone. Shadows floated between the crystals, darting away as Hale tried to hold his eyes on them.

"This is where the Qa'Resh live. They can't be on Bastion in their true form. You'll understand in a second," Stacey said.

"What are they?" Hale asked.

"They are the glue that holds the Alliance

together. They created the probe that saved so few of us on Earth. They are the ones trying to save this galaxy from the Xaros. And one of them is coming to say hello."

A blaze of white light rose from beneath the sled. Hale backpedaled into the railing, his hands fumbling for his weapon out of ingrained reflcxcs. The creature floating before the sled was enormous, several times the size of Elias in his armor. A dome covered in crystal plates held long tendrils that waved in an unfelt breeze. Glowing filaments rose and fell from the tendrils, rippling and shifting.

+Greetings+

Hale felt the word in his mind, reverberating so hard it felt like a vice across his temples.

Torni wiped a hand across her nose, and blood streaked across her glove.

"Too much?" Stacey asked. "It's sorry. Our minds can't process their communication very well. The AI on Bastion does most of that for us."

A tendril lifted from the Qa'Resh and slowly reached for Yarrow.

"Stop!" Hale moved Yarrow away from the glowing crystal tip and put himself between the fallen Marine and the alien. "What're you going to do? Tell me how you're going to get that thing out of Yarrow without hurting him."

"Ken, the Qa'Resh will do what it needs to. Don't expect it to explain itself," Stacey said.

"The hell it will." Hale jabbed a finger at the Qa'Resh. "You sent that probe to Earth and it let billions die for this war. You expect me to believe you won't kill Yarrow just to get at what's inside him?"

"They are our allies." Stacey's hologram walked in front of Hale and pointed a finger at his chest. "You're insulting them, I'm sure, by this macho nonsense. Now get out of the—"

Hale's hand snapped out and grabbed the ball at the center of the hologram. Stacey vanished and a muffled protest came from Hale's fist.

The tendril flipped over, tiny white filaments writhing like each had a mind of its own. The tip floated slowly toward Hale.

+Permission+

The word echoed through Hale's mind, a waning echo repeated by several different voices.

Hale didn't move.

+Touch+

The tendril bounced slightly.

"What do you think, Sergeant?" Hale asked Torni.

"It's a giant goddamn crystal jellyfish, sir. I don't know what to think," Torni said.

"Hold this." Stacey's angry face emerged briefly as Hale handed the ball to Torni. He removed a glove and slowly reached to the Qa'Resh's tendril. It felt warm, dry and rough like sandpaper. For some reason, Hale thought of the last time he saw his grandfather. He'd held the old man's hand while he lay in the hospital bed, his final moments nearing.

Everything vanished in a flash of white.

Hale blinked. Torni and the Qa'Resh were gone, and a new person was on the sled—a white-haired elderly man with bright blue eyes and wisps of hair. The old man wore a plain white jumpsuit, spotless and gleaming.

"Sorry about that, Ken," the old man said. "It's easier for us to communicate this way." His words echoed with the voices of many others.

"Where'd the others go?"

"They're still here. We're just talking privately. Now, may we remove the entity from young Mr. Yarrow?" His lined face widened into a kind smile.

"Can you do it without hurting him? I've lost too many good Marines and I don't want to rush … whatever you're going to do if there's a risk you'll hurt him."

"Your species is so contradictory. Save some, kill others. But we're not here to discuss philosophy. I can remove the entity, but there will be some lasting effects on Yarrow. He will be whole."

"Do you have a name? What are you?"

"We are who you perceive. We don't really bother with names. Now, may we?"

"All right. How will you—what the hell?" the old man vanished. Hale turned around and found him standing next to Yarrow's gurney, a hand held over the Marine's chest.

"This intelligence," the old man said, "has hurt so many innocent beings." Rays of golden light emerged from his palm and danced over Yarrow's body. "What it knows will aid us in the fight against the Xaros. Perhaps that will give it some manner of redemption."

Gray mist rose from Yarrow's eyes and mouth, coalescing into a small sphere just like the one they encountered on Anthalas.

"Billions of years ago," the old man said, his gaze on the sphere as it grew into the size of a baseball, "this species ruled the galaxy. They chose to leave, but they abandoned this one. Left it imprisoned on that planet. This one will tell us where they went, and how they got there."

"How does that help us against the Xaros?"

Ephemeral strands sank into the sphere, now nearly the size of Yarrow's head. A skeletal face pressed against the sphere, howling in silent, impotent rage.

"The Xaros are a tool, servants to something else. What controls them is after something more than a galaxy of their own. Something connected to this entity," the old man said. Hale blinked, and he was gone.

"Thank you, Ken," came from behind him. Hale looked around, and the old man stood at the edge of the sled, the glowing sphere suspended above his fingertips. "We would have saved more of humanity if possible. But if that sacrifice leads to victory, and survival, then it was an acceptable loss."

"'Acceptable'?"

"All life is precious to us, but we cannot save all of every species from the Xaros. More may be lost before we can end the war. This is our decision." The old man stepped off the side of the sled and fell away.

A flash of light overwhelmed Hale. He grunted in pain and pressed his palm against his head until his eyes stopped burning.

"Get back here! We are not your pawns and you're not going to throw us all away just because it suits you!" Hale opened his eyes to see the Qa'Resh floating in front of the sled, the full-sized sphere dangling between its tendrils.

"Sir," Torni had the hologram ball held tight against both hands, shaking and struggling to contain it.

"Let her go," Hale said.

"—will find a hot poker and ram it … what happened?" Stacey's hologram stared intently at the sphere.

"Where am I?" Yarrow groaned and pushed himself up on his elbows. He looked right at the Qa'Resh.

"Sweet Jesus!" Yarrow kicked away from his gurney, sending it and himself clattering against the sled. Yarrow scrambled away from the Qa'Resh and bumped against the force field surrounding them. He rolled onto his chest and looked down, over the edge of the sled and into the wide expanse of the planet's striped atmosphere.

Yarrow went prone, trying to grasp onto the sled.

"You OK, Yarrow?" Torni asked, she knelt beside him and put a hand on his shoulder.

Yarrow burst into tears and covered his head with his arms.

Torni gave Yarrow a reassuring pat. "I know, kid. It's that kind of a day."

Yarrow brought his head up and took a quick look at the Qa'Resh. "Sir, I know I said I wanted to join your squad for the experience … but God damn."

+Valdar+

Yarrow squealed and pulled into a fetal position.

"What about Captain Valdar?" Stacey asked. The Qa'Resh floated away, back toward the crystal city. "Why would …?" Her hologram looked around and swiped at a screen wherever she truly was. "Oh no, not the Dotok. We need to get back to the *Breitenfeld*, now."

CHAPTER 14

The sled skipped over the gas giant's upper atmosphere as it flew toward Bastion, carrying Valdar, Lowenn, Lafayette and Stacey's hologram.

Lowenn looked to space and gasped.

"A three-star system, how rare," Lowenn said, pointing upwards.

"There's only one sun up there," Valdar said. "Yellow, like Earth's."

"I see a white dwarf," Lafayette added.

"You all see the same security feature," Stacey said with a wave of her hand. "If you can't identify any stellar features, you can't trace your way back to Bastion."

"There are billions of stars in the galaxy. The Qa'Resh think one glimpse to the sky will compromise their location?" Lowenn asked.

"Take it from a navigator," Stacey said. "Every star in this galaxy is unique. If I know what the primary star, or stars, really are, and if I can see the star field through this gas giant's upper atmosphere, I can tell you exactly where in space Bastion really is."

"You've never tried to figure it out?" Valdar asked.

"Seems like a surefire way to get kicked off the station and on to the Qa'Resh's naughty list," Stacey said.

"Forget I asked," Valdar said. He looked back to the *Breitenfeld*, a grey bubble in the sky. He caught a glimpse of something beyond his ship, something that looked like another space station like Bastion. He looked closer, but it was gone.

Atmo playing tricks on me, he thought.

"There's a protocol to these conferences. Let me do the talking," Stacey said.

Bastion grew closer, layered domes of steel blue metal dotted with irregularly sized windows. Great spikes hung from it like a patch of icicles amassed over a long winter. A small circle of light opened against its bulk and the sled adjusted course suddenly.

Valdar and Lowenn grasped the handrails, their bodies reacting to what they saw and not what they actually felt.

"The other Karigole react the same way," Lafayette said. "Kosciuszko actually refused to take a sled to the pod that brought us to Earth. Steuben convinced him otherwise, and by 'convinced' I mean he threw our brother onto the sled and kept a boot on him until the trip was done."

"Why don't you have the same problem?" Lowenn asked.

Lafayette's metal fingertips tapped against the metal rising from the base of his skull. "My inner ear is bionic. Some improvements were made."

The sled shot into the open portal. A dark

gray metal tunnel blurred by, too fast to make out any features.

"Be right back," Stacey said. Her hologram vanished and the ball returned to its hole in the sled.

Valdar saw the end of the tunnel, interlocked metal walls that looked very solid and that were getting very close.

"Stacey?" Valdar asked. He looked around, his gaze returning to metal walls several times. "Stacey you want to open up?"

The sled continued on, its speed steady. The doors cracked open, and Valdar and Lowenn ducked as the sled shot through an opening barely wide enough to keep from knocking the upright Lafayette's head off his shoulders.

"My assumption is that they're showing off," Lafayette said.

"There's a fine line between arrogance and—whoa!" Valdar pulled himself to his feet, his jaw still on the floor.

A central dais rose from the center of the assembly, a column of rough stone perfectly flat at the top. The assembly stretched for miles around the dais, hundreds of small domes over round bases that floated in the air. Most were the size of an Eagle fighter, but others ranged from the size of a suitcase to one that was so large it could have held a destroyer with ease.

One pod rose above the others and the sled angled toward it. A door on the pod slid aside as they approached. Valdar saw a humanoid figure inside, obscured by shadow. The sled came to a halt at the door and the railing vanished.

The figure came to the door, Stacey Ibarra in a plain jumpsuit.

"Come on in. We're about to get started," she said.

Standing within the pod, Valdar couldn't see the dome he knew enclosed them, but he had a crystal-clear view of everything around them. He reached over the edge of the control panels, which were labelled in English, and his hand stopped where he thought the dome would be. He couldn't feel pressure against his fingertips as he pressed harder, but his hand would go no further.

"Nice to see you again, sir. In the flesh at least," Stacey said.

"Likewise," Valdar said, extending a hand to her. She tried to shake it, but her hand stopped several inches from his. A buzzer in the invisible ceiling sounded.

"That's right. No physical contact allowed. When the Qa'Resh first brought races together, there were a few incidents where ambassadors tried to … eat each other. Some of the species had warred before and letting old blood feuds play out wasn't very diplomatic," Stacey said.

Her face was different than he'd remembered, younger-looking. Tiny filaments of silver twinkled around her eyes as she smiled.

"Can we see them? The other ambassadors?" Lowenn asked, peering across the silver domes as they vanished into the surrounding darkness.

Stacey looked over her shoulder. "Hit the yellow and green button labeled VIEW." When she looked back at Valdar, her face was weary, more natural.

I need to see the doc when I get back to my ship, he thought.

Lowenn did as instructed, and the silver domes on each pod wiped to the side, revealing plain-looking men and women in dark jumpsuits in the pods.

"What? They're all human?" Lowenn asked.

"No, it's a projection to aide with relatability. They look human, but they aren't. … Trust me," Stacey said.

"I didn't come here to see mannequins. How do I see what they really look like?" Lowenn tapped buttons on the view panel.

"Don't say I didn't warn you. Chuck," Stacey looked up, "disable the filter."

The nearest ambassador looked like a hunched over cockroach, staring at the humans from three eyes mounted against a lupine skull and crystal, fanged teeth. Its jaws opened and a triple tongue wagged in the air.

Valdar turned around. Another pod held an alien that looked like a sphere of roiling swamp water. Another looked like a mass of black ribbons around a red hot ball of iron. Yet another pod moved closer, its occupants nothing but three black teardrops attached to stick-thin bodies.

"Oh boy," Lowenn said.

"Chuck, filter." Stacey snapped her fingers and the illusion of other humans returned.

"You should try having a conversation with the Dreggara. They're sentient pollen floating on a mat of seaweed the size of Asia," Lafayette said.

A light in the pod turned from red to amber. The ambassadors around them looked up toward the dais.

"About to start," Stacey said. "Captain, you should know that the Dotok were instrumental in getting a probe sent to Earth. If it hadn't been for their lobbying, we'd be extinct."

"Why are you telling me this?" Valdar asked.

"I only got the preliminary message, but I'm

pretty sure they're going to need us—the *Breitenfeld*." Stacey crossed her arms. "I'm not in your chain of command, and I can't tell you what to do, but please hear Pa'lon out."

The light switched to green and a chime sounded twice.

A huge hologram of a woman's face appeared above the dais. Her hair was deep gray, the lines around her lips and eyes on the verge of elderly. Valdar noted the set of her face, the same look he'd come to know from an entire adulthood spent in military service—determination.

"That's the Qa'Resh," Stacey said. "At least, that's what they look like to me when we're in here."

"Sentient beings of the Alliance," the Qa'Resh said. "A member finds their world under Xaros threat. This world should have been safe for centuries, but the facts are undeniable. The Xaros are there."

The face faded away and Pa'lon, in his true form, rose from the dais and raised a hand in the air.

A screen appeared above his head, showing a long, angular spaceship covered in dark lines that looked like roots had spread over its surface. The flash of laser bolts and brief explosions of dying ships surrounded the vessel. Fireballs burst along the ship's hull and the dark lines retreated toward the engines. The ship burst apart and the spreading fireball overwhelmed the camera, cutting the image off in a wave of static.

"This is what I saw on Takeni, one of the last few worlds we Dotok found after our home world was taken by the Xaros. This ship you see was once ... ours, one of the many colony ships that set out from our home world hundreds of years ago." The video rewound to the moment the ship exploded. The image zoomed in, and the outline of a Xaros drone that had survived the explosion was clearly visible.

"We don't know how, or why, the ship is fighting beside the Xaros. It was intercepted on the edge of our system and destroyed with great cost to our planetary defense forces. Our navy detected more ships—many more—just beyond the edge of our system. This fleet is on course to Takeni, my home. We have but a few days until it arrives.

"My people's only known colony is on that world. We do not have the time to evacuate them to the colony ships we still have in orbit, nor do we have the capability to open a jump point and get them to safety. I ask that the Alliance send a relief effort to Takeni, save what we can and learn about this new Xaros threat."

"Ibarra, you've never seen this before? Xaros allies?" Valdar asked.

"No. It's always been just the drones. For thousands of years since this war started, it's always been the drones," Stacey said.

"Then why this change?"

Stacey shrugged her shoulders.

"You cannot expect us to risk so much for a minor population center." A pod rose above the rest and floated toward the dais. Inside was a "man" with short dark hair and a patrician face.

"Here we go," Stacey said. "That's the

Vishrakath ambassador, an empire of dozens of systems on the edge of the galaxy. And if he's speaking, that means it's time to argue."

"Our numbers on Takeni are few, that is true." Pa'lon made his way to the edge of the dais, addressing the Vishrakath directly. "If the act of saving so many intelligent beings isn't enough for you, then consider the intelligence value of what we may learn. The Xaros are a formidable threat. Why would they seek aid?"

"Perhaps the better question is why your species is fighting beside them," the Vishrakath said.

"We lost our home world to the Xaros. We owe them nothing. There has never been a recorded communication with the Xaros. What we all just witnessed is a fundamental change in the paradigm. Why? Why are the Xaros in need of help?" Pa'lon asked.

"He's smart, appealing to cold logic of the longer war than the emotion of saving his family," Stacey said.

"Family? They have such a thing?" Valdar asked.

"The Dotok are mammalian, clan-based. Not that different from us." Stacey traced a symbol in the air and a picture of Pa'lon and his family inside an adobe home appeared in front of Valdar. The Dotok children were covered in short tan hair; the youngest one in its mother's arms had white spots running up and down its arms and legs.

"How many … how many children are on that planet?" Valdar's heart twisted as he recognized the look on Pa'lon's face, so similar to Valdar's own emotions from family photos—love.

"Chuck?" Stacey asked.

"There are 97,822 recorded Dotok on the planet Takeni. Recent losses in battle have not been measured," a neutral voice said from the control panel.

"There's no way I can fit that many on *Breitenfeld*," Valdar said. He looked up. "He said something about a colony fleet. How many ships do they still have? How many can they evacuate?"

"That information is not available," Chuck said.

"Lafayette, the jump engines can extend their reach beyond my ship, correct? How far into space can it go? Can we take other ships with us?" Valdar asked the Karigole.

"Sir, you can't be serious," Lowenn said.

"The energy demands would be enormous, but I could bring two or three more vessels the size of the *Breitenfeld* through an established wormhole … in theory," Lafayette said.

"Where's the microphone in this thing?" Valdar asked.

"Captain," Lowenn said, "we can't risk the ship for this. Earth needs it, the crew. The Xaros are coming back, remember?"

"I don't remember asking you," Valdar said. "How do I speak to Pa'lon, to them all?"

Stacey's lips pressed into a thin line. She turned away from her former commander.

"Lowenn's right. There's nothing on Takeni that can help Earth. The Dotok can send information back here long enough for us to figure out why that ship was fighting beside the drones," Stacey said.

"What? You said Pa'lon was the reason any of us are alive. Now you want to just hang him out to dry?"

"I'm being pragmatic, sir. Focus on the long war. If you go to Takeni now and lose everything, Earth will be that much weaker when the Xaros return. If you manage to save some of them, then the Earth gains almost nothing."

"Pa'lon managed to save an ember of humanity. We can at least *try* to do the same for him," Valdar said. "Let me talk to them."

"I'm going to regret this," Stacey said. "Chuck, wide address."

The edge of their pod turned yellow and rose next to the Vishrakath pod.

Stacey nodded to Valdar, who took a deep breath.

"Send us," Valdar said. The discussion between Pa'lon and the Vishrakath stopped. "I am

Captain Isaac Valdar of the Atlantic Union strike carrier *Breitenfeld.* I lost my family to the Xaros." The pod rose higher as it spun slowly, looking out across the assembled species of the Alliance. "If there is a chance we can save innocent lives, we will take it. Send my ship to Takeni. We could not save our own families, but we can save those on Takeni."

"Your ship possesses a jump drive," the Vishrakath said. "Manufacturing such a device is difficult, time-consuming and worth more to our efforts than every Dotok in this Alliance. What's more, Earth guards the only Xaros jump gate we could conceivably utilize. Your ship should return to your home world, protect that asset we risked so much to acquire."

"Billions of humans died so you could get that gate. Who the hell do you think you are to dictate what should happen to something we sacrificed for?" Valdar's pod rose level to the other ambassador's. He saw his angry face displayed on the giant hologram and forced himself to calm down.

"This display of yours is precisely why our probe had to trick your species into saving itself. Throwing away resources for something as useless as emotional triggers will not change the projected outcomes in our conflict with the Xaros." The Vishrakath spun his pod away from Valdar.

"Then you should know why my emotional triggers will tell you where to shove your projected outcomes!"

"Oh god, I'll never hear the end of this," Stacey said, her face in her hands.

The Qa'Resh's human mask formed over the dais.

"We will put the matter to consideration. Given the importance of the Xaros gate on Earth, all ambassadors have the right to vote. Vote for, or against, sending the human ship to Takeni," she said. Her face vanished.

Two lines, one red and the other green, appeared above the dais. Unique red and green symbols popped under each line as ambassadors cast their votes.

"Each ambassador has their own symbol. We can see who's with or against us on this," Stacey said. "Chuck, Earth votes for the motion." A green wire diagram of Earth added to the tally.

"Steuben?" Stacey asked the Karigole.

"I would be a shame to my namesake if I voted against this mission," Lafayette said. He spoke in his native language and a circle-of-fire symbol added to the green column.

As more and more symbols came up, the votes in the red column were decisively ahead. A last few votes trickled in, then stopped. The Alliance had voted against the mission by almost two to one.

"We're asking them to risk their own safety by losing the gate on Earth," Stacey said. "I'm not surprised by this." Her head sank to her chest.

"Damn it," Valdar said. He looked at Pa'lon, on the dais staring up at the tally in disbelief and horror.

The tally vanished, replaced by the Qa'Resh

woman.

"We thank each ambassador for their participation. The mission is approved. Coordinates to Takeni will be sent to the *Breitenfeld*'s jump AI and she will leave once the engines have recharged," she said.

Stacey looked up, as shocked as Valdar by the pronouncement.

Pods rose from field. Angry ambassadors converged on the dais, the conversion fields translating each species' outrage into shaken fists and shouted words that Valdar could comprehend.

The Qa'Resh's hand waved in front of her face and all the pods but Valdar's vanished.

"Why?" Pa'lon asked.

"The vote is for consideration, not decision," the Qa'Resh said. She looked at Valdar and cocked her head slightly. "We believe you can succeed, Captain Valdar. But our support comes with two caveats: you will discover the nature of the Xaros' allies and return that information to us, and the *Breitenfeld*'s jump engine will not fall into Xaros hands. Saving civilians is secondary."

"A captain always goes down with his ship. We will succeed or I will die trying," Valdar said.

A slight smile cracked across her face.

"We like you. Your determination has done much for us. Perhaps you will save the Dotok and become an inspiration to those species with such a concept. Hurry back to your ship. The Dotok need you. *Gott mit uns*, Captain Valdar."

"*Gott mit uns*," he said.

The Qa'Resh vanished.

CHAPTER 15

On the great pyramid of Anthalas, Xaros drones circled the apex. Fifty drones formed the first clockwise orbit around the pyramid. The second, counterclockwise orbit was twice that number. Rings of drones stretched beyond the horizon, alternating orbits flying so close that they blacked-out the sky. The General would have nothing less as his honor guard.

The General stood over twenty feet tall, its feet deign to touch the surface as he floated around the apex. Tight links of chain mail made of the same writhing metal as the drones enveloped its humanoid body. His shape was an affectation, a remembrance of its old form when it was constrained by flesh and blood. Red plates of armor hovered over the chain mail, shifting around it. One armor plate was affixed to its chain mail, a blank face mask with two eye slits that glowed with white light.

The General waved its hand over the Shanishol control panel, ephemeral fingers stretching through the armor, caressing the controls. It read the DNA presence of something that should not have been possible, something anomalous: humans.

The presence of a species that should have been extinct was beneath his concern. Such things had happened before during his long march across the galaxy. But their presence combined with the delay …

The General's body collapsed into a burning star and shot away from Anthalas with a blaze of light. Its beam of light sped toward the system's Crucible gate and it opened a wormhole harmonic that it thought wouldn't have been needed until his army stretched from one side of this galaxy to another.

It reformed, floating in a dark abyss. Strands of stars formed around the General as the Keeper brought its consciousness to bear.

You are early. That means you have failed. The Keeper's words resonated from the growing star field.

"I have not failed. There is an anomaly that we must address with the others. Wake them."

You have failed to cleanse this galaxy before our arrival. I will not disturb the rest to hear your excuses.

"The eradication of the infestation of all intelligent species remains on schedule. There is an anomaly that could jeopardize everything. I will speak with the others."

No. If you are contaminated by imperfection, I will not risk exposing them to you. Speak of this anomaly.

An image of Earth came into being beside the General. Recordings of television programs and waveforms from radio broadcasts orbited around the planet.

"My drones scoured this world with little effort not too long ago." The image changed to show Ceres in its new orbit around Earth with the Crucible. "Acceptable for our needs. The drones built a gate as per their programming. My attention wasn't required. All reports sent by the planet's caretakers during the construction were insignificant. The gate should have come online by now ... but it hasn't."

Stellar activity. Seismic disruption to the world that rendered the planet undesirable. I fail to see the relevance.

"The caretaker presence on an artifact world observed this." The images changed to show Hale and his team atop the great pyramid, Eagle fighters dogfighting with the Toth and crystal-clear images of the *Breitenfeld*. "The ship matches others the humans had when we cleansed their planet. They never attempted to colonize other stars. There is only one possible way that ship was on the artifact world: the humans must have captured Earth's star gate before it was completed."

You bring me conjecture. I require facts.

"The speed of light is a constant and a constraint. The nearest gate won't receive the final caretaker transmissions from Earth for years. One fact you should have grasped is that when the humans left the artifact world, they did not use our gate. They have jump drives that rip a hole in the fabric of space time. Jump drives that can cause the same disaster that drove us here in the first place."

The Keeper remained silent. The star field it chose to represent its intelligence wavered as it ran calculations.

There was no indication of this capability when your army cleansed the infested world?

"None. They were primitives."

They must have help.

"Yes. What's more, the humans took something from the artifact world. Something that might have aided our final objective." Drone footage of the sphere merging into Yarrow played, then cut as a quadrium round knocked the drone offline. "The artifact world held an intelligence unknown to us, a remnant of an ascended species."

You knew this but you did nothing more to secure it? Stars around the General burst into supernovae as the Keeper's anger grew.

"My role is to cleanse this galaxy, not pick through the ashes. Do not be so fixated on base matters, Keeper. The humans are an anomaly, one I wish to erase *now*. Awaken the Engineer. I require our jump gate technology. One jump of enough drones and the anomaly will be removed."

No.

"The risk is minimal." Light flared from the General's eye sockets as his patience waned.

No. The risk exists. The technology is forbidden. Handle the anomaly within your means.

"If I send drones to Earth from the nearest gate right now, it will be some time before they even arrive."

I am pleased to know you are capable of carrying out your function. Do not return until this matter is resolved.

The Keeper's star field pulled away, leaving the General in darkness.

The General raised a finger, and a star map of the Milky Way galaxy appeared before him. Most of its drones were on the leading edge of the cleansing tide, but it kept a sizable reserve at the star system where the Keeper and the sleepers would finally arrive. He directed a force of three hundred million drones through the Crucible gate system to a world the humans called Bernard's Star.

The invasion force would build him a command vessel, then set off to Earth. He would be there to grind the humans into extinction.

CHAPTER 16

A Toth command shuttle, the same that nearly collided with Durand's fighter on Anthalas, burst through a wormhole. Scorch marks from Xaros beams scarred its surface and its remaining engine flared out as fuel lines ruptured.

The overseer within the shuttle would have sighed in relief, if he still had lungs. He sent a distress signal and waited for the nearest Toth ship to come to his rescue.

The shuttle tumbled through space as the Toth home world came into view over and over again. The opal blue oceans filled ancient impact craters, each ringed by Toth cities that spread from the coastlines like an infection emanating from an untreated wound. The Band, the space station that circled the entire equator, was as busy as ever, creating new warships for the Toth fleet, receiving and processing raw material from the far reaches of the system.

A rune flashed on the overseer's control panel, a transmission from an overseer from a much weaker, and poorer, corporation. The overseer didn't answer the hail, letting the insult of not even bothering to reject the call hit home.

He may not have returned with the Omnium as contracted, but he hadn't returned empty-handed.

A new hail came in, one of the overseers that backed the expedition. Now he was being treated with respect. A mechanical arm attached to his tank opened a channel.

"Kren," the other overseer addressed him without mentioning his corporate rank, a mark of contempt, "you left with a much larger ship. Explain."

"Greetings, Stix. There were some Xaros

complications on Anthalas. I'm afraid we'll have to write off the cruiser as the cost of doing business," Kren said.

"Unacceptable." Kren heard the new voice, and the nerves within his tank coiled together in fear. "You assured the board that you could recover the Shanishol's Omnium technology without Xaros detection. You put up the bond. Consider it forfeit."

The controls on his ship were overridden and a hologram of five overseers filled his escape pod, each with tanks more ornate and elaborate than Kren's. The tank in the middle was covered in filigreed platinum and embossed with precious gems. The overseer inside twisted, no doubt anticipating just which of Kren's corporate holdings it would plunder first. The Chairman would go for his clone banks first; she'd grown hungrier and hungrier as age left her remaining body parched for fresh minds to consume.

"Wait … wait, Chairman Ranik. I've brought back something potentially more valuable than the Omnium. Something that will make us all richer than Doctor Mentiq and all the pleasures he keeps on his glorious world. Look at this," Kren said as he opened a freezer unit in the wall of his shuttle, revealing the body of Lieutenant Bartlett.

"A human? Where did you find that? The Xaros should have overran them by now," Chairman Ranik asked.

"It was on Anthalas, along with a Karigole that slipped through my fingers. It seems the Qa'Resh and the Alliance got to the humans before the Xaros. The humans have an incomplete Xaros gate, which is interesting," Kren said.

"Kren, you went to Anthalas with our shipyard's newest cruiser, the warriors from our finest gene line and more menials than I can consume in a month," the Chairman said. "You think this tidbit of information is worth more than Doctor Mentiq's menagerie of meat species?"

"No, certainly not. But this human is different from the ones we knew of. Its mind had enormous taste, but the body was far too young to hold such a feast. The humans found a way to mass produce themselves, quickly and without replication to dull the taste," Kren said. His nerves waved back and forth against his tank, too excited to keep his emotions in check. For far too long, Toth overseers had made do with bland clones to keep their minds alive. The human corpse represented a revenue stream that would make Kren wealthy beyond his wildest dreams, even if he had to assign a decent percentage to the corporation.

"Do you have this method?" the Chairman asked.

"No … no. None of the humans I encountered were aware of the flash-grown bodies with false minds amongst them. But they are on Earth, a location known to us. From what I gleaned off their minds, the planet's total population is paltry and their military is weak. An easy victory for us, yes?"

The audio from the Board cut off as the five discussed Kren's proposal.

"It is agreed. We will sponsor a trade expedition to Earth. Vice President Stix will head up the project as—"

"No!" Kren shouted. His nerves coiled around his spinal cord as the color within the Chairman's tank changed from red to deep purple. One did not interrupt her without consequence. "I invoke right of first refusal, as in our corporate charter, to exploit any new resources. Must I cite chapter and verse?"

"Kren," the Chairman purred at him, a dangerous tone that caused him to float against the back of his tank in fear, "Stix has led several raids, including the profitable expedition against the Karigole. Let him take care of the humans. You'll get your percentage."

Common sense dictated Kren cease his protest, but the thought of an unlimited supply of fresh, unique minds to sate his hunger was too much. As happened often in Toth history, avarice proved stronger than logic.

"I restate my claim," Kren said.

"As you wish," the Chairman said. "But even your wealth isn't enough to absorb the loss from *two* expeditions. Fail, and we will auction off the right to feast on your mind to cover your debts. And Stix will accompany you as a technical advisor. Liquidate your crew once your life pod has been recovered. No need to risk losing this secret to corporate espionage, now is there?"

"The terms are acceptable," Kren said. The warriors and menials crammed into his shuttle looked around at each other, their eyes widening as the implication became clear. The transmission ended.

"I'm sorry, everyone." Kren saw a space cutter through the windows, his rescue. His tank arms overrode the environmental controls on the pod. Being a nervous system suspended in fluid, he had no need for air.

"Your services are no longer required." Kren vented the pod's atmosphere into space. The death of every Toth around him was quick, but painful.

CHAPTER 17

The desk in Captain Valdar's ready room had a new decoration: a Toth claw pried from Elias' armor. The soldier, who had little use for possessions, gave it to the *Breitenfeld*'s master in appreciation for disabling the Toth ship and leaving it to Xaros mercy.

Valdar tossed an Ubi slate onto the desk and pressed fingertips into his temples. Speech writing wasn't his forte, nor was explaining to Admiral Garret why he'd take his ship into the jaws of the Xaros invasion of Takeni.

A chime sounded—someone at the door.

"Come in," Valdar said.

The door slid aside and Stacey's hologram entered, her projection around the floating ball. Commander Ericsson stuck her head into the ready room and cocked an eyebrow at the captain. Valdar waved his XO away and the door shut behind her.

"Thing about being a hologram," Stacey said, "you have the damnedest time opening doors. You asked to see me?"

"How soon can you get back to Earth? There's a lot they need to know," Valdar said.

"Days, at least. The Crucible is set to keep the gate open for *Breitenfeld*'s return, not an unscheduled visit by me. It'll take time for the gate on Bastion to charge up enough energy to get me through," Stacey said.

"It will have to do. You'll take my after-action review of what happened on Anthalas and my … reasoning for going to Takeni with you?" Valdar tapped the Ubi on his desk.

"Certainly. You don't need to see me 'in person' for that, though."

"No. The Toth, they kept going on about

'weed bodies' and 'false minds.' Do you know what they could be talking about?" Stacey shook her head. "I went over this with Hale, and the only other human contact they had was with Lieutenant Bartlett and the rest of his Rangers. The only thing that could be the 'weed bodies' and 'false minds' is them. I went through their records, but there's nothing unusual. None of the armor soldiers ever heard of Bartlett and the rest of his men and women."

"The army was a big place before the invasion. Don't tell me you knew everyone in the navy," Stacey said.

"No, certainly not. Stacey, I'm not in your chain of command anymore, but when you get back to Earth, would you look into this? Alert Admiral Garret that there's something wrong, something unnatural. And I'm certain Marc Ibarra is behind it."

"What're we talking about, clones? He was adamantly against the technology when he was alive. Sponsored all kinds of legislation against the practice."

"He's been playing a game with the rest of the human race for six decades. Do you think he's stopped?"

Stacey crossed her arms and looked away. "No, I suppose he hasn't," she said softly. "I don't even know if he's *him* anymore. Exactly how that probe preserved his consciousness is 'need to know' information."

"We're pawns, Stacey. I saw that at the assembly. All the races there will throw humanity to the Xaros if it suits them. Why clones? Do they think we'll be some kind of a slave army for them?"

"No, sir. Maybe you're reading too much into what the Toth said. If we really were pawns, would the Qa'Resh override the vote to send you to Takeni?"

Valdar pushed his chair away from his desk and frowned.

"They've played us, Stacey. Sacrificed billions to get a Crucible gate within reach. Don't tell me they won't let the rest of us go to save themselves. I have no misconceptions about how important my ship—my one ship—will be when the Xaros return to Earth. If we die on Takeni, it won't make much of a difference." Valdar stood up and looked over his uniform in a mirror.

"You should learn to trust, sir. It makes life easier," Stacey said.

Valdar tapped a photo stuck against the mirror of him with his wife and children around a Christmas tree.

"They're dead, Stacey. My family is dead because of the Qa'Resh and their plans. Don't talk to me about trust. Now, I have to go tell my crew what I just volunteered them for," Valdar said. He tried to sidestep around Stacey's hologram, but his shoulder passed through her image and distorted it with a tug.

Valdar found Ericsson waiting for him outside the door. He left Stacey alone in his ready room as the door closed behind him.

Stacey shook her head slowly. She waved a hand over the Ubi and drew out the final report

Valdar wrote for Garret and transferred it to her holo sphere. She took out the earlier drafts and sworn statements from Hale too.

She hated lying to Valdar. The man was a brave and talented officer that cared for his crew. He deserved better than canned answers and denial. Ibarra's plan for procedurally generated fighting men and women had to go forward. Without them, extinction was inevitable. Valdar would never know that Stacey brought the final neurologic programming code needed to create the proccies to Ibarra. No one could know that. Ibarra would absorb the backlash for their creation, not the Qa'Resh. Not Bastion.

Stacey walked to the door, which didn't open for her. She tried to push a key to open the door, but her hand slid through the wall. She looked up at the sensor atop the doorframe, which wouldn't read her presence.

"Ahh, seriously?"

****

Breitenfeld's flight deck was empty of planes, but full of sailors and Marines. Mustering the entire crew was rare, even in peace time. Thousands stood in formation, each individual section drawn up into a separate square of neat rows, facing a stage set up at the fore side of the deck, staring into the gray abyss Bastion kept around the ship. Low murmurs from those assembled rumbled like a crowd just before a performance.

"I don't like this," Standish said. "Anyone else not like this?" Bailey and Orozco, standing on either side of him, shrugged their shoulders. Torni, on the far right of the rank as she was the acting head NCO, rolled her eyes.

"What're you so worried about? You're the gossip center of this ship. Don't you know what the captain's going to tell us?" Bailey asked.

"I will neither confirm nor deny the existence of a junior enlisted information network. That being said … I don't know a damn thing. That's why I'm so nervous," Standish said.

"Settle down," Orozco said. "It's not like he donated all our organs to alien science."

"What? Where did you hear that?" Standish twisted around and repeated Orozco's supposition to the Marine standing behind him.

"Standish!" Torni's loud whisper snapped Standish back around. "I swear to God, I will jam my boot so far up your ass you'll choke on the steel-tipped toes. Will that stop you from yammering like a damn one-man knitting circle?"

Standish nodded furiously.

"Anyone been to see Gunney Cortaro yet?" Bailey asked.

"The lieutenant did, said he's in rough shape but he's stable," Orozco said. "I asked about Yarrow and was told he's in quarantine and 'don't ask anymore.'"

"Sarge," Bailey said to Torni, "you went with Yarrow. What happened down there?"

"Well," Torni said slowly, "this giant alien … thing …," Torni sniffed and wiped away blood seeping from her nose. "I'm sorry, what was I saying?"

"You were talking about what happened with Yarrow," Bailey said.

"What? Why would I do that?" Torni asked.

"You were down there with the LT, that's why," Orozco said.

"I was?" Torni winced and pressed a palm against the side of her head.

"Sweet Jesus, maybe the captain really did sell our organs to aliens," Bailey said.

A chief petty officer climbed a small set of stairs to the stage. The ship's crew fell silent as their attention turned to the stage.

"Crew! Attention!" the petty officer announced, his words amplified by speakers above the flight deck.

Thousands of heels clicked together and the flight deck went silent but for the thrum of air circulators.

Captain Valdar stepped behind a podium and looked over the men and women assembled before him, his face stoic.

"*Breitenfeld*," Valdar said, "our mission to Anthalas was a success. Our allies have everything they need to understand Omnium and that knowledge will go to Earth. But we're not going home. Not yet." He paused as crewmen looked to each other in surprise. "We have all lost. The Xaros took our families, everyone we knew. We never had the chance, or the choice, to save any of those we loved.

"A Xaros force threatens a small planet full of civilians. They won't survive unless we act. The women and children won't survive unless *we* save them. They're not our families. They aren't even human, but they need us. Our ship, our skill, our strength. They need heroes. They've got *Breitenfeld*.

"The Xaros would exterminate us, all intelligent life, from the galaxy. Let's rescue life from right under their noses. Let those robot bastards see that humanity endures, our light remains and that our survival defies them. We'll show them that setting foot on Earth was the worst mistake they've ever made.

"Get our ship ready to jump. Get our ship ready to fight. *Gott mit uns,* dismissed."

THE END

FROM THE AUTHOR

I hope you enjoyed The Ruins of Anthalas enough to leave a review and tell two friends about the Ember War Saga.

Sign up for my mailing list at www.richardfoxauthor.com for exclusive Ember War Saga short stories, spam free! As always, drop me a note at Richard.r.fox@outlook.com and let me know what you'd like to see in future novels.

87496670R10253

Made in the USA
San Bernardino, CA
05 September 2018